D1155351

**Praise for Ginnah Howard's first novel, *Night Navigation*:**

The strength of this story pulls Howard's readers along, unable to turn away from a fierce mother and son who are determined to negotiate the future.
– *New York Times Book Review*

A needle-sharp look into the life of a mentally ill drug addict . . . Howard's writing showcases the beauty that exists in the mundane, if we only open our eyes to see it.
– *Shelf Life*

Pitch-perfect . . . This is a book that will leave the reader reflecting on the life and death struggle of one family, only one among many.
– *Curled Up with a Good Book*

Fine writing.
– *Morning News*

What makes this novel shine is the writer's seemingly effortless ability to bring to the page living, breathing characters, each deeply flawed but trying . . . The story unfolds easily, though it is anything but an easy story. Yet in the abundance of evident pathology there is never a cheap shot: There's no attempt at tear-jerking, no poor-me-look-what-I've-been-through attitude underlying Howard's spare prose, which makes the telling all the more powerful."
– *Chronogram Magazine*

A powerful and singular work.
– WSKG.org

Harrowing . . . Howard's strength, besides lapidary language, is the ability to build scenes around quotidian activities . . . Stark scenarios will be cathartic for readers who have dealt with them firsthand, and profoundly cautionary for those who haven't.
– *Kirkus* (starred review)

*Night Navigation* will leave you breathless – a haunting, riveting debut.
– Kiara Brinkman, author of *Up High in the Trees*

In this bold debut, Ginnah Howard navigates the precarious lives of her people with searing compassion and devastating honesty, opening our hearts to the dark wonder of shared grief and the flickering hope of forgiveness.
– Melanie Rae Thon, author of *Sweet Hearts*

A gritty, unblinking, compassionate portrait of addiction – the deceptions, the exhausting repetitions, and most of all the agonizing dilemmas of parental love, which may or may not have the power to save but can never stop trying.
– Joan Wickersham, author of *The Suicide Index*

Howard's gripping tale lays bare the marrow of familial love – its messy desperation and its stubborn, enduring beauty.
– Maud Casey, author of *The Shape of Things to Come*

*Night Navigation* is unerring in its grasp of the multiple deceptions of the addictive relationship, the self-deceptions above all. You can't help getting furious at its characters. And you can't help loving them.
– Peter Trachtenberg, author of *The Book of Calamities*

I fully enjoyed and admired this sparely written, unsparing portrait of a deeply troubled American family. Ginnah Howard is a wonderful new writer.
– Hilma Wolitzer, author of *Summer Reading*

A gritty, realistic, powerful portrayal of the complexities of addiction and the strains it puts on a family.
– *Booklist*

Ginnah Howard

# Doing Time Outside

[ A Novel ]

Standing Stone Books is a division of Standing Stone Studios, an organization dedicated to the promotion of the literary and visual arts.

Mailing addresses:
1897 Route 91, Fabius, New York 13063, U.S.A.

Email: info@standingstonestudios.org

Web address: www.standingstonestudios.org

Standing Stone Books are available in both print and ebook formats.

This book is printed by Bookmobile, Minneapolis, Minnesota, and distributed by Small Press Distribution, Berkeley, California.

ISBN: 978-0-9836172-3-5

Library of Congress Control Number: 2013944187

Design by Adam Rozum

Standing Stone Books is a member of the Literary Council of Magazines and Presses.

[clmp]

Ginnah Howard

# Doing Time Outside

[ A Novel ]

Standing Stone Books
Syracuse, New York

**In Memory of My Mother**

*Norma Virginia Oles*

*1916–1986*

# Family Guide

If you are a family member or friend of a person incarcerated in a correctional facility, your life has changed in many ways. Some call this "doing time outside."

Whatever you may call it, this time can be painful and difficult for you. Changes have to be made in order to maintain the relationship with your loved one.

This handbook was designed to help you better understand the correctional system. We hope it will guide you as you cope with these changes in your life.

– Onango County Corrections, 2003
State of New York

*Doing Time Outside*

[1]

# Commence Lockdown

Carla pokes her daughter's thigh and grabs Queenie's collar. "There it is. You better slow ..."

Tess swings wide and makes the turn. The truck skids to a stop in front of the sign:

*Public Safety Building*
*Onango County Correctional Facility*
*State of New York*

"Any faster you'd have put me through the windshield." Carla stops clutching the door, lets go of Queenie's collar, and gives Tess a hard look. "Me, your own dear mother." She leans forward and squints at the sign. "Correctional Facility: You know I hate that, but it's better than parking by the razor wire." She gropes around in her pockets for loose change and dumps a fistful into the ashtray. "You might as well get rid of anything metal out here."

Tess does not move.

Carla shrugs out of her jacket and takes her driver's license from her wallet. "Got to have photo ID," she says. She pulls off both Velcro wrist braces and stuffs them and her purse under the seat. "I'm not putting anything in those lockers."

She darts a glance at Tess. "They won't let you in there in that sweatshirt. No sweatshirts with pockets."

Still no response.

Carla brushes the dog hairs from her good black pants and opens the door. "Those guards — I don't let them look at *me* through their bulletproof glass like I'm some … welfare person."

She takes a deep breath and then turns to face Tess, unmoving behind the wheel. "You mean it? Are you still saying you aren't going in?"

Tess puts an arm around Queenie and cozies the dog up against her thigh. She pulls her duffle over the seat and slides her *Comparative Anatomy* book out. "I'm still saying, 'Why are you stepping into the path of a tornado?'"

"Tess, Rudy is your brother."

"I'm saying, 'The siren is screaming … screeeeeaming. Time to take cover.'"

"You forget how he pulled you out of the brook when you went under."

"I know you can hear the warning blasts: 'Hit the ditch.'"

"How he wired you money when your truck broke down in Texas. We've all made bad decisions. You, too, Tess."

"I was seventeen. Rudy is thirty-five."

"Who else does he have? We're his only family."

Maybe the jut of Tess's jaw gives an inch on that plea. Maybe.

Carla takes hold of Tess's sleeve, tugs on it. "He sounded good on the phone. They've even made him a trusty for being so cooperative. Got him fixing their broken-down equipment."

Tess grips the wheel. No blast of any kind will eject her from this truck.

Carla leans over so she can look Tess in the eye. "It's like he finally gets it."

"Mamo, you know what he wants."

"What?"

"He wants you to come up with the money for the bail bondsman He wants you to get him out."

Carla pulls a tissue from her sweater sleeve, blows her nose. She gets out of the truck. She swallows and draws herself up. "I'm his mother," she says, and closes the door.

The lobby is cavernous, dim: no windows. Cold. Gray tile walls, gray chairs, the smell of disinfectant. Bulletin boards with a lot of boldface rules. The message: retribution. Rudy's third arrest. This time it's for assault, assault with a deadly weapon. Plus possession, of course possession. Rudy's always possessing something. Rudy claims the deadly weapon part is not true. First arrest you think, Well, maybe he'll learn from it. Second arrest you say to yourself, That's it; if he doesn't get it this time, I am not going to walk up to that window again, drop my license in the metal trough, say what my relationship to the inmate is. But here she is once more, sitting in a hard plastic chair, freezing. She should have kept her jacket on.

The guards, who aren't called guards — who are instead called C.O.'s, for Correctional Officers, though surely correcting is not what they're doing — stir about behind the big glass at the far end of the room. 2:56, but they will not begin the sign-in process until the little hand is exactly on the 3.

Two other waiting women on the other side of the lobby. One young, wearing a long black T-shirt imprinted with a bloody bolt of lightning that forks around her hugely pregnant belly, and flip-flops, even though it's only March. A dozen chairs distant, someone's mother, maybe in her fifties, about Carla's age, with about the same level of damage. Maybe they've been here before: They've left their coats in their cars too. But not recently: They've forgotten how cold it is.

Carla paces back and forth on her side, rubs her hands up and down her sweater sleeves to try to generate some heat. She does not want to have the blue-chatters when she begins her negotiations with Rudy. Okay, big thing is to leave no loopholes. Rudy, are you listening good? Have I got your full attention? I am considering … you hear that word "considering" because I'm only *considering* … first hint of any attitude and I am un-considering … I am considering trying to raise the money it's going to take to post bail. Put my house up for collateral, my house, which I could lose if you take off, with the police dogs tracking you down all over the county. So, maybe I'm going to try to raise bail under these conditions: (1)You have got to live at the house until the hearing because you're less likely to get into trouble, causing me sleepless nights and pain behind my eyes. (2) No phone calls, no drop-ins from … bad influences.

Larry Prager — especially that snake Prager. None of Smithy's old crowd. Because if I find any incriminating signs of drugs of any kind on the premises, including alcohol and marijuana, one needle mark on your body, one blackened spoon, even one spoon missing, I'll report you for violating. Because, Rudy, I am off the painkillers, off everything, even cigarettes, five and a half months, 165 days O-F-F, and all on my own: no AA, no rehab, no nuthin'. I didn't let Smithy's death knock me out and I am not going to have you shooting up in my bathroom. Or bringing trouble down on your sister's head. Your sister who is getting it together. Getting herself an Associate's Degree as a Veterinary Technician.

2:59. The first woman, the mother, heaves herself up and moves toward the window. The girlfriend pulls her T-shirt down and goes to stand jittering behind her. Carla lines up next and gets her license out.

There are at least five guards in the room behind the glass. Not a big room either and dim like the lobby. Several are drinking coffee, one watches a screen that shows what's going on in the dorms, one sits at the narrow counter directly behind the place where you register. Beyond this area, there's more glass, through which, if she has the heart to look, she'll see each of the men brought down by a guard when his name is called through a microphone. These guards — here's the thing that always gets her about these guards — almost all of them are fat-rolling-over-the-belt heavy, under the belt too, like they've a basket of soft dough balancing on their puffy thighs, and they are always yucking it up. This is a county jail, not a prison; a big, big difference, Rudy says. Elmira: a lot less yuck going on there. In fact, Rudy says that most of these C.O.'s are okay.

More women stream in: women with small children, infants, toddlers. More older women, women with their daughters, the sisters of inmates. They line up — talk, laugh. These must be people who've been coming for weeks. The shock and shame have burned off; the negotiations are over. Some of their loved ones may come down wearing fluorescent orange suits. Their hearings are finished: They've been convicted. At least for a while, these women will get no more calls in the night. And here's another thing that always gets her: It's rare to see a man in these rooms. How many fathers drop their photo ID's into the trough? Carla knows this isn't fair. If Rudy's father was alive, he'd be here. For sure, Steve would be standing in this line, leaning forward, ready to take on anyone who tried to stop him.

The first woman is signed in. She goes to wait by the steel door that leads into the small locker and metal detector area. The girl moves up.

"Name?" the guard says, ready to write it all down in a big ledger.

"Darlene Baker."

"Name of the inmate you're visiting."

"Charles Dale."

"Relationship?"

"What?"

"What is your relationship to Charles Dale?"

"Girlfriend."

"Photo ID?"

"No."

"No?"

"No."

"You can't visit an inmate without a photo ID."

"I don't have a photo ID."

"You can't visit an inmate without a photo ID."

The girl whirls around so quickly, she almost runs into Carla. "Fucker," she says as she veers away.

Carla resists reaching out to try to get the girl to slow down, to not step off into the heavy traffic of her next twenty years. Instead Carla moves forward and places *her* license in the trough. Behind her, low but distinct, from the far end of the lobby, the girl says "Prick" just before the entry doors shut.

The guard slides Carla's license out, compares the picture with her face, a picture taken so long ago it looks more like Tess. "Carla Morletti," she says. "I'm here to see Rudy Morletti. He's my son."

The guard writes down her address, her phone number. She hears them call Rudy's name. If she watches, she'll see him brought down, wearing the dark blue jumpsuit. If she watches, she'll see that his arms are bare — no long sleeves allowed no matter how cold. But she doesn't watch. She turns her back to the window. She waits behind the other mother for the buzzer to allow them to pull the steel door open. She does not watch because if she does, she knows she will cry.

▪ ▪ ▪

[2]

# Genetic Drift

> Analogous structures — structures that are similar in different organisms because they evolved in a similar environment, rather than were inherited from a recent ancestor. Example: the torpedo body shape of porpoises and sharks.

Torpedo — that's what she should have compared Rudy to — less random than a tornado. With her book wedged against the steering wheel and her notebook on top of Queenie's sleeping head, she can take half-assed notes, but she keeps losing her place, going back and forth at this awkward angle. No doubt Rudy will charm or guilt-trip Mamo into staying the full hour. Talk her into believing he wasn't even in Danford that night.

Cold, but she doesn't want to run the heater. Got to conserve gas. No doubt she'll end up driving her mother to Roscoe, the closest bail bondsman. Probably just as well that they did impound Smithy's truck, that her mother has no vehicle right now. Otherwise, when Rudy gets out, he'd borrow Mamo's wheels or commandeer them. Certainly he's not taking *her* truck — even though it means going to bed with her keys.

> Homologous structures — body parts which are similar in different species because the species have a common descent.

When she gets to the library, she's going to google all the parts of the male brain, compare them with the female brain. She and Rudy have common ancestors, but no question, they've got different circuit breakers.

Tess's eye is caught by the flash of the jail doors bursting open as a teenage girl explodes into view. Speaking of torpedoes. If the unborn can register rage, the baby in her belly just got a jolt of seismic proportions. Clear that for some reason the girl's been denied admission. Tess watches to see what's going to happen next. The girl begins to rocket back and forth on the sidewalk, chin skyward, her mouth going. Then she halts abruptly and stretches out her T-shirt enough to pull each arm inside to hug her body, so that now as she rams, she looks like a double amputee, with triplets on the way. Must be she's been dropped off and likely her ride's not due back until four.

Tess tucks her book and notes into her duffle and dumps it over her shoulder. Queenie opens one eye. Tess rolls her window down and sticks her head out enough to yell. "Hey, want to wait in the truck? Cold out there."

The girl looks her way, but makes no moves of assent.

Tess opens the door and steps out, walks within non-shouting range. "My mom's visiting my brother. I'm going to be here for a while. You're welcome to sit inside until your ride comes."

Tess knows the girl is assessing her, taking in her tangled dreads — no doubt smelling faintly of cow shit from morning milking. Taking in her almost elderly status — hell, she's a good ten years older than this kid. No way to impress this teen that she's known "cool," not that long ago was the lead singer for the Texettes. "Best keyboard player the Wayside ever had" the local paper said.

No expression on the girl's face beyond a pissed sour-puss, but she does begin to advance. Tess slides back in and opens the passenger door. She lifts Queenie's warm bulk onto her lap. This girl may need a push from behind to lever her up, but you wouldn't want to venture to help unless asked. She starts the truck and flicks the heater fan on low. Take some time  before any warmth is going to blow out of those vents. From the girl either most likely.

The girl manages to lift herself up. Then she pulls her arms inside her shirt again. Her thin blond hair's skinned back so tight it's got to be pulling and her jaw is clamped down so hard Tess expects to hear the grinding of teeth.

"I'm Tess," she says, "and this is Queenie." She lifts Queenie's paw to make a small wave. Maybe Queenie's meditative calm will absorb some of the fury.

The girl huffs out a great blast of breath. "Fuckers won't let me visit. No fucking ID. No fucking photo ID." And then, she begins to cry, terrible cries that fill the truck.

Queenie rises and begins to nuzzle one of the girl's empty sleeves. Tess reaches under the seat for the paper towels and places one on the shelf of the girl's heaving abdomen.

The girl pulls her arms free, and after a few more shuddering moments and some delicate nose-blowing, she says, "Me not showing up like I promised will probably upset Charlie so much, he'll get himself into trouble. Already a couple of guys in his dorm are giving him the business."

"That's got to be rough," Tess says.

Finally the girl turns toward Tess and places her hand on Queenie's head. "I'm Darlene. I appreciate you letting me wait here. My friend's not coming until four and it was fucking freezing out there."

Tess ups the fan to maximum. Not much else she can offer. "Likely I'm going to be here 'til then."

"The really rough part is he's going to try to call me, but my brother's phone's been shut off and my brother's so pissed about everything, he's kicked me out. Phone's going to ring and nobody's going to say hello. Jail-call computer probably won't stay on long enough to talk to the 'number not in service' computer."

"Jesus," Tess says. Got to get the vet tech degree, save up the money to go somewhere warm, walk along the beach with Queenie. Get a job at some exotic zoo.

"Thing is, even if I put a letter in the mail today, Charlie won't get it until Tuesday — three days of thinking something bad happened to me."

She is not going to ask this girl — Darlene — if she has a place to stay. She's not even going to tell Mamo Darlene's desperate plight. Mamo, Rudy, Darlene, and looks like any minute, this baby — all living at the house. No.

As though Darlene has read her mind, she says, "Until Monday I'm staying with the friend who's picking me up — her father says not a day beyond that — but first thing Monday morning, I'll go to Social Services. They'll take one look at me and find me a place in a shelter or something. Somehow I got to let Charlie know I'm okay and that he's not to get into any trouble at the jail. I tell you, one more thing turns to shit and I am going to lose it."

Seems like a totally rational next response.

Darlene's face brightens. "Say, you think your brother might call you today or tomorrow and you could tell him, if he sees Charlie — Charles Dale — to give Charlie a quick rundown of what's happened?"

Likely from here Tess is going to be taxiing her mother around trying to rustle up the five hundred to pay the bail bondsman. Plus all depends on Rudy's mood as to whether he could even be counted on to do a good deed.

Tess takes a breath, closes her eyes, and makes the leap. "How about this? I'll go in and give Charlie your message right now."

"You think they'd let you in to see him? You'd do that?"

Tess pulls her sweatshirt over her head. "They won't let me in there in this. Put that over you because I'm going to have shut off the truck. Smells like cow manure because I work on a dairy farm." She gets her license from her bag and throws her keys under the seat. Trusts Darlene more than the lockers. She steps out. "Anything else you want me to tell him?"

"No, I'll write him a long, long letter."

Just before Tess gets to the entrance, she hears Darlene yell, "Tell him I love him."

No point in turning around to shout back, *Don't.*

Tess moves down the aisle toward the one inmate without a visitor sitting opposite him on the other side of the Plexiglas barrier. "Darlene," she mouths across the distance to his wary expression.

Carla and Rudy are next to Charles Dale, with one empty place between. When Carla sees Tess, she gives a welcoming smile, but Tess passes her by. "I'll explain later," she says.

The guard shifts his walkie-talkie to a more alert position. He runs his eyes up the row of eight inmates and down the other side. All of these men are young and dressed in blue, like they're on the same sports team.

Tess doesn't look at Rudy. Instead she keeps her focus on Charles Dale, who's gripping the edge of the counter with both hands. Charles Dale's face, a chubby face that doesn't look old enough to cause anyone serious trouble, gets ready.

The visitation room is divided down the middle by a low Formica counter about three feet wide, with a dozen or so attached stools on either side. Inmates and visitors are separated by a plastic window bolted to the center of the counter. Children must remain in the lap of the parent. The visitor and the inmate may embrace at the close of the visit by standing and leaning toward each other over the divider. The visitor may leave at any time within the hour, but the inmate must stay until the visitation period is over at which time he will be strip-searched, including a gloved finger up his rectum to make sure no one has slipped him any drugs or weapons.

Carla and Rudy stop talking. Neither turns, but both watch from the corners of their eyes, both cock their heads toward Tess, listening, listening. The guard speaks quietly into the walkie-talkie, then once again leans against the wall.

As soon as Tess reaches Charles Dale, she says, "Darlene's okay. She's sitting in my truck in the parking lot. They wouldn't let her in to visit because she doesn't have a photo ID." In order to be heard, she must lift herself up a little to throw her voice over the divider.

Charles Dale's hands let go of the counter.

Now Carla does turn. "Good for you, Tess," she says.

Tess motions *stop* to cut Carla off. The guard drifts along behind the row of inmates, a bit suspicious.

To Rudy, Carla says, "The girl in the lobby I told you about."

Tess sits on her knees, so her voice can reach Charles without raising the volume. "Darlene's brother's phone has been shut off, so you won't be able to call, but you'll get a letter Tuesday explaining everything."

The clock says 3:59.

Charles Dale lifts his head and looks at Tess straight on. "Tell her I'm okay. Tell her not to worry and … thank you."

"She says to tell you … she loves you."

"Ahhh," Carla says.

Charles takes in a gulp of air and then he laughs. "Well, tell her I love her, too."

"Time," the guard says. "Time."

Rudy rises, hugs Carla, waves to Tess. "Hey, Sis, long time no see."

Tess turns to leave. "Not since Papo's funeral four years ago," she says.

"Don't bother calling until the latest you can," Carla tells Rudy. "If I don't accept the call, you'll know I'm still working on getting bail."

The visitors all line up. The door to the lockers slides open, then closes slowly behind them once they're all out. They pass through the metal detector. A little girl with pink barrettes totters against Carla's leg while her mother gets her things. The girl looks up at Carla, studies her with large dark eyes.

"Oh," Carla says, "break my heart."

The buzzer sounds and the big steel door unlocks. They file through. No one says anything. Carla and Tess push out into the March wind. They shiver.

The truck is empty. One less complication to further tangle in the wreckage.

"What a shame," Carla says. "Now you can't deliver the message. I hope that poor girl has got somebody good to take her in. Did you get some sort of contact number?"

"No," Tess says. "No, I did not."

▪ ▪ ▪

[3]

# Other times I can barely see.

Carla zips her jacket until the zipper scrapes against her chin, then turns up the heat as far as it'll go. "I'm going to reimburse you for the gas as soon as my check comes," she says.

Maybe Tess nods. Maybe she didn't even hear. She seems to be far, far away. Her all-grown-up daughter, who ran off to Texas when she was eighteen to sing in a girl band. All her efforts to be a better parent, but in the end, Tess seems as angry with her as Carla was with her own mother all those years. Ran away from home herself at fifteen. She and her friend Vickie, sneaking off in the night. From Newark to Monterey. Hitching with truckers. And now her mother's coming from California to stay with them for a few months. Her mother who she hasn't seen in such a long time she can't remember when.

Carla watches Tess's profile as she drives. What's she thinking? Maybe seeing Rudy look so good, so clean, broke through. She turns a little in the seat to better gauge Tess's mood and eye the speedometer at the same time. Fifty. If the needle goes up one more mile on these windy roads, she's going to protest.

She tries again — "Well?" — and when Tess doesn't respond, she flashes a hand past Tess's dead-ahead gaze.

"I'm here," Tess says.

That's it: two words.

They bump along the dirt road in silence for a while, but when they reach the main highway, Tess makes the turn so fast, Carla has to once again grab the door. She presses her foot down hard on the truck floor, the nonexistent brake. As if Tess registers her panic, she slows and relaxes against the seat.

Tess scratches her head, stirs up a whiff of barn. If she didn't twist it into that ratty mess, she's got the loveliest hair, just like Carla's before it started to frizz up gray. Carla can't figure why Tess doesn't have a boyfriend, nobody after Mark Merrick and that was so brief, maybe it didn't even happen. And herself, except for these months since Smithy's death … since she was fourteen, almost twenty years married to Steve … has she ever been without a man?

"Well?" she says again, upping the volume, and when Tess still doesn't respond, she adds, "Then just tell me this: By any stretch, would you call a baseball bat a deadly weapon?"

In answer to this, Tess raises her hand from the wheel as if to ward off anything further.

"Tess, you think that girl, Sonny, is mixed up in any of this? Sonny … girl with the nickname of a little boy, girl with a name like that's bound to cause trouble."

"Woman. Sunny's at least thirty-two."

"Girl … woman, whichever, she's been running around with Rudy for years. Must be she's not a very good influence either."

Tess gives her a long one-eyed look and tightens her grip on the wheel, "What? Now you're going to blame Rudy's behavior on his girlfriend?"

"Thing I'm wondering is why didn't he call *her* instead of me?"

"Maybe when she saw the jail number on her caller ID, she had the good sense not to pick up the phone."

"Also I'm wondering why haven't I had one glimpse of this Sonny in all these years — not since she graduated from high school. Not since she was that sweet-looking girl who played the trumpet, holding it right up high in the front row? Remember … that same concert when you sat up there on the stage and played the piano. Your father and me not even knowing where you learned such a thing."

Carla pulls out a ragged spiral notebook: old lists, emergency numbers. "You got something to write with?"

"In with my registration."

The glove compartment is tidy. At least one good habit she's passed on to her daughter. "This little stub of a pencil. That's it?"

Tess gives her another look.

On the inside cover of the notebook, Carla writes "William Granley, Stanton," the name of the lawyer Rudy said one of the trusties told him is a pro at getting felonies reduced. But how's she going to come up with the money for even the bail bondsman, let alone a lawyer? No disability check for two weeks and anyway she needs every cent of that to pay the electric, the rest of the bills. And she is not, she is not going to ask Tess to dip into her student loan funds.

A folded square of greasy paper falls from between the pages. The sheet Mark Merrick gave her way back in October when Tess was driving him to rehab. Mark? No news of him in a long time. Carla unfolds the paper even though she knows what it says by heart.

"R.E.B.T.": Rational something. She never did know what the E.B.T. stood for.

1. You are responsible for your own emotions and actions.
2. Your harmful emotions and dysfunctional behaviors are the product of your irrational thinking.
3. You can learn more realistic views and, with practice, make them part of you.

But it's number four — highlighted and underlined twice with wobbly lines — that still feels like some distant town she's limping toward:

4. You'll experience a deeper sense of acceptance of yourself and greater satisfaction in your life by developing a reality-based perspective.

She's doing better than she was, but "satisfaction" isn't the word she'd use to describe it.

"Tess, you ever hear anything about Mark since he went off to halfway?"

"Nope."

"You think he's going to make it?"

Tess shrugs.

Carla presses hard on both sides of her nose. Already she's got a terrible pain behind her eyes and Rudy's not even out yet. Plus both wrists ache, an ache that goes all the way to her elbows. She pulls her braces from under the seat and adjusts the Velcro bands so they're not too tight.

Can't ask their old friend Nooley for a loan. Not after what Smithy and Rudy did. At least she's pretty sure it was them. Stole Nooley's marijuana harvest money right out of his garage. Can't ask Del Merrick — that's for double sure — never paid back the five hundred Del loaned her for bail years ago when Rudy got busted at a Dead concert. The pain's worse behind the right eye. Hot lights explode. A migraine coming on.

"You got any Tylenol?"

"Ibuprofen."

"Can't do that to my stomach."

"See," Tess says, and speeds up again, as though the weight of her foot on the accelerator is the measure of just how angry she is.

"But doesn't he look good?" Carla can't resist pushing a little more, with one eye again on the speedometer. "He always was a beautiful child. You, too, Tess."

Tess takes a deep breath and eases back to forty-five. "You know what they say."

Evidently she's decided he's not worth careening over the bank for.

Carla lightly takes hold of Tess's shoulder, jiggles it a little. "Tell me the truth: Doesn't it hurt your heart to see him in there and maybe for something he didn't even do? Public defender's doing nothing for him. Three messages on his machine, but he never gets back to me. I need to fill that man in on what Rudy's never going to tell him."

On that one, Tess leans a little her way. "What?" she says.

"I need to tell him Rudy's got a diagnosed mental illness."

"Are you saying that lets Rudy off the hook?"

"I'm not saying that, but that's part of it and his lawyer ought to know." She taps Tess's knee. "But at least right now there's no wild look in his eyes."

Tess shakes her head. "I'm sticking to my original warning: Take cover."

"Sometimes I wonder if Rudy really is crazy ... bipolar like that psychiatrist said. The not sleeping, the thinking everybody's out to get him, the being ready to go off at the drop of a pin. And a few weeks later, he seems as sane as you and me."

Tess laughs at this.

"What? Why are you laughing?"

Tess makes the turn toward Stanton, much slower this time.

Carla's body eases down a notch. "And here's another thing, Tess. Your Gramma DeLuca called last night. Maybe she's going to come and stay for a few months, get her strength back. Chemo about did her in."

"She's coming to *our* house to recuperate?"

Carla rests her forehead against the cold window. Her mother: almost no contact since Carla left home over thirty-five years ago. Except for the fake Christmas phone calls: "We're fine. How are you?" The thank-yous for the presents. Yeah, it has been over twenty years since her mother's seen Tess or Rudy. When she and Vickie ran off, she didn't even leave her mother a note. Well, she's paying for it now.

All along the highway nothing but black snow and the leavings of winter, the hills hopeless and gray. Falling-down barns, trailers with a lot of junk in the yards. Welcome to Upstate New York. March — whenever she complains about March, Tess tells her somebody or other says April is the meanest month, but for her vote, March wins, no contest. And where *is* she going to get the money for the bail bondsman?

They take a right onto Main. Tess finally turns her way, an honest-to-goodness look of concern. "You want to stop at the store for Tylenol?"

Queenie straddles Carla's legs, pushes her nose against the window. Air, she wants air. Easier to read Queenie's mind. "Oh, Tess, you can't fool me."

Tess laughs. "Mamo, you be fooled up one side and down the other."

"The thing is, I've got to come up with the bail. I believe him. There was no baseball bat."

They pass the Edgewater Bar & Grill; its sagging porch still leans toward the brook. The Edgewater, where Carla used to bartend, ten, fifteen years ago, listening to men one-upping each other. Same busted Coors sign blinks in the window.

"Stop," Carla says. "Stop right here."

▪ ▪ ▪

*Doing Time Outside*

[4]

# Society has decreed that you be in our custody.

Rudy sits as far away from the other trusties, the crap blasting from the TV, as he can. He presses both hands against his ears to better hear the last part of his letter:

> Sunny — All Im asking is that you let me know your ok even if you dont want to let me know where you are. The sadness Ive caused you — you who have already had so much of that — Im sorry. But I hope you sometimes remember the good days. Those are what I keep turning back to in this dark time.

He crosses out "the good days" and writes in Portland, Toronto, the city. Or maybe he should say: "Remember, Sunny, the time on our way to Blue Mountain Lake when it was raining so hard we had to leave the motorcycle in the ditch. 'I can't believe it,' you kept saying when we found a lean-to with a stack of dry wood and a double sleeping bag wrapped in plastic, pinned to it a note, 'Please leave me for the next wayfarer in trouble.' 'That's us for sure,' you said."

So many trips … following the Dead when Garcia was still alive. All this past couple of years. On and off. Off and on. Of course he won't mention how so many of their other trips ended in his drug-fueled detours.

He scans the letter again. Does he really want to say "dark time"? So pitiful. But it's true, the darkest time he can ever remember. Main thing is to make no excuses. "No more excuses, Rudy," the last thing she said. Does she know about his fight with Keegan? That he's in jail?

He fixes all the missing apostrophes. The places where they ought to be flash at him as he moves along the lines. What lessons have you learned? I finally get fucking contractions. He changes "agresive" to "angry." What he needs is a dictionary instead of shelves full of wanky Westerns. He can hardly call out "How do you spell?'" to any of these miscreants. "Miscreants": one of Aaron Merrick's favorite words.

Speaking of same, Kendrick shouts over the TV's blare, "What you doing, Morletti, writing the judge to say you're sorry?"

Going to have to wait until he's back in his cell to finish this. Otherwise his desire to take Kendrick by the throat is going to pulse its way into the words proving to Sunny once again that he *is* trouble. Plus cause him to lose his trusty status. And goodbye forever to any hope of bail.

Rudy folds the letter. Of course no pockets, so when the C.O. isn't looking, he tucks the paper into his jail bootie. Kendrick eyeballing him all the while, but knowing if he calls that out to the C.O., Rudy *will* get even.

One streak of light in this darkness is that since fixing the jail's antique dishwasher, he's been made a trusty with a work assignment. This got him out of the dorms where definitely the shit was about to go down. He was starting to get the bewaries, which always meant the white-coat swat team would land soon to give him a double shot of Thorazine. Or maybe in jail they'd just Taser him. No question his mental health's much improved by having a cell of his own and only three other thugs to be pals with in the rec area.

He returns the pencil to the C.O. and goes to the jail call box *again*. Dials. Again he turns his back on his fellow trusties who now track him like he's their favorite reality show asshole.

Ring. Ring. Ring.

His hope for a human Hello dies. So … why doesn't he hang the fuck up? But no, he's into self-inflicted agony; otherwise why would he wait for the machine's computer message in case, in case, against all odds, his mother's rushing up the walk, down the stairs to reach him?

"Please leave a message after the tone."

He waits for the jail computer recording, ready to wrap the phone cord around his throat as he listens to it one more time:

"This is a collect call from" — "Rudy," he says — "an inmate at the Onango County Jail. No custom calling features allowed. If you have any questions, please call 888 236-8444. The cost for this call is … one dollar and seventy-six cents … for the first minute and … eighteen cents … a minute after that."

"Rudy-Tootie, you going to suck on that phone all night trying to get your mommy? Don't you got a little girlfriend you could call instead?"

Rudy turns to face Kendrick, but keeps his ear tight to the receiver, "Fuck off, Ken-Dick."

"If you do not wish to accept this call, please hang up. If you do wish to accept, please press zero now."

Rudy replaces the receiver. "Because if you don't, I'm going to tell you a few things about *your* mama."

The floor officer looks up from his acrostic book, raises his pencil in warning.

Rudy does his air-guitar routine: Every Good Boy Does Fine. His practiced fingers hit the fantasy chord full and true. Kendrick laughs and settles back in front of the idiot-box with the other two trusties. The officer nods and returns to circling letters.

"You really think someone's going to bail your ugly ass out of here," Gaugan says. "Got you tucked away … out of their hair. Not a chance."

Rudy goes over to the table, deals himself five cards off the bottom. He sings, soft and low: " 'Watch each card you play and play it slow, wait until the deal comes round, don't let that deal go down.' "

"Whoa, take it on the road, Morletti. You and Eminem," Gaugan yells.

Not a single pair. Highest card an eight. And no way he can get a letter to her anyhow: Whereabouts unknown. Sunny's gone. Aaron's gone too. Gone gone.

Kendrick surrenders the remote to the new guy, O'Hara. "Tomorrow you'll be pushing the mops around with the rest of us, delivering the trays," Kendrick says.

"Money on it …"

Once again the C.O. looks their way.

Rudy sinks down in his chair, waggles his fingers. "Tomorrow: empty space where me and my music used to be."

Forty-four steps between the TV and the phone. Forty-four times at least fifty trips.

"You're going to wear a groove in the floor," Kendrick says.

All the rules and regulations are posted on the wall behind the call box. Improve your reading skills while you wait. Get your *d*'s and *p*'s and *g*'s all turned in the right direction.

Once again Rudy dials the number and waits for his mother's machine.

> **2. Inmates are required to submit to a search of their person at any time.**

Waits for the "This is a collect call."

> **6. No sheets are to be tied to the bars to cover going to the bathroom.**

Says his name.

> **10. Entering any cell other than your own is not permitted.**

Waits for the computer to say "press zero now."

> **31. The staff does not carry keys that will allow you to reach outside the facility.**

Hangs up the receiver.

> **8. Wearing a disguise or possessing one is prohibited.**

10:30. Almost time to commence lockdown. Bail is more and more in doubt. Proof that being justified is no guarantee.

"You can give it another go tomorrow, Morletti, after your duties are done," the C.O. says. "Time to line up for the count."

Goin' down that same dark hole … Gotta claw back up … You still thinkin' I'm a fool … Gotta dig back out … To a world that's sweet an' cruel … back up, back up. His callused fingers play the chords: A, C, E. Minor, all of it minor.

And it's a lie that he only wants to know she's okay. What he wants is find out where she went, so he can knock on her door, try one more time not to fuck it up.

Rudy folds the jumpsuit, places it in the bin, pushes the bin beneath the bed. He sets his booties side by side, tucks the letter under the mattress. He pulls the blanket all the way up against the cold. The jail is always cold. This is a jail. A jail is a jail. His cell door clanks shut. The clang of cells being locked echoes through the building.

Lights down, but never all the way out. Never darkness. The camera is always watching. The C.O. running the monitors sees you lying on this bed. Does he believe what it says in the rules?

> … that each person here is an individual and possesses
> the dignity inherent in every human being.

▪ ▪ ▪

*Doing Time Outside*

[5]

# Crawl Space

Tess slides the paper out of Mamo's bag and then closes her mother's bedroom door without making a sound. Let her sleep. Up half the night, vomiting in the bathroom. Have to google "migraines," see if they're one more thing she may be in line for. Start a list of her predispositions: bipolar disorder — or whatever they're calling wacko this week — substance abuse, heart trouble, breast cancer … At least it looks like she's managed to duck arrested development.

She holds the paper up to the kitchen window to make sure it's the right one. Yep, bail bondsman's unreadable flourish at the bottom, his stamp of guarantee. Everything all set with the jail anyway. Unless the guy was talking into dead air on the phone last night. He looked legit, nothing sleazy. Though it took forever to track him down, which meant coming home in the middle of the night to the hysteria of a million jail calls on the machine. Frustration level for Rudy always was minus-ten.

Queenie's curled in the chair by the stove.

"Get any closer, Queenie, you'd catch on fire."

Queenie's ears twitch, but her bulldog jaw stays between her paws. Sun's not even up yet for godsake.

"At least we don't have to go milk, ehh?"

Queenie does open her eyes to this news.

Tess rakes the coals forward and loads the stove. That they have a box full of seasoned, dry wood inside, plus three or four face cords under cover on the back porch this late in March, is proof she and Mamo have finally got the upstate-winter thing knocked. A world without Smithy or Rudy.

She pulls two bananas free and takes her mother's sweater from the hook. Might as well not go in there smelling like a barn. "Rise and shine, Queen, if you're planning on going."

She and Queenie step onto the porch. Red sky beyond the bare black trees. No wind. The smell of mud, spring heading her way. The sun'll be up over the hill any minute. She backs the truck out, feels the give of winter ruts.

Her mother's blinds are still down. No point in both of them going to get Rudy anyway. Besides, with Rudy a captive in the truck, she can do some exploratory surgery, see if he's really had a change of heart. Or is he still blaming the world for all his shit-luck? And she is not going to ask about Sunny: less she knows about that, less chance the mess is going to mess with her. Funny though that as long as Rudy and Sunny were together, they never had a baby. Proof Sunny's got some sense.

She shifts gears. "Here we go, Queenie, heading for bad weather."

8:15, and already Tess has been standing at this reception window for close to an hour while one guard takes a trainee, hunt and peck, through the whole out-on-bail computer process. No call has been put through to anyone beyond this area to advise them that Rudy Morletti is about to be released.

Tess leans toward the window. No opening to speak into, only the inch-high access to the metal trough to make thin exchanges. Though larger items — say a suit and tie for your trial, if your family can purchase such a costume — may be placed in a steel compartment in the wall after this outer compartment is buzzed open. Once the clothes are screened for explosives, the inner door can be unlocked, your suit delivered.

"Excuse me," Tess says to the bent heads. "Would it be possible to let my brother know I'm here? Otherwise he's going to call and call my mother. She's going to think there's been a catastrophe."

Both men look up. Shake their heads.

"She's ill and this anxiety will only make it worse."

"Once the paperwork's done and you've signed, we'll move on to the next step," the guard with the American flag insignia says. Both men return their focus to the computer screen.

8:30. The trainee gives all the forms one last check. Then he pushes a carbonized pad into the trough. "Sign on the line," he says.

When this is completed, the trainee gives Tess the white copy. "Like it says at the bottom: The inmate's hearing date is at 4 p.m., April 6, 2003, in the Town of Danford Court. If Rudolph Morletti fails to appear, bail is forfeited. The Order of Protection is still in force."

"Is that it?" Tess says.

Town of Danford Court. Her boss, Hoop Dawes, the honorable judge. Small world justice: Always the speculation has been that Rudy might be the father of Hoop's daughter Katie's kid — back before Rudy took up with Sunny. A kid that's got to be ten or eleven by now. If that's true, she'd bet money it's a child Rudy's in complete denial about. Anyway, how can someone be called the father or the mother of a child they've never even held?

As she nears the exit, she resists doing a Darlene. Outside, she lifts herself into the truck and restrains the urge to bang the door shut. Why damage her own property? "If it wasn't for you, Queenie, I'd throw a fit."

Tess stares out at March: a flat gray sky that says 'Get through this, you can get through anything.' She pulls the course description for Wildlife Handling VET 260 AZEW out of her duffle. A zoo where the sun shines almost every day of the year. Apes or cats? She can't decide which.

One hour later the jail doors crash open and Rudy catapults through. She starts the truck, gets ready. She knows his first burst will contain the word "fuck." He's all in black, your standard Hell's Angels get-up. Probably Papo's leather jacket, same worn ridges she remembers. A bandana holds his hair back and his face is hairy. He's got Papo's build as well. And yes, there've times been when he had some of Papo's goodness. But not lately and not now. A beautiful child maybe, but right this minute, he's a compacted hunch of anger coming at her.

Queenie leaps into the back. Just before impact, step aside.

Rudy rips the door open, hurls himself into the truck. "Where the fuck have you been?" he says. "Got a cigarette? A shot of whiskey?"

Tess adjusts her rearview and backs out.

"Mamo said you left before dawn. Five more minutes and I'd have taken that fat fucker Kendrick by the throat. I need a cigarette *now.*" He holds his shaking hands up for her to observe. Papo's hands, too.

Rudy leans forward, presses his fingers against the dashboard. "Jail," he says. "Remember the time I locked you in the crawl space? Forgot you there all day?" He raises his hands in excitement. "Pull in at that gas station."

She does.

"Would you go in? Cheapest full flavors they've got. I'm not ready for the public."

Tess doesn't move.

Rudy opens the door. "You got five dollars?"

Tess turns the truck off.

Rudy takes an envelope from his pocket. He pulls out a check and holds it up for her to see. "Commissary refund. Five dollars and thirty-two cents. But I can't be using that in there. No ID for one thing."

She hands him a pen. "Sign the back." She counts out five ones, three dimes and two pennies.

Rudy gives her the check and steps out. "Is that how it's going to be?"

Tess nods.

He starts for the store. She watches him gather himself together. Her brother.

Soon Rudy's back outside. He lights a cigarette, walks to the edge of the highway, turns toward the open fields. Smokes. Smokes.

Maybe she has the energy to tell him she doesn't want him smoking in the truck. Maybe she doesn't. And now their grandmother's coming to stay for a while, a person she and Rudy know only through Merry Christmas calls. Tess's chest tightens: one more knot in an already tense tangle.

In a few minutes, Rudy gets back in. She turns toward home. Four cords of wood on the porch. Her tuition paid for this semester. Her job at Hoop Dawes's. Hunker down and try to stay out of the storm.

Rudy closes his eyes. Queenie climbs into the front, settles on Rudy's lap. He strokes her ears. "Queenie," he says.

That's it. His only words for thirty miles. Finally, when Tess turns the truck up Cobb's Road, Rudy comes to, begins to look around. Across the field, the brook, Del Merrick's stone house. "They living there?"

"Rented out," she says.

"Mark?"

She shrugs.

Rudy's alert now, seems to tense up at any changes they pass: new houses going up, the old barn by Grat's Bend finally in full collapse. All this since her return to living home in November, a few weeks after Mamo broke her leg and they drove Mark to rehab. And Rudy's maybe not been up this road since before Smithy O.D.'d. Maybe not since he stole Smithy's truck last July.

Rudy hums a bit of an old Dylan song, one of Papo's favorites. She whisper-sings it, can't help herself. Rudy joins in: "And too much of nothing can make a man a liar. Cause one man to sleep on nails. Others to eat fire."

She turns onto Chicken Farm Road, pulls up to the house. She and Mamo have cleaned up the yard, fixed the steps, taken down the broken swing. Only thing left: the Maverick. Got to get her mother to give up any hopes for that junker. Send it off to the crusher. There's smoke coming from the chimney, a good fire going. Mamo has fed the stove.

Rudy pats the rear bumper of the old car, kicks one of the tires, then he turns to face her. "You hear anything about where Sunny went?"

She shakes her head.

"All that karma shit, Sis — you were right about that."

▪ ▪ ▪

*Doing Time Outside*

[6]

# Wings of a Dove

Tess stops to scan the big arrival/departure screen just inside the Continental terminal.

"Plane's on time," she says. "Concord C, Gate 40. It should be landing in about twenty minutes."

"And how may I ask do you know that?"

Tess tilts Carla's head toward the schedules and points: "See halfway down: Flight 2465, 3:50. The escalators are this way." She steers Carla in that direction.

"How come we can't see any planes?" Carla takes hold of both sides of the escalator and plants her foot right in the middle of the moving step. "Good thing you're here or I'd be running around like a chicken. I tell you I'd take a Greyhound bus before I'd ever go up in one of those things. Especially these days. Somebody getting on with a bomb in his shoe."

"You think it's safer to hitch with truckers or ride on the back of a Harley cross-country?"

A skinny person … maybe a girl, maybe not … all visible surfaces tattooed with snakes, begins to press into Carla. If the person had a siren it'd blare on at full volume.

"Your house on fire?" Carla says.

The head swivels, the eyes flash. Tess places her arm across Carla's chest to clear a path and in one bound the person is up the steps and gone.

"You ever see *The Exorcist?* If that one sat down next to me on a plane, I'd have to cancel my trip."

When they get to the top, Tess turns toward a row of leather benches.

"No, no," Carla says, "we got to be right there when she gets off. She sounded so weak on the phone, I'm thinking we may have to practically carry her to the truck. Not that she ever was any ball of fire. 'Lay down and walk all over me' her main position."

"You sure this woman's really *your* mother. Hard to think you swam up out of the same gene pool."

"Ha, ha. Main thing is I was determined. Determined not to be like that. A rag doll some man could shake any old which-a-way. We better find Gate 40 quick."

"This is as close as we can get." Tess sits down on one of the benches and pats a place beside her. "Anyone going beyond here has to have a ticket and go through security. All arriving passengers will be coming through those doors. Luckily we don't have to go to claim any bags since she already sent her luggage UPS."

Carla sinks down and begins to root around in her large pocketbook.

"Tess, I haven't really given your grandmother the full rundown on Rudy, so I'm thinking we can kind of let her get clued slowly after she's had a chance to settle."

"Yeah, if you'd given her the unexpurgated true-crime story, she might have chosen to fly to Hawaii to recuperate by the sea, rather than be on hand for visits from the narc squad."

"Tess …"

"Reality, Mamo. Rudy keeping it together … well, we'd have to call it a long shot."

"Another thing: sounds like your Grandmother's gotten very religious in the last few years. Mass, Confession, the rosary, the Hail Marys … Why are you laughing?"

"Who knows maybe she'll get us all cleaned up and converted. Get Rudy narrow and straight."

"I thought you just said 'reality,' Tess. Anyway if I get much straighter, much more reformed, you can poke me through the eye of a needle. You, too. No vices, unless you're up to something undercover."

"Mamo, twenty years since you've seen your mother. Maybe you won't even recognize her. She may not know us either. I figure I was about eight the last time she came to Danford. Right after your father died."

"Don't get me started on *that* man." Carla pulls what was once a large tinted studio portrait out of an envelope marked 1961. Half of the photo has been cut away. The only evidence there was originally another person in the picture is a large hand, draped across a woman's right shoulder.

Carla holds the severed photo out so the two of them can study it. "My mother, Angela DeLuca, your age, twenty-eight. I was about eleven when this was taken. Your uncle Bobby was ten. T.J. nine."

A lovely woman with a mass of dark hair and a shy smile. A woman who looks so much like the women looking at her, it startles them.

"You're the one who cut your father out of the picture?"

Carla nods.

"When did you do that?"

She counts on her fingers. "He died in '82. A few years before that, I took the scissors to him. I'm not nearly as angry with him as I once was." She tilts the picture a little more toward the light. "See those scars across his knuckles. He got those riding his bicycle too close to a speeding train. He was eight or nine years older than your grandmother. A stroke. Just like your dad."

"And Papo? Are you still as angry with him."

"Oh, no. I always loved your father. Even when I hated him."

"So what do you think made it go so wrong?"

Carla tears up. Maybe she's looking for the answer to that. Maybe not.

Just then a lot of people begin to stream through the archway. Carla and Tess rise, start to search for a woman who may still look something like both of them when they get to be seventy, plus or minus the chemo treatments and years of submission.

And then, there's someone being pushed along in a wheelchair. A frail woman, a pale woman, wearing a terrible black wig. A wig that makes them both want to turn away.

She sees them. "One moment," she tells the airport attendant. Then she rises up and moves toward them, her face a glow of joy. She takes them both in her arms. Who would think such thin arms could encircle so much and with such force?

"Here we are at last," she cries. A laughing cry. She kisses Carla on both her Italian cheeks. Then places her hands on her granddaughter's face. "Tess, sweet Tess, what a beautiful child you are."

▪ ▪ ▪

[7]

# Daily Bread

*"If you love him you'll forgive him … Stand by your man …"*

Who can believe Tammy Wynette is still giving that advice? Carla eases the twelve-pack onto the bar. Same tired done-me-wrong songs on that juke box as when she worked here in a previous life. Or if not the same, the same. What she needs is "You just kinda wasted my precious time" instead of this "And he beats me too" hooey.

Carla pushes the beer, one bottle at a time, into the ice at the far corner of the cooler. The pain in her wrist is worse than a toothache, but shoving the bottles from this side is the only way to do it until Dirk gets the door on the other section fixed. Don't hold your breath.

Willie Jones gives her a bleary look and a wan wave. Willie Jones, in his permanent slump at the end of the bar. The day she looks up and sees that stool empty will be the day she sends a condolence card to his family.

"What can I get you, Willie?" Of course she knows exactly what, but throwing a question at him now and then sometimes forces him to surface.

But no, he's past the point of contact. All he can muster is a small push of his empty glass in her direction.

*"Give him two arms to cling to … When nights are cold and lonely …"*

She'd like to give the guy who keeps playing this song a karate chop. She glances over her shoulder to see if anybody needs a refill. Ollie Burke and Ron Luger swivel their eyes away from her rear. Time was she might have felt a stir of heat in response, but all it means now is maybe a few more dollars in tips: the sooner she can pay off Dirk's five-hundred advance for the bail bondsman.

Business is so slow, it's a wonder Dirk could take the risk she'd be good for it. And no question, given her aches and pains, the hassle of lining up rides to and fro, well, it's a semi-miracle she hasn't missed a day of work yet. Though she has to be careful not to rack up too many hours or she'll end up losing her disability. She hefts another twelve-pack onto the counter. It's a little easier loading into the front corner.

She catches Willie in her periphery. His next order will be in code: two taps of his glass thunk thunk on the bar, which means "and give me a shot of Jim Beam, too." If Willie was driving, she'd have to shut him down. No question tending bar can be depressing.

One good thing at least: she's pretty sure so far Rudy's staying clean. She checks his pupils every chance she gets. Still no response from the public defender beyond one visit with Rudy in jail. Secretary says he's got all he needs for the hearing. If only they could afford a lawyer who'd put some energy into getting the felony counts reduced to misdemeanors, and it'd be good if the court would make Rudy go to the Chemical Dependency Clinic. Somebody who does that Rational thing. Her old counselor Joy was good, but mostly she just listened. What Rudy needs is a team of wild horses that'll drag him to CDC. That and some med that will about knock him out.

Carla closes the cooler and rubs her wrists. She downs three Tylenols.

But Rudy's got to get himself a job right after the hearing if he doesn't end up going to jail. She can't keep buying him cigarettes. Though Rudy with money — well, easier to step off into trouble. Her mother's not quite as bouncy as she appeared at the airport, but definitely one good thing about having her with them now, Rudy has become her special concern. Maybe she can wrap that rosary of hers around his neck and hang on.

"Carla, any chance you could rustle up a burger, something for a hungry man?" Ollie Burke says.

Kitchen's closed is the correct answer to this.

*"And show the world you love him … Keep giving all the love you can …"*

"Tell you what, Ollie, you make sure that song never gets played again, and I'll fix you a hamburger. How you want it?"

She takes the meat out of the fridge and gives it the smell test. Right on the brink of take-it-home-for-Queenie. She breaks off a hungry-man hunk, still got that dyed-red exterior, but the center's going gray.

There's the bang of the front door out in the pool room. She checks the mirror above the stove. Jesus Christ. Prager. Larry Prager. First she's seen him since Smithy's funeral. And looking like he's on something for sure. Looking like if you crossed him, he'd let you have it right between the eyes. He glances back to the kitchen and heads straight for her. She flips the burger, pushes the bun into the toaster.

Prager leans against the door, lights a cigarette.

"I hear Rudy's staying up at your place. Must be your phone's not listed. Tell him to give me a call if he'd like to come back to the mill. I could pick him up mornings. John's short on help."

She uses the big knife, chops it down hard so it thuds into the board. The onion slices fall away, thick and white. She doesn't look up, but it's like she can feel some of the darkness lift. The front door slams. Prager is gone. Tell Rudy about the job: when hell freezes over.

■ ■ ■

*Doing Time Outside*

[8]

# Gone

Tess goes through the list again out loud: "Adaptation, Genetic Drift, Gene Flow, Mutation …" She pulls her truck in beside Budd's old Jeep with five minutes to spare. The Dawes's barnyard is always model farm: no broken equipment rusting on the periphery. Everything painted and clean.

She rests her head on the steering wheel and closes her eyes. She needs a nap. Doing barn chores and milking weekends, plus the afternoons she doesn't have classes, is laying her low. She'd like to put together a girl band, do a few of the college bars, some Chicks covers, some Alison Kraus, but no time for that. Anyhow no way she can buy a keyboard. And no money in college bars anyway. Truly it's all a long time gone.

She slips her inhaler into her pocket. The ambiance of a barn, the hay, not the best thing for her asthma.

"Up and at 'em, Queenie."

She readjusts her study sheets under the St. Christopher statue her grandmother insists she keep on the dashboard. One thing for sure: Christopher anchors her notes so she can read while she drives back from Marwick on I-88.

The cows are already down from the upper pasture. Tess slides out. When Queenie doesn't rouse, she rolls down the window and lets her go on sleeping: oh you lucky dog.

Hoop Dawes waves to her as he backs the manure spreader away from the barn. Hoop is about the biggest man she's ever seen out in the real world, not so much fat, but big like a giant. As if a couple of huge oak trees got together and produced a boy. And his wife Betty's no Little Miss Tiny either. Del Merrick told her Betty was a great model for their life-drawing group, said all bodies are beautiful without clothes. Betty … nude? Well, Tess can't quite imagine that.

She goes around the corner to the side door of the barn. She resists grabbing her nose. Even after all these months of helping with the milking, the smell of ammonia when she first steps into the warm darkness still gives her the gags. She pulls on her coveralls and barn boots and stuffs her dreads up under the wool cap. Mark's old barn hat. Mark's in Florida. That's what Rudy heard.

Budd's at the far end of the barn, busy pushing up hay, with the radio blasting some right-wing propaganda. Budd's deaf as a post Hoop says, but Tess thinks he's faking. Budd, the Daweses' hired man for the last hundred years.

"Of course it's appalling, ladies and gentleman, but the peaceniks are already saying there are no WMDs. Our brave men and women are risking their lives in this Shock and Awe operation and this ElBaradei's busy setting our great country up for another terrorist attack …"

Betty appears in the door of the milk room. "Tess, go tell Budd to change to the oldies station. My boy over there in Iraq. Does he think I want to be listening to that? Cows won't let their milk down with that madman raving."

Betty's son, Tommy, is a sergeant or something. Tess's first boyfriend back in sixth grade. Only a few years older than Tess, maybe thirty now, and his forces are advancing on Baghdad. Only thing *he* ever did with a baseball bat was hit one over the fence. He's promised to email his parents.

Before Tess gets to Budd, he switches to Merle Haggard, which is only a little better but proof he can hear as well as the rest of them.

She gets down the jar of udder cream and then mixes a little soap with warm water in a clean pail. Suddenly half a dozen barn cats appear, hoping to get in on a squirt of milk. She steps into the first stall and, ever mindful of the big Holstein's back leg, pats the cow's warm side. "Afternoon, Dolly." Dolly gives her a look and then returns to her feed with a hard swish of her tail that smacks Tess in the shoulder. "Bless you, too, my dear," Tess says.

Betty Dawes blinks in surprise over the top of the stanchion and goes around to lift the milk machine into place. "Bless you?" Betty says.

"My grandmother's influence." Tess begins to clean Dolly's teats. "I'm trying to change all my 'Jesus Christs' into something that doesn't send her scurrying to pray for me. That woman would be on her knees night and day trying to save our family."

"How's she doing?" Betty says. "My mother went through chemotherapy, radiation …" Then she stops, clearly decides not to go any further.

"Yeah, well, she's not too exhausted to bless us all through the making of the sauce for the ziti. Put some meat on our souls. Her name isn't Angela for nothing. She already planted a bunch of tomato seeds in little pots in all the windows."

Pots that used to be the starters for the family marijuana crop.

"And she's keeping her hand on my brother, giving him a lot of encouragement and Hail Marys."

Betty laughs and wags her finger at Tess. "Don't you be forgetting I'm a good Baptist myself."

Now would be the time to broach the subject of would the Dawes possibly need somebody part time on the afternoons when she has classes. But it's tricky to bring Rudy up. Rudy was part of the bad crowd their daughter Katie used to hang out with. Plus there's the rumor about Rudy maybe being the father of Katie's kid. They never mention Katie. Something bad, something sad, going on with her. Plus Hoop is going to be the judge for Rudy's hearing in April. Plus does she really want to risk recommending Rudy when more than likely he's going to screw everything up?

Betty turns on the milk machine. Both of them listen to the build-up of pressure.

Tess rubs some udder cream into her fingers and palms to cut down on the friction and then wraps each hand around a teat to squeeze first with the left and then with the right to bring down the milk.

"Keep a special eye on Dolly's milk before you put on the cups," Betty says. "I thought her udder looked a little red this morning."

Tess checks the milk as it squirts toward a waiting cat. "I don't see any clumps. The udder doesn't look inflamed." She prepares the other two teats and then puts the suction cups in place as Betty hands them to her.

Hoop steps into the barn and comes up close to Betty. "Any word?"

Betty takes hold of his arm, closes her eyes. Shakes her head no.

Imagine you're in the middle of an invasion and you email your mother a hello *or* you don't email your mother a hello. Which would be worse, your kid calling from jail or from some desert battlefield? That's it: she is not going to have any kids. A puppy maybe, but no children.

▪ ▪ ▪

[9]

# Desperate Hope

Rudy's got the front of the Maverick rolled up on two planks he pried off the falling-down barn. He's got the planks resting on two piers of cinder blocks he borrowed from a man down the road, some city guy who, when Rudy knocks, only opens his door part-way — Rudy not looking like a Jehovah's Witness, the only other strangers who'd pop up unexpected because certainly this neighbor is not someone Social Services is investigating. Or maybe the man's suspicious because he's heard talk at the P.O. that he's got a jailbird, a possible maniac, living within robbing distance.

So — Rudy gives the man his best attitude, his "I'm trying to get my car started, so I can get to work" story, which is not a total lie, because if he had a car maybe he could line up something, though not something probation would approve. Which means probably not, since who else but people like him are going to hire people like him?

But the neighbor semi-buys it or simply doesn't want to be in bad with a maniac, so next he trundles the fucking blocks, in Papo's wobbly wheelbarrow, half a mile back up the road through the muck and wind, and now and now, every slither he makes under the car, Gramma DeLuca tracks him, her skinny chicken-legs moving when he moves.

"Gramma, go back inside, " he calls, his head only a foot from a pair of Tess's old high tops that his gramma must have dug deep to find in the closet. "It's too cold for you to be out here. The car's not going to fall down on me." And what the fuck would she do if it did? Like Mamo, she believes she could lift the car up to save him.

"I'm not cold," she says. "The fresh air's just what I need. Tell me what sort of tool you want from this box and I'll give it to you. Keep you from having to crawl out. You know, you say scalpel, and I'll slap it in your hand."

Scalpel? What the Maverick probably needs is a new transmission. Plus fifty other things. At least he knows it isn't the battery. Piece-of-shit car's actually got a semi-new battery. Somebody, in some moment of desperate hope, maybe Smithy before he left this world for good, has messed around with trying to get this clunker going again.

Of course he's got the wrong wrench for loosening the starter bolts, so he sticks his hand out by his grandmother's foot. "Okay," he calls, "slap me with the wrench that's got a hole the size of a penny. Probably it'll say '9/16' on it." And within half a minute, she places the instrument solidly in his palm. "That'll do it," he tells her. "Now, really, you can go back in the kitchen. Once I can get this bugger off, then I'm done for now until I get the part."

Her feet stay fixed.

"Best thing you can do is throw a log in the stove and start up some high-test coffee."

A moment of hesitation, but finally her bony, blue-veined calves disappear and he hears the kitchen door slam, the only way they can get it to close.

No doubt his gramma is in there offering up prayers, bead by bead doing her rosary, believing between the two of them, the Maverick can be resurrected. But he knows, should Tess find him under here when she gets back from milking, she'll offer up her usual comments: "Fu-tile. Fu-tile. Be like the reptile. Shed your skin. De-friend the bend. Get yourself out to look for a real job." Just what he's supposed to use for wheels never part of her nag.

And maybe there are miracles, because once he gets the cables off, and after some hard turns with the wrench, the rusted bolts drop off in his hand. He shoves them in his pocket, pulls the starter free, and inch by inch wiggles out. He sets the starter on the front seat ready to take with him for exchange. He lights up the half a butt he's got left and takes what comfort it offers all the way down.

Somehow he's got to hitch a ride to Cooper's Salvage to get a used starter. If he can at least get the car running, he can figure if a fix is worth even thinking about. Anyway, nothing else for him to do until his hearing, see if he's going back to jail. Better than sleeping all day like he's been doing and writing "Where are you, Sunny?" letters half the night. If only he could find a way to get a message to her. Working on the car helps calm the itch of his craving. 'Cause any minute some narco might buzz in from narco-land and give him a piss test.

Just as he turns the knob to go in, the back of his grandmother's bald head bobs into view, a plucked chicken with ears. He almost falls off the step, his recoil so sudden. Startled, her hands clutch at her head. First time he's seen her without the dead-black wig, a wig so pitiful he veers off when he meets her face on. Poor Gramma DeLuca. But her baldness is even more terrible. He hesitates, gives her time to pull the witchy-wad back on. Instead, she turns to face him through the glass, her fingers flared over her skull. Her cornered-rabbit eyes. No way to turn away now.

He opens the door. The stink of burned hair. Smoke. In the sink a wet blob of black.

"Oh," she says. "Oh." Her hands still cover as much as they can. "I bent over to light the gas. The flames exploded. Set me on fire. My wig, set my wig on fire." With that she sits down. Silent crying. The worst kind of crying.

"Aw, Gramma," he says. He pulls his bandana, his best red bandana, from his pocket, stowed away from the grease under the Maverick. He lifts her hands and looks her over good. Then he sets the bandana on her baby-bald head, pulls it down over her ears, tucks in the point of the triangle and ties a neat knot at the nape of her neck. He lifts the little mirror above the sink and holds it before her like the hair dressers do. "There," he says, "there, red, much better than that black thing. Red, just right for an Italian lady like you."

▪ ▪ ▪

# *Doing Time Outside*

[ 10 ]

# Strata

Carla watches Dirk's truck lights disappear down Chicken Farm Road. Dirk's a nice man, but no matter how grateful she is for the loan of the bail money, for the job at the Edgewater, she does not have to put up with him plunking his hand down on her knee.

She makes her way around the mud ruts to the walkway. What in God's name is Rudy doing with the Maverick? Whatever it is, it looks dangerous. Still it's better than him in bed all day with the blinds down. If only Tess would try to get Rudy some part-time work at Dawes's, maybe helping Hoop get the equipment ready for spring planting. Surely there's no law says he can't work for the town justice. But no, Tess won't go out on a limb; Tess always thinking mostly of Tess.

Carla turns the knob and then twists to give the door a big push with her rear. Everything around this place you've got to either slam or crash into for it to work.

A terrible smell. She plugs her nose. "Sweet Jes ... what in the name of ... what's that stink? Like somebody threw a dead rat in the stove."

Rudy puts his finger to his lips. "Cigarettes," he says, and when she sets the pack on the table, he rips off the top of the box.

Angela appears at the back door, a load of wood in her thin arms and her head still done up in the red bandana.

"Rudy, least you could do for your grandmother is to ..." But Rudy's already transferring the logs from Angela's arms to the box by the stove.

"Carla. Dinner's almost ready." Angela's fingers flutter about her head. "Maybe you're wondering about my ... new look." And with that, she strikes a pose as if she's ready for the flash of the cameras. Rudy laughs. She dumps the pasta into the colander. "Rudolph, please set the table and then go call your sister."

"Well," Carla says, "yes, I am wondering ..."

"Rudolph convinced me these are a lot more ... modern." So saying Angela lifts a stack of neatly pressed and folded bandanas from the shelf.

Steve's bandanas that he left here on a child-visitation laundry day fifteen years ago.

"Mama, if there was any around, I'd say you were into the hooch. Are you going to tell me what's going on?"

Tess comes in, one of her heavy textbooks under her arm.

"Here." Rudy hands her the stack of plates.

"Oh, tell her, Grammy," Tess says. "Otherwise she'll be ferreting around, going at me to divulge."

There's a flurry as Angela hands people food to put on the table: the ziti and sauce, the salad, the garlic bread. "Sit. Sit," she says.

And they do. Angela stretches out her arms on either side of the table to reach for Tess's hand and then Rudy's. Carla's fingers flash up in surprise, but then they settle and join the circle.

"Our father, bless this food and keep us ..."

Just then there's the roar of a motorcycle and it sounds like it's going to come right through the house.

Carla rushes to the window. The yard is dark. But all of them know it's not a gift from our lord and savior. She turns on the porch light. Prager, dismounting, two inches from the back steps, his nasty red eyes leering up at her. She grabs the knob and yanks, but the door doesn't open.

Tess ladles more sauce onto her pasta and opens her book to "Natural Selection."

Rudy steps up behind Carla. "I'll take care of this."

"Rudy, don't you go out there. You and I have an agreement. You promised me. I swear to God if you go back to jail, I ..."

Rudy reaches over and switches off the porch light. One hard wrench and he's out the door, closing it firmly behind him.

Once again Carla pulls on the knob. When the door doesn't open, she gives it a kick.

"Carla," Angela says.

"Oh, don't tell me to do nothing. Look the other way like you always did when my father …" With that Carla leaves the kitchen, her feet pound up the stairs, her door slams above them.

Tess looks across the table at her grandmother's stricken face. "Eat, Gramma. Eat. Got to keep your strength up. Be hard-shelled like a trilobite. Look the other way as much as you can."

▪ ▪ ▪

*Doing Time Outside*

[ 11 ]

# Long, Strange Trip

Something wakes Carla. She listens. There it is again. A soft pawing at her bedroom door. She lifts one corner of the shade. It's light outside. One of these days she's going to get herself a goddamned watch. "What is it?" she calls.

"Are you awake, Carla?"

Her mother, and this is definitely right up there with one of the dumbest questions anyone can ask. "Come on in," she says, though her mother is the last person she feels like talking to right now. At least there's this: Prager didn't stay long, and though she couldn't hear Rudy's words, his tone was steady. Then for a long time afterwards she heard the back-and-forth rhythm of her mother and Rudy talking in the kitchen below. The longer that went on, the more she calmed down. She must have fallen asleep because she never knew when they came up the stairs to go to bed.

Her mother backs her way in. Two cups of coffee balanced on the bread board. She sets the board on the table and closes the door. At least she didn't bring her breakfast in bed, knew that would really piss her off. Her mother has got on a fluffy pink robe, with a lavender bandana on her head, one of Steve's favorites.

Carla pushes herself up to sitting. She feels downright ratty in comparison. She takes a sip of the coffee and sees that it's just right.

"May I?" her mother says, and sits down on the end of the bed. "I want to talk to you about the lawyer."

"The lawyer?"

"Prayers are not going to be enough." Her mother takes a deep breath and squares her shoulders. "I've got some money saved up and I want to use it to get Rudolph … to get him that good lawyer. He should only be punished for what he did."

"And what does Rudy say he did?"

"He did have drugs on him. He did knock that man down … more than once. But that man hit Rudy in the face the night before. And there was no baseball bat. Rudy thinks the emergency squad report ought to prove that. That man only just got out of prison and he's been known to lie to the police." She stops for one quick breath. "Rudy should only have to suffer for what he did wrong. Otherwise he'll keep seeing himself as a victim. He needs a lawyer he can believe in."

Carla clamps her jaw back into place. "Well, that's the speech you could give to the jury."

"Yes," her mother says.

"And you believe Rudy?"

"I do."

"Any idea about how much money this lawyer will charge?"

"Two thousand dollars is what his friend told him."

"Mama, this so-called friend is somebody Rudy met in jail. What's he doing in jail if this lawyer's so good?"

"He doesn't have any money and what he did is really bad and he really did all of it."

"And you can do this without getting yourself into money trouble?"

Her mother nods.

"Is that the truth, you swear to Jesus?"

"Yes. And Rudy says if he doesn't go to jail and he can get someone to hire him, he'll pay me back a little at a time."

"And you believe *that*?"

Her mother shakes her head. "And he says he'll think about going to Mass with me."

Carla's laugh is so sudden and loud it surprises them both.

Her mother responds with a giggle, then says, "But he told me it's unlikely he'll go to Confession. I told him I'm going to keep, from time to time, seeing if he'll change his mind on that."

"And what happened with Prager?"

Her mother rises, picks up Carla's empty cup from the table.

"Did he say anything about a woman named Sonny?"

Her mother balances the bread board on her hip and then carefully reaches for the doorknob. "Could you call the lawyer today? Make an appointment. I want the two of us to go see him first, make sure we think he's going to be the lawyer Rudy needs."

"You mean you and me? Rudy's willing to have his mother and his grandmother …"

"That's the deal. Confession's negotiable. Me meeting this lawyer first is not."

▪ ▪ ▪

[ 12 ]

# Good Behavior

As soon as he hears the approach of Prager's motorcycle, Rudy slams the door and walks out to the road. Prager has sworn on his mother's grave that he's licensed, registered, and insured. Rudy checks his pockets again to be certain he has everything he needs and zips up. No gloves. He inherited his father's jacket, but not his gloves. Where did those go? Probably Mamo's boyfriend copped them. Toward the end Smithy was selling most anything that wasn't nailed down.

Rudy shakes his head. That is anything he himself, Mr. Rudolph Morletti, hadn't already hocked.

Prager's wearing a helmet, even has an extra, strapped on the back. He yells something that Rudy can't hear. Bike's either been revved up or one of the mufflers is going. Rudy swings on and adjusts Tess's backpack so it's settled securely on his shoulders and makes sure the strap's snug on the helmet. Best to avoid a head injury, knock out what brain cells he's got left. Hard to tell what sort of shape Prager's in beneath the goggles. Prager, definitely right up there on the Miscreant Roll Call. Last fucking thing he needs is for them to get stopped by a sheriff for some stupid-ass infraction. No doubt somewhere on his person Prager's got something illegal. Lead me not into temptation, ehh Gramma.

Fortunately, they can take the Back River Road and only have to be on a main highway for a couple of miles to get to Stanton. Prager hangs a left at Grat's Bend. The ideal thing, if he doesn't end up going to jail, would be to go back to working at the sawmill. But doubtful probation would allow that, or John either. Have the narcos sweeping in unannounced.

He motions for Prager to slow down. Be good not to get killed. Burn in hell no matter how many candles Gramma lights. They're going to have to pass the Dawes farm, but no way Tess can be back from dropping his crazy mother and grandmother off at the lawyer's — though why the fuck they are going to his office when his machine says he's out of town … Anyhow, so what if Dawes sees them; he's not doing anything illegal. No restrictions on his associations — other than Keegan. Not until after the hearing anyway. Hoop Dawes may be something of a hard-ass, but he's not a prick.

As they approach the Dawes outbuildings, Rudy once again extends his hand where Prager can see it, tamps the air down, down. There are no vehicles parked by the house or the barn.

Prager actually stops at the stop sign at Bellow's Corners and once again at Dry Brook Road. Indications that he is not totally wasted. And there it is: Cooper's Salvage. Same trailer. Same neat rows of vehicles that still have good parts ready to be further dismembered. And Cooper will know right where to find the best starter for the Maverick. He's got it all on a computer. Fortunately it doesn't have to be an actual Maverick match. Probably no salvage lot in the country still has an actual Maverick anywhere. Maybe the only one remaining is jacked up in their yard on Chicken Farm Road.

Rudy slides off as soon as Prager brakes and lifts the old starter out of the backpack. Prager extends a Camel Rudy's way and lights them both up. "You know, I can get you a little something if you're interested," Prager says.

It would have been less risky to have gotten Tess to bring him, but he couldn't stand the thought of having to listen to her disapproving silence all the way over.

▪ ▪ ▪

[ 13 ]

# Tepid souls shall become fervent

"Here's Maple Street. Which way?" When no one answers, Tess makes the turn that takes them past the Catholic church, past the statue of the Blessed Virgin, her hands crossed over her heart.

"Oh, I didn't know there was a church so close to the lawyer. Our Lady of Sorrows." Angela squints and leans toward the words at the bottom. "Father Alberto Rios. Well, that's reassuring."

"What's the number on Maple?"

Carla digs around for the notebook at the bottom of her purse.

"Mamo …"

"Won't he have a nice plaque someplace with his name on it: William Granley, Attorney at Law?" Angela says as she adjusts the black bandana and smoothes the front of her winter coat while Carla struggles to pull the notebook out of her bag.

"The number, Mamo …"

"Chill, will you, Theresa. The spiral's caught on something."

"There, there it is." Angela points to a weathered sign that's fastened at a slight tilt to the front door of what looks like a converted garage, a tier of scaffolding set up along the front, the painting job-in-progress at the scrape-off-the-currently-peeling stage.

Tess pulls the truck around a stack of boards at the end of the driveway.

For a minute Carla and Angela sit and stare at the building, the "William Granley, Lawyer" sign.

"I hate to think this is his office," Carla says.

"Gramma, Mamo, you want to know what I think?"

"Yes, we do," Angela says.

"After I swing by Daweses' to let them know I'm going to be late, I think you should let me run you both back to the house and wait until you can actually reach this lawyer on the phone. Maybe check with CDC; see if they know anything about this guy. The mental health clinic. Call the Better Business Bureau or Legal Aid. Let's face it, by the clues collected so far, William Granley's legal opinions appear not to be ... much in demand."

Carla gives the notebook a yank, which causes half the spiral to unwind, but which finally frees it. "Your decision, Mama. Your money, your call."

"You may be right, but ... I want you to drop us here and pick us up later as planned." Angela opens the truck door. "First, I'm going to take a peek in a window and then see if the priest at Our Lady of Sorrows knows Mr. Granley."

"Wait." Tess slides out her side. She takes hold of her grandmother's arm and steadies her until Angela gets both her Sunday-shoes solidly on the ground. Then Tess pulls the seat forward so her mother can scramble out on her own.

Angela has already ducked under the scaffold to get a good look in the window.

"Where do you want me to pick you up? It's going to be at least two hours, five o'clock at the earliest before I finish barn chores."

"Better hope they don't have a Neighborhood Watch in Stanton. You come back to pick us up and we aren't here, check the trooper barracks on 23."

"Mamo, where should I pick you up?"

"The Edgewater, of course. The Edgewater Bar & Grill. I'm going to need a shot of Tequila after this."

"How about at the church?"

"The Edgewater."

Tess slowly reverses onto the street. Waves, but both women's backs are turned: Carla banging on the door; Angela up on her toes, fingers gripping the ledge, forehead pressed to the lawyer's front window.

Must be William Granley's not worried about his electric bill: he's left his desk light on. When there's no response, Carla goes to the window also. "See anything incriminating?"

"Carla, let's not to come to hasty conclusions … based on circumstantial evidence. Can you tell what that is on the chair by the desk?"

"Circumstantial evidence? I think you've been watching too much *L.A. Law.*" Carla grabs the ledge and jumps to try to get a better look, but all she can see for sure is that the desk is a mess, stacks of stuff all over. "Well, he definitely doesn't have a file clerk."

"We need something to stand on." Angela points to a pile off in the weeds. "Those'll do."

Carla drags two cinder blocks over and pushes them together. Mud smears the cuffs of her good black pants, but of course Angela insisted she look her best. Carla tests to make sure the blocks are level. Now she can see the entire room.

"On the chair?" Angela says.

"Joseph and Mary …"

"Carla, I wish you didn't always …"

Carla laughs and steps down. She takes Angela's elbow and boosts her up. "I want you to eyewitness this for yourself."

A chain saw, "Black and Decker" on its bright orange exterior, the biggest chain saw either of them has ever seen, and positioned on the chair, its chain blade gleaming, like it's all ready to tell its side of the story as soon as William Granley returns.

▪ ▪ ▪

[ 14 ]

# Shelter from the Storm

In the last light, Rudy gives one final turn of the crescent wrench. Rest of the Maverick may fall apart, but this mother of a safety switch is never ever going to loosen. He crawls out and, standing on one of the planks, puts the hood up. The oil stick reads full and not too black. Plenty of water in the radiator. Since Smithy gave such serious energy to getting the car to run, chances are he put coolant in as well. Otherwise, the block will be cracked and then of course Tess's "fu-tile" will be one more item for her "I told you so" list. He unscrews the cap and upends the last of the mower gas, a couple of gallons, into the tank. He listens hard: the tank doesn't sound empty.

Once more he searches the glove compartment for the missing key, unloads all the junk onto the seat even though for sure he knows that's fu-tile. All of this an empty ritual to put off the final verdict. He bangs the dash. Shit, probably have to go through the whole hot-wire hassle, but first try the old screwdriver trick. He locates the slotted screwdriver under all the crap, slowly inserts it into the ignition, and twists. The engine catches, starts to sputter. *Yes.* He hops in and pumps the accelerator. Sweet Maverick-baby holds a rough idle.

Well, it's a long way from actually shifting into drive and rolling down the road, but who knows, if he keeps messing with it, maybe, just maybe. Get Gramma DeLuca on it, doing all those mystery chants. A vehicle and a good lawyer: turn his fucking life around.

Just then Tess's truck pulls in. Him looking a little silly sitting in this car that's jacked up on planks. He taps the accelerator, lets the engine rev a little for Tess's benefit.

Tess motions for their grandmother to wait and then heads his way. He rolls the driver's window down. She's grinning. Not often she sends a smile in his direction. "Well, you got her going," she says, tapping the hood.

"Found the part I needed at Cooper's. Have to take her off the blocks before I'll know if there's any real hope …"

"Yeah, but still, I never … never thought I'd hear that engine turn over again. Better go on inside. Gramma insisted you be present to hear what she found out about the lawyer. We couldn't jimmy out even a hint from her all the way home. When I picked them up at the Edgewater, she was in the process of converting half the rummies at the bar."

They all troop into the cold kitchen. Right away Mamo starts up. "Rudy, you might at least have kept the fire going …" Then she begins to stab the coals with the poker which results in filling the room with smoke.

"I'll do it," Tess says. "You start some coffee. And lay off a little why don't you."

Her mother's eyes widen. True, it's been a long time since Tess has defended her brother.

Meanwhile her grandmother has seated herself at the table, all ready to tell her tale. "Oh, don't worry about that now, just sit, sit, Rudy, all of you, Tess, Carla, so we can talk over what we found out about the lawyer."

"What you found out," Mamo says. "Your grandmother hasn't told us anything. Made me sit out on a bench while she grilled the priest at the Catholic Church. Said she'd get more of the 'inside story' if she went in alone."

Rudy laughs. "Tess said you were also whooping it up with the boys at the bar. Well, out with it."

"Whooping it up? She ordered us both Shirley Temples and then made me help Dirk stock the coolers. What I want to know is: Are you for this William Granley or not? Me, I have serious doubts."

"You decide, Rudy," Grammy says. "Here's what we have so far. Though Mr. Granley is not a devout, church-going person, the priest says he always donates generously to all the fundraisers and he's good to his mother. Takes her to Florida every year in March. That's where he is now. Be back April first. Father knows that because he heard Mr. Granley arranging to have his mail held at the post office."

She stops there and looks around the table. Easy to see where Mamo gets her flair for drama.

"Good to his mother," Rudy says. "I'm with you."

"He may have been good to her, but she sure didn't teach him neat and tidy. His desk is piled to the ceiling."

"Also Father Rios said that William Granley was once an assistant D.A., district attorney, in Ulster County, but he decided to move upstate to have a practice that didn't require a big office and a secretary … More of a low-end practice …"

"Low-end? Is that what he calls working out of a garage?"

Tess and Rudy and Gramma all three give Carla the look that says, Put the lid back on.

"Okay. Okay, but do tell them about the chain saw."

"Also he came upstate because his ex-wife lives here and he wanted to be near his son."

Mamo pours them all coffee. Sets a box of sugar donuts on the table and a pack of Camels. "Your grandmother's treat."

"Now, for what I learned at the place where your mother works. First of all, I'll have to admit I wasn't expecting to gather much reliable information … well, at a bar, especially from people who would be there so early in the day when most would be out working … but I was wrong. One of the men, Oliver Burke, is a carpenter and he said that William Granley is a lawyer who's willing to represent people who … well, I think he said who aren't 'fancy-pantsy,' and that he knows what he's doing, and that Mr. Granley got his nephew's bail lowered and all the charges against him reduced … considerably."

"Burke. Break-in Bobby Burke. Yeah, I heard he did okay," Rudy says.

"Robert Burke who used to ride our bus? Remember what he said to you? 'Rudy, you ought to be nicer to your sister, otherwise …'"

"Yep," Rudy says. "That's him. Break-in Bobby. He broke into JAKE's. And The Inn. And Stanton Market …"

"Drugs," Mamo says.

Her grandmother pats the table. "Be that as it may — a couple of other men at the bar corroborated."

Her mother throws up her hands. "Corroborated. Meaning they all had kids who'd had their charges reduced. Like who else said that?"

"The point is Mr. Granley is an experienced lawyer we can afford. And they all said that Mr. Canon, the public defender who's been assigned to Rudolph, is a lawyer who mostly handles people's estates."

"Are you going to tell them about the chain saw?"

"So Rudy, my suggestion is that you call now and leave a message saying you have a hearing April 6th and you'd like to make an appointment as soon as possible after he returns."

"Mama, you're giving up your plan to look this lawyer over first?"

"Be better for you, Rudy, to not have me and your mother trotting in there, making it look like you can't handle your own affairs. And here's something else that might be of interest to you. Parked in the back of his office, under a tarp, which I carefully lifted up so as not to disturb anything, is a huge motorcycle. A Harley-Davidson motorcycle. All shiny and well cared for. Reminded me of the one your father had long ago."

Rudy squeezes Gramma's shoulder. "Thanks. And I suppose you told Father … Rios he'd be seeing us at … Mass?"

Tess knows now is not the time to ask Rudy how he'd managed to get to Cooper's Salvage.

▪ ▪ ▪

[ 15 ]

# Cosmic Insights

The three of them detour around the Maverick, now off the planks, its back end blocking the front walk.

"Rudy, why'd you leave this wreck smack in the middle …"

"Not going to be there long … once I put in a new transmission."

"A new transmission? Where do you think the money for that's coming from?"

Tess gives her grandmother a thumbs up. "You two — wave goodbye. You know she's in there trying to make up for the rest of us."

Rudy and Carla turn. Sure enough Angela is watching from the kitchen window. She gives them a peace sign and mouths what is probably a "Good luck."

"Thanks," Rudy calls, and opens the truck door.

"I'll sit in back," Carla says. "If you're going to ask that priest for a reference, you'll be getting out first."

Tess pushes the application for the zoo internship under the St. Christopher statue.

"What're you doing that for?" Carla says, catching Tess's eye in the rearview.

"So I can think about the questions before I talk to my advisor."

"Jesus, you better not let your grandmother see you doing that, reading while you're driving."

As they near the house of the neighbor who loaned him the blocks, Rudy leans forward and motions to Tess. "Stop here for a second." When she does, he rolls his window down, looks all around, and then pulls a newspaper from the man's *Morning Sun* box. "Go," he says.

Carla grabs Rudy's shoulder. "Are you out of your mind? Stealing that guy's paper."

Rudy opens to the classified section. "They're away. Papers piling up. Their 'look-like-we're-here' light comes on every night at six."

"Sounds like you're casing the joint."

He passes the paper back to Carla. "Read me anything in jobs where they might hire a jailbird like me for a few weeks. Yard work, unloading … nothing where you handle money or need a security clearance. Not likely I'm going to find anything in Stanton. They know me there."

"And how do you think you're going to get to Marwick? Why are you looking for a job now anyway? Seems like you'd wait until after your hearing. Only seven days. Better to find out what that lawyer thinks you should do when you see him."

"I need money to work on the car. Start paying Gramma back for the lawyer. Buy my *own* cigarettes."

"You still didn't tell me what that lawyer said on the phone."

"He said, 'three o'clock next Tuesday.' Sis, if I find something in Marwick that fits with your classes, could I ride with you? Unlikely I can hitch."

"You're sure you don't want me to talk to Hoop? He's got an engine head that needs to be changed."

"Maybe after the hearing if it turns out okay. But I doubt he'd take me on anytime."

"Katie?" Tess says.

Rudy nods.

Carla shakes the newspaper to get Rudy's attention. "They need night shelvers at Walmart. A cashier at the Stop & Go. Everything else is for social workers, substance abuse counselors, violence intervention … Evidently we're not the only dysfunctional family in the area." Carla turns to the horoscopes. "You want to hear what the astrologer predicts for your day? I'm Cancer. The crab."

Tess laughs. "And you make fun of Gramma and the Mysteries?"

"You think it's funny, but I tell you there's something to this star connection stuff. When I used to follow it regular, it was often right on the money. Here's what it says for me: 'Something good that happens right now starts off a domino effect of good fortune, so get ready to run with what life presents you.' Well, I tell you it's about time the dominoes would fall our way. I am oh so ready to run. You want to hear what it says for you, Tess?"

"No, and I hope you aren't going to get into that nonsense again. Remember the trouble it caused the last time." Tess takes a left at Nina's Pizza, then stops for the only light in town.

"What's my star connection?" Rudy says.

"Aquarius."

He turns toward his mother. "Hit me."

"'Don't bank on anything until you see it in black and white. Nothing can be set in stone until you tidy up the loose ends, so there is no time to waste.'"

"You want me to drop you at the church?"

"No, I'll get off by the grocery store."

Carla passes the paper back to Rudy. "You aren't going to see the priest first?"

Tess pulls into the Stanton Market lot.

Rudy sets the paper on the dash. "Read about Iraq while you drive. I could sign up for that, but they don't take people like me either. At least not until a lot of the up-and-standing return home in boxes. I'll come by the Edgewater when I run out of places to go. You'll be back around four?"

Tess nods. She and Carla watch Rudy stop in front of the big silver ice machine, check his reflection. His clean-shaven face, his recent Gramma DeLuca haircut. His pressed Dickie work shirt and newly washed hoodie.

"Break my heart," Carla says. "Let me out here, too. I'll walk to the Edgewater." She leans over the seat and pushes the truck door open, maneuvers her way out. "Good fortune falling our way. Wouldn't that be nice?"

Tess waits until her mother reaches the sidewalk. Then she backs into the street. At the red light, she reads Aries out loud: "'You've worked hard and been committed to achieving your dreams. Very soon this diligence will pay off. Now that Mercury, the planet of recent events is coming back in phase, good news is on the way.'"

▪ ▪ ▪

[ 16 ]

# Something's burning, Baby.

The tired-looking woman at the register is Dara Moore's mother. Dara: the first girl he ever took to a drive-in, first girl he ever smoked pot with. "Borrowed" the brand-new-to-them Maverick when no one was around. Fourteen. No license. "Is the manager here?"

The woman eyes him bottom to top. "He's in back."

Chances are the manager's somebody's father or even somebody he went to school with. That's how it's going to be. There's a skinny, balding man putting packages of hamburger into the meat case. His glance is none too friendly either. "Are you the manager?"

"Back room."

Rudy passes the shelves of soda, the bags of chips and jars of salsa. Six-packs of beer. When he looks up, he sees the hamburger man's image in the big mirror set up to check this aisle. The man's standing still, watching him. He resists the twitch to give this sorry-ass the finger. Through one of the windows of the big back room's swinging doors, he sees the fat behind of a man lifting a crate of lettuce onto a makeshift cart. Rudy knocks on the glass and pushes the door open. "Excuse me. Are you … ?"

When the man faces him, Rudy sees it's Fletch Wheeler, the long-ago star of the Danford High basketball team, a guy he once slammed against the gym lockers for calling him a druggie greaseball.

"What do *you* want?"

Rudy lets the door swing shut, moves past the rows of dog food, cat food, cleaning supplies. Make a real clatter if he reached out his right hand and took it all off as he went by. Outside he lights up his next to last cigarette. He turns into the park behind the fire department, sits on the bench. Smokes. Lights up his last cigarette. He hums, moves his fingers to the frets for the chords: No woman, no job, and no car. A lotta jail time pending. Troopers got me walled in and radared. Nothing left worth defending. Think this mess got me depressed? Yeah.

Well, maybe he will go see the priest. Got nothing to lose. Though it might be better to wait until after Sunday Mass. Let the priest see him with his grandmother.

He sits and watches the town. People going into the bank, the post office. People coming out. The church looks quiet. Quiet. One good thing: been a while since he couldn't sleep, since his brain was sending him messages in scrambled tongues, since it felt like a piece of hot metal was scraping along his nerves.

He carefully stubs out the cigarette, places the butt along with the other one in the now empty pack. He folds the pack and puts it in his pocket. What he needs is money *now.* And piss tests aside, what he wouldn't give for the sweet pleasure of a little homegrown. Not the rush of something speedier, not the dark forgetting of smack. Just a quiet hum, a low-flyin' high.

There's the roar of a motorcycle with a hole in its muffler. It stops for the light. Rudy rises — yes, he knows, he knows full well he may be asking for trouble, but he moves out to the street and waves his arms back and forth anyway. Here's the answer in black and white. Hitch a ride to the mill, see if John'll take him on right now. Get a small advance for cigarettes, maybe even a good used transmission.

Prager pulls up to the curb. Rudy mimes the need for a cigarette. Prager hands him a pack of Camels. When Rudy goes to give it back, Prager sticks the pack in Rudy's pocket. Rudy fastens the helmet and swings on. Phone the Edgewater from the mill. What's the best way to tell her? "Don't worry. I'll just be working there for a few days. Get enough to fix up the car, so I can find a steady job after the hearing if things go my way." But no matter how he wraps up all those loose ends, he can already hear her screaming. Well, better to have the blast coming at him down the wire than to hit it head on.

Prager takes it slow by the bank, the Stop & Go, the laundromat where the local constable sometimes does the speed-trap lurk. Prager the model citizen, until they hit the open road.

■ ■ ■

*Doing Time Outside*

[ 17 ]

# Domino Effect

Way up the street the bank clock says 1:48. Carla's actually early. She could walk back to the corner. Maybe see Rudy, find out how it went at the market, try to talk him into getting a reference from the priest if it didn't go well. But no, Tess is right: She does need to lighten up on the nagging. She digs down into her bag for the bar keys.

Willie Jones is already on the Edgewater porch, sitting in the swing, next to the blinking Coors sign, waiting for her to open up. Willie Jones is always sitting in the swing next to the Coors sign waiting for her to open up. The Edgewater was once a nice little cottage on the edge of the Onango Creek and rumor has it that Willie Jones's family lived here long ago. Willie Jones practically lives here now.

Carla nods to Willie, who shuffles up to wait while she steels herself to struggle with turning the key to the exact angle, a little to the left, while she pushes in on the knob. Why is it that every goddamned door in her life requires a goddamned formula to open? To her surprise the bar door gives way without the usual hassle and she practically falls into the pool room. Good fortune or Dirk has finally given the lock a generous squirt of WD-40.

She switches on the light. Willie makes his way around her and takes his usual stool at the end of the bar. She sets him up with a draft.

She turns on the juke box and the lights behind the bar, automatically scans the Jim Beam and Tanqueray Gin bottles to see if she needs to go down to the basement and bring up more liquor from the lock box. This is mostly a beer-and-shots bar. Rare she has to do a mixed drink. Maybe an occasional screwdriver, but a martini, with a pearly little onion — no way.

"You've got a nice mother," Willie says, and tips his glass up in tribute.

She gives this shrunken, sad little man a smile. "Yes, I do." Though there was a time when you couldn't have pried those words out of her mouth even if you choked her. A time when she wanted to scream down the stairs to that bleating creature in the kitchen below, "Scratch his eyes out." Once she even called the police, said "My father is killing my mother." Stood with her two little brothers at the window in the upstairs hall and listened while her mother answered the door and told those police, "Nothing's wrong. There must be some mistake."

"You're lucky," Willie says.

Lucky? "Well, like the rest of us, my mother's learned a thing or two along the way. Willie, are you by any chance related to Sonny Jones?"

"My brother's granddaughter. Real name's Shannon. Pretty girl who's had a lot of trouble."

"Woman. She's a woman. She still live around here?"

Willie shakes his head and puts down his glass like it just got too heavy. "Up and left and nobody knows where to." He turns his face and drinks.

Another sad story. And does she really want to hear another one of those?

Carla shifts the rack of glasses to the other side. Next she needs to check to see how much beer she's got to bring in from the back room. Might even wait until Rudy comes by. Have him do the hefting, not get her wrists throbbing for the rest of the night.

She leans down to examine the gleaming beads on the left latch of the beer cooler. "Sweet dear Jesus." The hinge on the cooler has been welded. She lifts up gently on the left panel. Not even a squeak of complaint. Plus the cooler is full. Dirk doing her a good deed before he closed last night, not a man to get even because she removed his hand from her knee. Or this weld job, the WD-40, is him charming her up for another attempt.

So slow if she had a book she could fix herself a cup of coffee and catch up on her reading. A good steamy story like *Lady Chatterley's Lover,* which she never did return to Del Merrick. None of the loans: *Middlemarch. Madame Bovary*. She could give Connie Chatterley and her gardener another go, but not that Bovary woman. She couldn't stand that Bovary woman. Del laughed when she told her that every other page she felt like giving Emma a back-and-forth smack. Del. She misses being friends with Del, talking to her. Rudy says she and Mark are both in Florida. Though the other day she saw a van pulled up at the stone house like Del's tenants were moving out.

"I'm going to make myself a cup a coffee. You want one, Willie?"

"I'll take another draft," he says.

She turns his glass at the right angle so there's no head. Fills it almost to run-over full. After all, this is the only pleasure Willie has. She puts a couple of heaping tablespoons of coffee in the maker and pours in enough water for two cups. Going to be a while before the regulars drift in.

Then she searches under the bar for an old *Morning Sun*. Check another horoscope. See if the crab has some love interest heading her way. It's been a long time, a very long time. Smithy dead almost a year. Get a good astrologer to do her chart, let her know what Zodiac sign will be most compatible for a lover. This time she's going to be more careful. Pass the next prospect through her own security clearance. The astrology reading she got right before she met Scorpio Smithy gave her some warning: It said, "intense chemistry locks these two together." She does not want dull, but she doesn't want to be cuffed to wild and crazy again either. True, Steve was a good man mostly, but somehow, eighteen years together, they just seemed to wear away at each other until there was nothing left. Who could've known Steve's heart would give out before he was fifty. Him dying in another woman's arms.

The phone.

Right away that catch in her chest, a streak of light behind her right eye. Only people who call the Edgewater are wives looking for late husbands and it's much too early for that. She lets it ring and ring.

"Phone," Willie says.

Ring and ring.
"Carla, somebody's trying to get you on the phone."
What life presents you. She picks up the receiver.

■ ■ ■

[ 18 ]

# Complex Social Lives

When Tess turns into the Daweses' driveway and parks in front of the house instead of the barn, Queenie rises and expresses some interest. A new adventure.

"Sorry, Queenie. You better stay here. I'll only be a minute." She sticks the folder with the reference form under her arm and gives herself a quick check in the rearview, runs her hand over her head.

Before she gets halfway up the walk, Betty opens the door and beckons her in. "Tess. Why, look at you. I hope nothing's wrong."

Probably they're on the brink of a lot wrong now that Rudy's back working at the mill, getting rides with Prager, but certainly she won't tell the Daweses about that. "I just wanted to see if you and Hoop might give me a reference for the zoo internship."

"Of course we will." Betty reaches her hand toward Tess's head, then stops. "Come on in. But I tell you it's about all I can do not to run my hand through those curls of yours. I have to say I prefer this hairdo to all those ... tangles. Some nice young zookeeper's going to try to capture *you*."

Tess rolls her eyes.

"You're one of those dark beauties. And a good worker too. What's the occasion?"

"It's for my interview. Gramma DeLuca's handiwork. Only way to get rid of the knots was to cut them all off. Now I know how your sheep feel."

"Come on in and have some dinner. We just got an email from Tommy, so we're in high spirits."

"Oh, you don't have to do the reference right now." Tess opens the folder and lifts out the top sheet.

Betty takes her arm. "Be good if you fill us in on what the zoo's looking for before we do it. We're having chicken and biscuits. Won a blue ribbon at the Onango County Fair." Betty looks toward the truck. "And bring Queenie in. She'd never forgive me such rudeness."

Hoop and Budd are already at the big table, with Betty lifting a huge pan out of the oven, when Tess and Queenie get to the kitchen, clearly the center of the Daweses' house. Grandchildren's drawings cover the giant refrigerator. Shelves and counters are loaded with every kind of machine that dices, mixes, steams, or broils.

"Look who's here, Hoop. Tess wants us to write out a reference so she can work at a zoo this summer."

Hoop smiles and pulls a chair out for her.

"But like I said, I'm hoping to get a schedule where I can still do either morning or night milking here."

"That's going to be fine for us. Right, Mother?" Hoop says, patting Betty's backside as she goes by.

Hoop calling Betty "Mother" always surprises Tess. *Her* mother would certainly do a number on that one.

Budd remains his usual mum self, all his focus on the chicken and biscuits, his napkin tucked in his shirt and his fork and knife at the ready.

"I forgot you have your big meal at noon or I would've come by later."

"Earlier or later I'd be out in the field or under some greasy machine. This is perfect timing." Hoop begins to load up the plates that are stacked in front of him.

Tess passes the first one on to Budd, who actually gives her a friendly duck of his chin. "About a third that much for me," Tess says. "I had a huge breakfast." One cup of nasty coffee at the college cafeteria.

"So what sort of thing are they going to let you do if you get the zoo job?"

"Well, it's more like training. I'm not going to get paid. Not all that different from barn chores really: feeding and cleaning up. But I hope they'll let me assist the primate keepers … especially the ones who take care of the chimpanzees."

"You want to care for monkeys. I think I'd choose the tigers or the lions," Betty says. "Though I suppose monkeys, even those big ones, are a lot less dangerous."

Budd gives a cough and then he speaks: "Chimpanzees aren't monkeys. They don't have a tail."

They turn to look at Budd. Several sentences all together is a once-a-year event.

Good and loud, Betty says, "That a fact, Budd? Gorillas, orangutans, chimps …"

Tess jumps in. "They're all called great apes. I want to study them because they're so much like us. Chimpanzees …" Tess knows she should not go any further with this, but she does, "chimps and humans have ninety-eight percent identical DNA."

Betty laughs. "I don't have any problem accepting that. Big males, humans or apes, a lot of them strutting around beating their chests for power. Look at this Shock and Awe Iraq thing. 'Course I'd never say that to Tommy."

Hoop laughs too. "And you'd never say it in front of Reverend McCauley either, would you, Babe?"

"Oh, Tess, our Baptist minister, half the congregation, get themselves in a real stew if you get anywhere near evolution. But if you work on a farm …"

Hoop interrupts. "It's all a mystery. And for sure it didn't *all* happen in seven days. Humans are animals who know how to get themselves in a lot more trouble than our cows."

"For sure," Betty says. "But church, well, I love the hymns." And with that Betty lifts up her generous arms and sings, "Morning has broken, like the first morning …" Then she reaches over and takes Hoop's hand. "Oh, I don't believe a lot of it, but every time I think of Tommy down in one of those tanks, I whisper, 'Dear God, Dear God, keep my boy safe.' And Tess, your mother's saying the same thing for your brother Rudy."

▪ ▪ ▪

[ 19 ]

# Own Recognizance

Prager comes to a stop a few feet from the new mill. An eight-foot log is already set up on the skids. "There she is," Prager says. "Came all the way from New Zealand."

For a few minutes Rudy says nothing, simply walks around the swingblade sawmill, inspecting it from every angle. "Got both high and low tracks. That's an advantage." He crouches to check the blade out from below. "Twenty-seven horsepower. Very nice. Just this one winch?"

Prager steps forward. "Yep, you can lower and raise the bed by pushing these buttons. But the big thing is you can double cut without turning the blade."

"Maximum cut?"

"With this eight-inch blade, eight by eight. Double cut eight by sixteen. DVD says one man can pack it up and load it in the truck alone. Unload and set it up in less than twenty-five minutes. Half that for two. All the parts together, eight hundred pounds."

Rudy lightly fingers the controls, runs his hand across the bar. With something like this, he could go into business, spend a lot of the time in the woods. Out of harm's way as Gramma DeLuca's always saying.

"Manual says two men can cut this log right here into boards in ten minutes, very little waste. On the demo we watched two guys on this same Peterson swing mill do just that. 'Course we only fucked around with it a little yesterday right after we picked it up. John as shaky with care as if he was doing brain surgery."

"It's a beauty. What about the kerf?"

"A bit wider than with the bandsaw."

"How much you figure John paid for this baby?"

Prager shrugs. "I'm guessing over $35,000."

"Where the fuck did John come up with that kind of money? Must have had a mighty fine harvest last year. Prime pot to have cash like that in the till."

Prager laughs. "Oh, something a lot more lucrative than that. Speaking of which, maybe you'd like to get in on it ..."

Rudy steps away and shakes his head. "I got a hearing in four days. A meet-up with the lawyer Tuesday. What I want to get in on is a reduction of the felony counts. I'm interested in not having to line up my booties under my little jail cot for the next few years."

Prager comes up close, looks around, and lowers his voice. "There's going to be practically no risk on this one. Big money."

"Yeah, right." Prager and Gramma both watching too much drug-bust HBO. Prager — who's so fucked up for sure, one day he's going to hit the wall and take all near and dear down with him. "No need to wait for John to get back. Let's do this log," Rudy says.

He hands Prager a face guard. They both tie on the leggings. Rudy adjusts the earmuffs, pulls on some gloves, and goes to the end of the track.

The motor fires up, the winch lowers the bed. Prager slowly pushes the mill to take off the top layer of bark to prepare the log for the first cuts. As Prager pulls the mill back, Rudy gets ready to step in to lift that strip away.

Forward and back, forward and back, the smell of hemlock, the blackberry canes all around the yard thorny and red, reaching out to grab hold. Thing is not to back into them or the big double cut blade. Or Prager. Thing is to be careful.

▪ ▪ ▪

[ 20 ]

# Fires on the Moon

Carla heaps the clean laundry on the kitchen table and starts to fold the towels. Angela pulls her own things from the pile. The last time these two women folded laundry together Carla was fourteen, already plotting with Vickie to run off. All those years ago, but they've never talked about it.

Angela peels several pairs of Tess's bikini underwear off her nightgown. "Your father would've made you burn undergarments like these in the trash barrel."

Carla stops folding and glares at her mother. "My father ..." She skids to a stop right there.

Angela skins another pair from her robe and holds them up to the light: pale pink with little flowers. "But really they're pretty aren't they? And maybe proof that when Tess isn't so busy, she'll find herself a good man."

"Good luck," Carla says.

"That's what Rudy needs."

"What?"

"A good woman."

"Mama, would you wish Rudy on a good woman? Any woman?"

An electric spark zaps Angela on her next pull. "You know, if you'd stick a couple of Bounces in the dryer, you'd have a lot less static."

Carla gives her mother a double huff on that one. "I'd have a lot less static if I lived in a convent. Especially if I'd had the good sense to go there before I had Rudy."

"Carla. Maybe it's good for Rudy to be working at the mill until his hearing. Idle hands … Besides, he says he'll try to put some of what he earns toward paying me back for the lawyer."

"Don't be so naïve. If the cops did a search and seizure on that place, you think they'd come up with lollipops? That Prager … he's the last person Rudy should be anywhere near. He's already been in prison. Plus he's not right in the head. A full-blown paranoid."

"Rudy knows that."

"Knowing and doing. Two different things. Speaking of the money, how're you going to handle paying the lawyer the two thousand. I'm sure Granley has to get paid when Rudy sees him tomorrow."

"I've got the cash here. I'll give it to Rudy."

"You're going to give Rudy two thousand dollars in cash tomorrow? Please."

"Well, we'll have to get to the bank for a cashier's check first. I'm not as naïve as you think. Rudy says once he has the hearing, if he doesn't go back to jail, then he'll be on probation. The probation department won't let him work at a place like that."

"If … if. Rudy has serious drug problems. And though his brain doesn't seem to be in overdrive at last look, those revved-up episodes crash in out of nowhere. There aren't enough beads on that rosary of yours to clean up the mess the devil will stir up if Rudy starts using again."

Angela sits down. "I'm tired."

But Carla jackhammers on: "And it's not like this is some new twist in our family drama: your husband; your son; me, with the Vicodin … even Tess had a little go-round when she was a teenager." Carla places the folded laundry in the basket and sets it by the hall door. "Want some coffee?"

Angela nods and then gets up and goes to the closet, starts to fumble around in the dark. Carla sets a couple of cups in the microwave and sticks two cinnamon buns in the toaster oven.

The kitchen fills with the smells of why it is that families keep pushing the big stone up the hill. She sets their little reward for a morning of housework on the table and begins to dig down in her purse.

"Come on. Before it gets cold. What are you looking for?"

"Your ironing board."

Carla dumps the contents of her purse beside her plate. "Oh, here it is." She opens the little horoscope book, *Your Personal Guide to the Future*. "Come sit down. I don't have an ironing board."

Angela takes a place across from Carla. "Well, I guess I can use the table or the counter."

"I don't have an iron either. Nobody irons clothes anymore."

"What's that?" Angela says, pointing to the little book.

"It's horoscope readings for the month of April. Let's see: your Zodiac sign is the same as mine. Cancer."

Angela starts up. "Cancer?"

"Yeah, I don't like the sound of that either. Or the symbol: we're both crabs. Want to hear what it says for you?"

"Carla, I'd just as soon not go near anything to do with that word. Signs of the Zodiac. It sounds a little like bowing down before idols."

Carla laughs. "You want to talk about idols. No place are there any more idols than in the Catholic Church. Mary here and Mary there. Why the Stations of the Cross alone …"

Angela puts her hand up, palm spread in a "stop right there" signal.

"Okay, okay … I take it back. Just let me read you what it says for *me* in the section for 'The Stars and Your Love.'"

Once again Angela raises her hand.

Carla puts the book down. "Love. After Steve died, even after all those years of him being with somebody else and me too … well, I mean after my father died, even after all those hard years, did you … ?"

"Oh, Carla, look."

Just beyond the big maple, a trooper car. Two troopers starting for the house.

"Dear God, Dear God," Carla says.

They both get up from the table.

Angela takes Carla's arm and moves her toward the kitchen door. "Best we open it before they even get here. We've got nothing to hide." She wraps one of Carla's hands around the knob and places hers on top.

They plant their feet and pull.

One of the troopers steps up on the porch. "We're looking for Rudolph Morletti."

"He isn't here," Carla says. "I'm his mother. What's this about?"

"There's a charge that he violated the order of protection. It's alleged that he was seen in the vicinity of the alleged victim's house. One of the neighbors says he saw him too. Can you tell us where he might be?"

Both women hesitate.

"We just need to talk to him," the other trooper says.

"He's working," Angela tells them

"And you are?"

"Rudolph's grandmother. Angela DeLuca."

"Working where?"

Angela looks at Carla and when Carla doesn't answer, she says, "Working at a sawmill."

"Where is the sawmill located?"

Carla steps forward. "It's off Route 12, a mile or so out of Stanton, on the way to Marwick."

"Thank you," the first trooper says.

Angela and Carla watch the two men get into the car, the car pull away.

"See. See," Carla yells, her arms in the air.

"Call the sawmill," Angela says. "Call the sawmill right now and let them know that the troopers are on the way."

"Mama …"

"You've got to, Carla. You have to right now. Or I will. Then one of us has to call the lawyer."

▪ ▪ ▪

[ 21 ]

# Special Problems Not Listed Above

He steps into the cell. Neither of these C.O.'s looks familiar.

The fattest one places several sets of clean underwear, a laundry bag, sheets, a blanket on the bed. "You'll be in lockup for seventy-two hours. You've already been given your one free phone call. You'll have no more privileges until after booking's completed and you go up to the dorms."

"Remove all clothing," the other C.O. says.

He sits down on the bed and begins to untie his boots. Do not give off any fucking attitude. Make it worse than it already is. Piece by piece he steps out of it all and stands there naked. He knows what's coming next, but he waits to be told. Make no sudden moves.

"Place your hands against the wall and spread your legs. I'm going to check your rectum for weapons or contraband."

He does as he's told. He hears the snap of the rubber glove as it's placed on the older C.O.'s hand. Always a shock, but quickly it's done and with no extra jab. One sign-in to a lockup is all that's needed to register where anyone is on the Prick Scale. Next test: Will they let him cover his body before they inventory his clothes and have him sign the property list?

They do not. He stands and waits while the younger C.O. lists each piece of clothing on the sheet that's fastened to a clipboard. Then he waits while the officer once again checks every pocket and then places each item in a plastic bag. He wills his body not to shiver, not to cover himself with his hands.

Finally the officer gives him the clipboard and a pen. "Look over the list of your property and then sign at the bottom where you see the *X*."

He starts to sign.

"Look it over as instructed before signing. No shortcuts. It's my understanding you're not new to these procedures."

Needle going up on the Prick Scale, Prick. He pretends to skim the list, which is basically unreadable given the lousy handwriting. He signs and hands the clipboard back.

The officer lifts the clip and passes him a white booklet: *Rules & Regulations*. "Can you read?" the officer says.

He nods. No doubt somewhere on his rap sheet the word "dyslexic" is scrawled across some blue line along with psychotic and drug addict, alongside assaulter with a deadly weapon and dealer and violator of orders of protection. He takes the booklet.

"You are to read this carefully after you dress and before you make your bed."

The two officers exit and lock the cell. He watches their bodies as they walk away. Thing is, you fat fucker, you are going to get yours. Because no one is more practiced in Prick Karma than the incarcerated. He pulls on underwear, the blue jumpsuit.

It's all going down the usual black hole: No hearing now until the fourteenth. On the edge of looney tune time. Zero chance he'll get bailed out again. Dawes so pissed he upped the bail another five thousand. One more strike against him if Sunny hears that he's been picked up again and that it involves her ex, Keegan. Who does he have to back up his alibi that he never went near Keegan's house? Prager. Prager, who's already done time in Elmira for armed robbery. He drops the booklet into the storage bin and kicks it back under the bed. Unfurls one of the sheets, then freezes at the sound of a clack, clack, clack along the bars.

"Well, lookee here, who's joined us once again at the County Hilton," Kendrick whispers, pushing the mop past the cell. "And no calls to Mommy for ever so many hours."

Rudy turns and begins to make his bed. The hot scrape along all the circuits now. That black scream to smash all of them. All of them. The fucking liars. All their fucking lies.

▪ ▪ ▪

[ 22 ]

# Captive Species

> *Gestures:* Chimpanzees also use many gestures to indicate needs and they will beg other chimps for food by approaching them with open hands. Friends may hug and kiss. A worried chimp makes a lip-puckering face.

Tess twists the rearview her way and puckers her mouth. Yeah, this is a gesture she can feel her face making a lot lately. And why not given the subgroup her double whammy bad luck has landed her in? Stress level always Code Red. Like having to tell Hoop she couldn't work just now because … because of a family emergency. And even though she knows they'll still keep her on and it won't affect their zoo reference, being in the middle of the whole mess makes her press her lips tightly together ready to attack. What did Hoop say? I can't discuss this case with you, Tess — like she even wanted him to — but I recommend your family get your brother a very good lawyer.

She pushes serenely dozing Queenie over a bit so she can, for the fiftieth time, slide her hand into the side pocket of her duffle to make sure the money for the lawyer is still there. Of course it's there. Maybe she better add obsessive-compulsive disorder to her medical conditions after all, because who or what might have stolen the money away during the ten minutes since she last looked.

She lifts the St. Christopher statue up to turn the "Chimpanzee" page to the other side. Wikipedia stuff when what she needs to be reading are Goodall's essays on Gombe, but it's too awkward to balance the book on the dashboard. Got to watch for the back-way turn for the jail now anyhow. Last thing she needs is to miss meeting up with the lawyer to give him the cash before he has his first session with Rudy.

Rudy? Did he go near Keegan's house or didn't he? Gramma DeLuca says no. Mamo says it figures. But she can't decide, because it doesn't figure at all. Just as things are starting to turn around for him, why would he do something so stupid?

There it is: Wolf Hollow Road. Loud enough for the whole goddamned world to hear, she says, "Well, I'm telling all of you this: I do not care if there are five family emergencies tomorrow, this truck and I are not going to miss my interview at the zoo in the morning." With that, she turns so sharply onto Wolf Hollow, Queenie almost falls off the seat. Tess checks to see if Queenie puckers up when alarmed. She does not, only gives Tess a puzzled what-in-gods-name look. "All I'm saying, Queenie, is how much good news has Mercury delivered so far? Zip. N-O-N-E, which spells nada."

At a lurch that knocks St. Christopher to the floor, she peers hard at her truck hood through her dirty windshield, then rubs the window with her sleeve, her good red jacket sleeve that Gramma told the lawyer she'd be wearing for ID purposes. No question: steam. She checks the temperature gauge. Boil-over red. "Shit. Shit."

She pulls the truck onto the shoulder and looks around for a rag. Have to use the chimp notes. She lifts the hood and with one hand holding it up, steps back and shields her face with the other. As soon as most of the scalding steam clears, she puts the bar in place to hold the hood, then wraps the sheaf of papers around the radiator cap, presses down, unscrews, and then leaps away from the boil-up. She looks under the seat, then walks to check the truck bed. Why does she do this when she absolutely knows there is no emergency container of water anywhere in her world?

She takes the money and a pen from her duffle and removes her keys. "Come on, Queenie." She rolls the window up tight on the greasy bunch of papers so they flap in the wind and locks the door. Across the top sheet, she prints "GONE FOR WATER." For a minute she just stands there trying to decide. No houses for as far up Wolf Hollow as she can see. Little chance she'll be able to hitch a ride on this deserted road, but walking back to 23, what are the chances there? And even if someone stops, what's she going to say, "Please, could you give me and my dog a ride to the jail?"

With that she turns and starts up the dirt road. Tears. Full crying now. And of course nothing even vaguely like a Kleenex in her world either and no fucking way she's going to make it in time to meet the lawyer now unless there's a miracle.

She walks and cries and Queenie follows close, with an occasional woof that says "We can do this." And then, not too far along, she hears the sound of an engine coming on. She wipes her nose on the underside of her sleeve and sticks her thumb out. An old truck, the grill gone, and no question an exhaust system that'll be dragging soon. Dented and rusty makes it more likely the person will stop. Better than pristine and snooty.

The truck pulls over and she and Queenie run. The passenger door swings open. Tess leans in to be heard over the rumble. "Have you got any water? My truck back there boiled over. It's an emergency. I'm late for an important appointment."

"No water. Where are you going?"

"The jail."

"Me, too," the man says. "Hop in."

She and Queenie scramble up. The truck pulls back on the road and gathers speed. "Hang on," he says. "It's 3:45. What time you have to be there?"

"Four."

"Me, too." He turns into the curve so fast the tires spin on the gravel. "And with luck we're going to get there right on the minute. Don't you remember me?" the man says. He turns a little her way, with both eyes still on the road.

For the first time Tess gives him a full inspection. More a boy than a man. "Sweet Mercury," she says, "Charles Dale."

"Yep, and I'm on my way to meet my probation officer."

She wants to ask about Darlene, but maybe that's not a happy topic.

"Our baby's due any minute. Darlene's back at her brother's. Not enough money yet to get us a place, but now that I've got a job stocking at Walmart, we ought to be able to put together something soon."

"Good for you. Hard to get a job … under the circumstances." There's another thing she'd like to ask Charles Dale: knowing that Rudy is never going to tell the lawyer that he's been diagnosed with a bipolar disorder, should she mention it? Maybe the rages are related to that. I mean would Charles want his sister to tell his lawyer? Tess gives a quick swipe at her nose. She desperately needs some tissues. Once again she searches in her pockets.

"There's paper towels under the seat," Charles says.

But then what if Charles ends up going back to jail and he tells Rudy? Tess pulls out the roll. "I'm going to take a bunch. In case I have another freak out."

"Going to see your brother? I thought he got out on bail."

"Re-arrested yesterday. Charged with violating the order of protection. I'm on my way to give some money to his new lawyer."

"Who's the lawyer?"

"William Granley."

"Buddy of mine had him."

"And?"

"Granley got all the counts reduced, but then my buddy really didn't do most of it. Word at the jailhouse is that he's a good guy all around. You know, for the underdog."

Tess hangs onto the door on the next turn.

"We're going to make it."

If they don't go over the embankment and land in the gully below.

*Public Safety Building*
*Onango County Correctional Facility*
*State of New York*

"If you want to hang out in the lobby of Social Services — that brick building across the way — I'll help you find some water and give you a lift back to your truck. It might be your water pump's busted."

She and Queenie jump down. "When Darlene got in my truck, she said, 'If one more thing turns to shit, I'm going to lose it.' Well, that was me on the road until you showed up. Thanks." She closes the door.

A Harley pulls in and parks by the fence with the razor wire. The rider removes his helmet. A tall man in a three-piece suit, wearing aviator glasses, his hair pulled back and held by a neat braid that goes halfway down his back. He takes his briefcase from the saddlebag. He sees her, smiles and waves.

William Granley, Attorney at Law.

▪ ▪ ▪

*Doing Time Outside*

[ 23 ]

# Thorns, and Also Thistles

Carla rips out the pages of *Your Personal Guide to the Future* and scrunches them into little balls. Next she throws the whole lot into the cold stove and touches a match to as many wads of guidance as she can reach. She watches the future flare up. Dominoes turned out to be loaded with TNT: BOOM, BOOM, BOOM. Next she builds a real fire. April, but raw and dreary. What would it be like to live where the winters aren't six months long?

4:20. Tess promised to call the minute she hands over the money to the lawyer, promised to give her gramma the lowdown on this guy. Bound to be a payphone handy. Doesn't she realize her grandmother's waiting?

Carla listens. Not a sound from upstairs. Not even the low hum of her mother doing the beads. Rudy's last champion and maybe even she's given up.

Then she hears movement, her mother's slippered tread coming slowly down the stairs. She puts on the kettle. What they both need is a couple of shots of tequila. Now that she's given up drinking and drugging and smoking, what's she supposed to do for escape? Maybe she can take up eating. She presses her aching wrists to her head where a migraine is lurking. Then she pulls a brownie mix from the cupboard.

Her mother stops in the doorway, something in a shopping bag pressed against her chest. She's still in her bathrobe. She hasn't even bothered with a bandana. It's not as shocking as it was. Her head is now covered with short gray fuzz like a baby bird just getting its first feathers. Last week she was starting to have some color in her cheeks, but the pale of the chemo is back.

"Sit, Mama, I'm making us tea. And maybe a batch of brownies if we have eggs."

Her mother sets the bag down and then uses the table to lower herself into the chair. "I wanted to be down here for when Tess calls you about the lawyer."

"Oh, I'm going to give the phone straight to you. Like I told you last night, if it'd been me, I'd have let Rudy go back to using that public defender. Saved the money or used it to help Tess go on to a four-year college."

"Carla, you're just saying that."

"When I heard they'd charged him with possession. Well, that was it for me. Maybe what he needs is some real jail time or to go into one of those alternative drug treatment programs."

"You really think being in jail will help him become more stable?"

"Well, what *is* going to knock some sense into him?'

"Carla, just like I already told you: when he called to ask me to contact the lawyer to tell him he was in jail, he said he didn't go anywhere near that man Keegan's house."

"You believe that? What about the drugs?"

"He'd just smoked some marijuana, but he swore he didn't have any drugs of any kind in his possession."

"Please," Carla says.

"I believe that, too. We weren't able to warn him about the police. It's not like he got ready for them."

"Maybe if you'd been living with Rudy, getting his phone calls all these years, you wouldn't be quite so trusting."

Her mother pulls a large, flat book from the bag and turns it toward Carla: *Blue & Gold 1989*. "I found this under Rudy's pillow when I went in to make his bed." She opens to the page that's marked by a flattened origami crane and tilts the yearbook toward the light. "Is this the girl

Rudy's been trying to find?"

> Shannon Jones: Always a smile when you're feeling down. Cheerleader. Band & Chorus, Class Secretary '89, Book Buddies volunteer, soccer and swim team '86-'89.

Below the photo, in neat script: "For Rudy, who was always willing to listen. Love, Sunny."

S-*u*-n-n-y — all along she's had the wrong name. This girl, this eighteen-year-old girl with the long blond hair and the lovely young neck, is looking right at Carla with a grin that Carla knows she couldn't get her own mouth to make even if you offered her a thousand bucks.

"Because if this is Sunny," her mother says, "we should help him look."

Carla turns away from the photo and cracks two eggs on the side of the mixing bowl. She turns the oven to 350. She may have to use olive oil instead of real butter, but in about forty minutes she's going to pull a pan of brownies out, and even if she burns her mouth, she going to down half of them herself.

The phone. Her mother pushes herself from the chair and picks up the receiver. "Your grandmother speaking … Yes, Tess, we're right here, and I want no sugar-coating. Can we count on this man to do the best for our Rudy?"

▪ ▪ ▪

[ 24 ]

# This is a smoke-free institution.

The lawyer is already there when they bring Rudy in. Small gray room, table, three chairs, dim light — just like the interrogation rooms on all the cop shows. But no handcuffs, no officer sitting on the periphery.

The lawyer rises as soon as Rudy enters. A big man, tall. A suit with a vest and a braid down his back. Double agent? Need to stay sharp.

"Bill Granley," the man says, and extends his hand.

Rudy hesitates for a telling second and then puts his hand forward. His first response to this alien ritual is to step back. Maybe it's expected for him to say his name and some polite bullshit, but he doesn't. And definitely he's not going to mention Sunny as part of the mess with Keegan.

Granley sits and gestures for Rudy to take the chair opposite.

Rudy eases down, works on unlocking his neck.

The man gives him a direct look, but not tense. No rush to fill up a talk bubble.

Rudy breathes, breathes. Let this guy come out of his corner first.

Granley doesn't pull a pad and pen out of his briefcase — not going to do the usual "I'm in charge; you're the flunky" routine. Instead he sits back, stretches out his legs, and folds his hands across his chest. "Main thing," he says, "main thing, is for you to tell me what happened right from the beginning. Take your time."

Rudy moves forward, leans his arms on the table. The cold table. "All right," his mouth puts out the words. Voice steady. His fingers open and close, and finally land palms down like he's told them to shut up. "I'm not sleeping," he says, "so if I look ragged, that's why. That and withdrawing from nicotine. Probably I'd sell my grandmother right now for a cigarette."

They both laugh.

"No, you don't want to sell Angela DeLuca. If you were going to have a jury trial, which we certainly do not want, your grandmother'd be a real plus in your defense."

"Yeah," Rudy says, "she's a pistol."

He takes in a chestful of air and then lets it go. "Okay, first thing I need to say is this: I beat Pat Keegan with my fists. I beat him up until he went down on the ground, until he stopped moving. Maybe I knocked him out, but there was no baseball bat. Nothing but my hands. Not even a kick. And this beating was because the night before in some drunken thing over … over a woman …"

The lawyer shifts forward, turns up the electric on his focus. "A woman?"

"Some woman." No, Mr. Lawyer, I'm not going there. "This Keegan came up in the parking lot of the Eagle and smashed me in the face. Then took off in his truck. A lot of blood from my nose. There were a couple of equally drunken witnesses who saw this. None of them up-and-standing citizens who'd be a plus in the box."

Granley nods like he's taken that all in. No more press on the woman.

"My beating of him the next night happened by his mother's garage in Danford. Around eight o'clock. I was waiting for him when he got out of his truck. It was dark. No lights in the house. I doubt if anybody saw the fight. By the time I got a few blocks away to where I'd parked the motorcycle I'd borrowed, the firehouse sirens were already screaming. I took off and got picked up a few hours later at Larry Prager's girlfriend's apartment in Stanton."

Rudy takes another a deep breath. It's clearly a story he's gone over and over in his head, one, two, three. Granley motions for him to continue.

"Troopers took me for blood tests and to the Danford Court. Judge Dawes set bail at five thousand, then the troopers brought me here, charged me with assault with a deadly weapon, possession of a controlled substance, with the hearing to be April 6th."

"The blood test?"

"Going to be positive: crack. Cops busted in real unexpected. Found a few vials in the lining of my jacket. No question I was certifiable at the time."

"Enough to be suspected of dealing?"

"Probably not."

Rudy sits back in the chair and twists his neck a few times, then plunges into the freezing water again.

"'Course I say nothing when they give me the 'Just tell us what happened and you can go home.' A public defender, guy named Canon, came to see me once. I told him pretty much what I've told you. I was in jail for five days and ten hours before I finally got bailed out about two weeks ago. During those two weeks I used no hard drugs though they were handy-dandy. Seven days ago in order to make enough money to buy cigarettes and maybe a used transmission, I went back to work at a sawmill where I've had a job off and on for years."

"What about the violation?"

Rudy says with disgust, "Violation. At no time since I was released on bail have I been anywhere near Keegan's mother's house. I haven't even been in the town of Danford. All trips to the sawmill, to Stanton, to Cooper's Salvage on 12 have been by the Back River Road. Keegan and his neighbor are lying or they're so paranoid they thought they saw me. I've heard that the whole town got into a panic when the whistle went off, the troopers and the ambulance came screaming up. Keegan going around saying I tried to kill him. You know — maniac on the loose."

Again Rudy stops, unclenches his hands that have turned into fists. He rubs where his nails have cut into his palms.

"Tell me all about the arrest for the violation."

"Just prior to the troopers picking me up, I smoked a joint which no doubt will show up on this second blood test. But I did not have any pot or any other controlled substance on me. No paraphernalia. The troopers did find a bag of capsules tossed in the bushes right behind me. No doubt belonging to one of my … compatriots. That bag was not mine and there's no way they can prove otherwise."

Granley leans forward and opens his briefcase. "Anything else you can think of?"

"Pat Keegan is no up-and-standing either. He's done time in Elmira for dealing. He's been charged with giving false witness at least once that I know of. He's known as a troublemaker in town about on the same level as me. We went to school together and pretty much since junior high there's been no love lost."

Granley scans his appointment book and closes his briefcase.

"Anything more?"

"Any chance you can get my bail lowered? Jail … well, it's very bad for my mental health."

Granley looks Rudy straight in the eyes, a long look with a squint of sizing it all up.

Rudy allows this.

"All things considered, I'd say you're doing okay. Your new hearing date is in a little over two weeks, April 20th. I could approach the judge, but given what you've told me, I don't think he'll budge. Anyway my advice to you is to sit tight. What we want is for things to calm down. Time will help drain the energy out of this situation. Remember, we don't have to prove anything. The assistant D.A., Stan Murphy, is going to have to do all the proving: the baseball bat, the possession, the violation. He's going to have to put together the case: EMT and hospital records, witnesses, blood tests, fingerprints. I know the assistant D.A., and what he's going to want is for everything to cool, for you to do some 'good time served.' If this Keegan's a bad actor, someone who's given false witness, Murphy is going to be on that. Main thing is we want this case to remain in town court, not go to county. Keep it local."

"Are you saying the hearing might get postponed *again*?"

Granley nods. "Yes, and hard as it is for you to think about an extended stay here, letting things drag on is in your favor."

Rudy flinches and ducks his head like he's been hit.

Granley gives the table a slow-it-down tap. "Meanwhile, I'll be talking to the assistant D.A., the judge. I'll get back over in a few days to let you know how I think it's likely to play out. Anything comes up, you can call me." He takes a card from his pocket and hands it to Rudy. "Mornings are best. I'm in court most afternoons."

Granley rises. Rudy does too.

"You meet my grandmother?"

"I only talked to her on the phone. She said to tell you she'll be over to visit Saturday. I did just meet your sister out in the parking lot. Seems to me she's going to come around. Always good to have a few believers in the stands."

▪ ▪ ▪

[ 25 ]

# Boundary Patrol

Tess makes her way around a group of mothers and their children, backpacks and strollers and kids jumping up and down pointing at a mass of white fur and claws stretched across a cliff above a deep pool.

"But when will the bear get to go back to his home in the North Pole?" asks a little boy with very red cheeks who's straining against one of those child leashes, the halter cutting into his heaving chest.

Tess doesn't hear the mother's reply, but she's pretty sure she doesn't tell the unvarnished truth, which is *Never*. That's the one part she dreads if she ends up getting the internship. Seeing a Siberian tiger pacing back and forth, back and forth … no matter how "rich the environment." It may be too depressing. Still, how she loved the class trips to the petting zoos when she was a kid, feeding the baby goats bottles and letting curly lambs nibble the zoo food from her palm. She opens and closes her hand, remembering that breathy tickle.

Tess makes the turn at the sign that says "Tropical Core," which seems a bit esoteric for zoo goers looking for chimps. Funny, but the only chimpanzees she's ever seen have been in the movies. No chimps in a zoo, none of the great apes. All she knows are what she's read about them, what she's seen on short zoo videos these last few weeks since she started thinking they might be a key to understanding some of the strange behavior of her own family. Good luck.

She glances at the info sheets the director gave her and then stuffs them in her mother's bag, her own duffle deemed too ratty when she had to muster up for her grandmother's inspection before her departure this morning.

Have to get a TB test and tetanus shot soon if she gets the internship. And well, depending on the competition, it feels like she's got a good chance: high grade point, bravo references from Hoop and her Animal Care professor, her "Why I want to work at the zoo" essay sincere and without error. Not so sincere that it told the total truth: I want to get the hell away from my own environment.

No question she passed the "ability to stand, stoop, climb, and lift up to fifty pounds" test. Sitting across the desk from somebody you've never met before, it was hard to prove the other requirements: "flexibility and a good sense of humor." Glad she didn't have to get Mamo to sign off on that one.

Tess stops, senses that she's under surveillance: dead in the sights of a droopy-lidded dromedary. The camel is too far back to spit in her eye, but it's that kind of look. A Rudy-stare that always said, How can you be so dumb? Probably the keepers will tell her that it's best to assume a submissive posture, but well, that's going to take some serious reconditioning. She moves a little closer to the railing, gives the King of the Negev her best "Make Me" face. The camel's long eyelashes seem to flick in surprise, his nostrils flare. Then he leans as far over the fence as he can and smacks his loose lips, bares his big yellow teeth in what looks like a smile.

"Better watch out or he'll fall in love with you. Make it harder for me to give him his daily pedicure," a man's voice says.

Tess moves to the side to see around the camel's bulging girth and big frame, which has got to be at least seven feet from ground to hump. A man, in the standard zookeeper uniform that looks like surgical scrubs and a bulky sweatshirt, is breaking up a bale of hay into the bin at the back of the camel enclosure. A man maybe about her age, a black wool cap pulled down over his ears.

He approaches the camel, with a handful of hay. "This is Jabbar, our Arabian beauty."

Beauty is not the first descriptor she would have picked for this beast of burden. "Haughty" seems more apt.

Tess leans in closer to Jabbar, checks him from a different angle. "You think there's anything to the story that once a year, in order to get along with his camel, the driver had to take off all his clothes and let the camel stomp all over them?"

The man grins. "Well, I might just give that a try. But maybe not this very minute." Just like Jabbar, the man looks *her* over. "By any chance are you here about a Primate Enrichment Internship?"

It's Tess's turn to blink. "Yes, but how did you know that?"

"Mostly we get parents and kids this time of day. One of the great things about a zoo that's free. Amanda said she had an interview scheduled this morning. Somehow you look like a person who'd like to work at a zoo."

They both laugh.

"I'm going to take that as a positive. My name's Tess. Tess Morletti. Maybe you could report back to Amanda that I've got a sense of humor, one of the requirements to get the job. Are you a keeper?"

"Gary Simms. A first-year veterinary student at Cornell, doing my own internship here. You in vet school?"

"I wish. No, I'm getting a two-year technician degree at Marwick Community. I'm thinking I might like to work in a zoo, work with primates."

"Primates. They've got a pretty good setup here. The man in charge is into doing it right. As right as you can for any creature in captivity." Gary has turned his face up toward Jabbar, who is nuzzling his neck and cheeks.

This Gary has nice cheeks and she'd bet money a nice neck too.

"Jabbar has got some serious hoof problems. I've had to bond with him to get him to let me handle his feet every day. I'm wanting to work at a zoo also," he says, looking into Jabbar's eyes like they are bosom buddies. "Do rehabilitation. Help animals who were injured learn to go back to the wild. Have you already had your intern tour?"

"No, the director had to send me off on my own. Some emergency involving a rhino."

"So where are you headed now?"

"Over to see the chimpanzees."

"If you'd like to be able to go into some of the restricted areas, I could take you around — where you would've gone for your tour."

"Well, yeah, I'd appreciate that."

"I'll meet you inside the chimp house in about fifteen minutes. Take the next left. There's a big sign that says "Great Apes." Gary gives Jabbar a pat on his broad side and goes off at a trot toward the back of the enclosure.

Tess rolls her eyes at the camel. She is not going to tell Betty about her meet-up with this vet student, this Gary Simms. She'd never hear the end of it.

There are no chimps behind the huge glass that fronts their indoor enclosure. Lots of ladders and viney-ropes for swinging, a few nests made of branches about fifteen feet up in the piping. Seems like it'd be better if it was all more natural. Lots of objects are scattered about: ten-gallon cans, several tires, blocks — nothing like the green world she's seen in the Jane Goodall books. Must be the chimpanzees are outside in their open area. And truly that's where she'd rather see them. Behind this great glass wall she's face to face with how far away from places like Gombe these animals are. She starts to head back to the entry to catch Gary Simms there so they can observe outside, when there's a dart of movement in the upper platforms.

A chimp swings down. Probably a male since it looks like it's between eighty and a hundred pounds. The creature moves toward her. Not fierce looking, but not quite what she thought from the pictures, certainly not goofy like the movie sidekicks. He's dark and hairy, with a much lighter face, a large bony ridge for a brow that appears to be frowning. His eyes are deep black and suspicious. He walks slowly toward her on all fours, supported on his knuckles. She wants to back away, but she doesn't. His hands are surprisingly human, with pale pink palms. About five feet from the glass, he stops, squats, and stares at her. Gives her a beady squint. She returns the stare.

And then it happens. Muted howls explode from him. He bares his teeth. He bounces up against the glass with both feet, then bounds back and forth between the two side walls, leaping against them, and then runs around the whole area. She retreats when he bangs the thick Plexiglass so hard it actually vibrates. Perhaps her lack of submission, her failure to cast her eyes down, has caused this surge of rage. She lowers her gaze now, but he continues to careen and scream. At this point he looks very like Rudy when he's in a manic state.

"I'm sorry," she whispers.

Just then a hand on her shoulder. "Well, something must have really set Jo off. Chances are she's going to continue this display for another fifteen minutes."

"She? She? This is a female chimpanzee?"

"Amazing, isn't it. One of Jo's displays always gives me pause when it comes to thinking about marriage."

▪ ▪ ▪

[ 26 ]

# Pleasant as Possible Under the Circumstances

"Hello."

Shit. Why couldn't it have been his grandmother, or even Tess.

"This is a collect call from" — "Rudy" — "an inmate at the Onango County Jail. No custom calling features allowed. If you have any questions, please call 888 236-8444. The cost for this call …"

He should try again later. But for the first time today no one's near the phone.

"If you do not wish to accept this call, please hang up …"

No dial tone. She's going to take it. Two wannabe thugs from his bunk section have drifted over to the magazine rack.

He presses his mouth to the receiver. "It's me."

"I know it's you. Why are you whispering?"

Any closer and he'll swallow the phone, but he can't turn his back. "People are listening."

"I can barely hear you. Anyway, Rudy, I'm so upset by you getting picked up for violating and possession, I almost didn't accept this call."

"Those are false charges. Why can't you believe me?"

"Why can't I believe you? I can't believe you're asking me that."

Now the guy from the next bunk section is eyeballing him instead of the TV. They're all messing with his head.

"Could I speak to Gramma?"

"Your grandmother isn't here. She's at the doctor's."

"Could I speak to Tess?"

"Tess drove her to the doctor's. Probably you're so concerned your next question is going to be 'Why did she have to go to the doctor's?'"

"I need to get out of here. Trouble's looming. I haven't slept for days."

"Rudy, there is no money for bail. You know that. Anyway your lawyer says it's best for you to stay right there until after your hearing."

The volume on the TV goes up a notch. Two of the most recent miscreants close now, singing their little song, "mommy, mommy, mommy."

Then, the dial tone.

Someone has been in his bunk area. He can feel it. The writing paper and envelopes he left lined up on the shelf have been moved. His pillow is not where he placed it and the clothes bin is several inches off center. At least he's got a lower bunk. That's important. Much less open to attack from below, much easier to get to the main aisle if he has to. And it looks to him like this bunk has been angled so it's almost out of the monitor's view, like the C.O.'s are in on it, plan to look the other way.

He'd like to check to see if his letter to Sunny is still hidden in the bin, but it'd be too obvious. They're all watching him now. He's going to have to take them on. Goodbye good time served.

▪ ▪ ▪

[ 27 ]

# Prohibited Acts II

Tess almost misses the turn for the jail. She swings her arm over in front of her grandmother when she pumps the brakes. Queenie braces herself.

Carla leans over the seat. "This isn't how you went last time. Visiting hours probably started already."

"Shortcut," Tess says.

Angela is holding her new photo ID up to the light, turning it this way and that. "I can't believe the old woman in that picture is me." She lifts the plastic card for Carla to see.

"Oh, Grammy, you don't look like that mug shot," Tess says, skimming her hand over the top of Angela's head. "You're going to have curls any day now. Looking pink again now that you got the okay on your mammogram."

Carla hands the ID back. "Unbelievable all the crap you had to go through to *get* that ID. Your birth certificate. Having to get mail in our P.O. box. Other cards that say who you are. They should do so well ID-ing terrorists bringing their box cutters on planes. Tess, on the way back, can you stop at the P.O. before you drop me at the Edgewater? I'm expecting something. Something important."

"If there's time after you two visit Rudy. I *have* to get to the Daweses' by five." Tess points to the side of the road and veers off a little. "Right here's where I got the hitch with Charles Dale. Look: a bunch of first yellow flowers. Spring."

"April, but it still feels like March to me. Mud and dirty snow. You think that Darlene girl had her baby yet? And don't tell me *she's* a woman, Tess. Can't be a day over sixteen."

Angela turns in the seat so she can see Carla. "Sixteen. I wasn't much older than that when I met your father. You weren't all that much older when you had Rudy."

But Angela can't catch her daughter's eye. Carla's forehead is pressed to the cold glass. "Headache," she says. "Sometimes numbing helps."

*Public Safety Building*
*Onango County Correctional Facility*
*State of New York*

Angela opens the truck door the minute Tess stops.

"Wait, Gramma."

"No, I can manage. Going to have to go back home before too long, be on my own." She slides down, using the door handle to steady herself.

Tess moves the seat forward for Carla to angle out. Then she reaches back to get her anatomy book so she can study since Rudy can only have two visitors.

Carla doesn't move. "Tess, *you* have to go in with your grandmother. I'm going over to check on my Medicaid."

"Mamo, it's Saturday."

Angela is looking back at them now, one hand resting on the hood.

"I can't go in there. I can't. I can't stand to see him in there again. He sounded all paranoid on the phone. Hung up on me. He's going to have that crazy look in his eye."

"Mamo ..."

"He's going to plead."

Tess gives her mother the look. Then she breathes in, gets out her license, and turns to place the duffle on the seat beside Queenie. "*I'm* going to be on my own very soon too," she says.

Carla grabs Tess's arm, crying now. "Don't let Rudy talk her into bailing him out. Something terrible could happen if he gets out now like he is. I can feel it."

Tess closes both doors and takes hold of Angela's arm. They begin to walk toward the jail entrance. "Rudy can only have two visitors. We decided you and I have the best chance."

"Best chance of what?"

"Not detonating any mines."

Tess guides her grandmother into the jail lobby. The dim damp of a tomb and the powerful stink of Lysol. Seeping through it all: something rank that cannot be expunged. "Numb up as much as you can," Tess says. "I've got your back all the way."

2:55. Several C.O.'s are moving about behind the big glass. There's one man fidgeting at the head of the line, drumming his hand against his leg, and two young women after him, one with a baby swaddled in her arms, a tiny perfect nose, a fringe of black hair, surely a newborn.

Angela smiles at the baby, the mother.

"I'll go first," Tess says. "Just watch me. They'll ask your address. It's right there on your ID. They'll ask you your relationship to Rudy." Once again Tess slips her arm through her grandmother's.

Angela tucks her other hand under Tess's sleeve. "Cold in here. Giving me the shakes."

They wait. Then one of the C.O.'s sits down ready to sign people in. Older, with a gray buzz cut. Here they go.

"Name?" the C.O. says to the man in front.

And in a voice so loud it echoes, the man says, "Prager. Larry Prager."

"Oh God," Tess says.

Angela stiffens. "Tess …"

"Shh, first mine."

"Address?"

"It's on my license."

"Address?" the C.O. says again.

"I'm here to see Rudy Morletti."

There's a long pause. Then the C.O. stands and pushes the license back into the trough. Two other C.O.'s appear at his side. Beefy men, their mass fills the window.

Tess and Angela take a few steps forward, strain to hear.

"Rudolph Morletti does not have visitor privileges today. And Mr. Prager, should you wish to see Mr. Morletti another time, I suggest you come when you're clean and sober or your request will be denied. Next."

Larry Prager remains frozen before the glass for what seems like a long time. Nobody moves. An intake of held breath. Finally, he turns, his face pulled down and terrible.

He moves back along the line, looking at each of them as he passes. Tess shields her grandmother. Prager hesitates when he comes to her. Takes Tess all in. "You're Rudy's sister," he says. "Tell him he better call me."

Angela has pulled her beads from her pocket. Her eyes are closed.

▪ ▪ ▪

[ 28 ]

# Mea Culpa

Jesus Christ, Prager, and he's headed toward the truck. Her first impulse is to duck behind the seat. But then he turns off toward a motorcycle parked on the other side of the drive. After several angry attempts to get the bike started, he roars past, spewing black exhaust and kicking up gravel until he becomes just a smudge in the distance. Rudy can only have two visitors and Prager's not going to be one of them. At least there's that.

The pain at the base of her skull is so bad, she has to lie down and shut out the light. Nausea. Both wrists throb as well. But she can't call in sick again. She pushes Tess's bag to the floor and curls around Queenie's warmth. One hour to go and already she's got the chatters. If only she could conk, wake up when it's *all* over.

Something is out there.

She lifts up enough to look through the windshield. Tess and her mother. Bad news coming her way. More bad news. She sits up. Gets ready.

Tess helps her grandmother in, starts the truck, and backs out.

Carla waits.

Tess catches her eye in the rear view. "For some reason he's lost his visitor privileges. That's all we know. They wouldn't tell us anything else."

They drive in silence for miles.

Finally Carla reaches forward and touches her mother's shoulder. "You'd think he would've called to tell you, Mama."

Her mother turns. Her voice is weary. "We think he lost the privilege to make phone calls too. Otherwise he would've called to tell me not to come."

Carla resists her urge to scream, to bang her aching wrists against something. Her aching heart. Mother of God, when will they reach the bottom? The only sound now is the soft click of her mother's rosary. Carla knows if she could see her face, her eyes would be closed, her lips moving.

Finally, Tess comes to the Danford turn. "I'm going to run Gramma up to the house before I drop you at the Edgewater. Do you still want me to stop at the P.O.?"

Before Carla can decide, her mother says, "I don't want to go to the house. I want to go to work with you, Carla."

"That'll be fine. Willie Jones'll be happy to see you." Carla has a vision of her mother measuring shots while she rests in one of the booths, a towel across her eyes.

"Good idea," Tess says. "And I'll pick you up on my way back from chores."

The car behind them honks. Tess goes ahead and makes the turn. "What about the P.O.?"

"It can wait," Carla says.

Her mother turns to look at her again. "Let's stop at the post office. There may be a letter from Rudy to tell me not to come, to let us know what's happened."

"Mama, Rudy …" But when Carla sees the hope on her mother's face, she doesn't say it. She doesn't say that Rudy's not a writer, that ever since his fifth-grade teacher took her red pen and turned every *p* and *g* and *d* and *b* in a different direction in his story about becoming a composer of songs for his own rock band, ever since she marked the story an *F* and wrote "Sloppy work like this is unacceptable," Rudy has never written anything. Instead getting her or Tess or Aaron Merrick to do the writing while he dictated. Had her go to the school to insist that all his tests be given in a private place, with someone he trusted to write down what he said. Bloody. She made it all bloody, he said when he brought the story home and burned it piece by piece in the stove.

Tess parks across from the post office. "I'll get it," she says. "Need anything from JAKE'S?"

"Advil," Carla tells her. What she'd really like would be a double hit of Oxycontin. Knock herself completely out.

"Your head?" her mother says, reaching her hand back as though to soothe her.

"Yes."

They watch Tess sprint across the street. She looks like those muscular marathon runners, her own dark head bent into the wind.

"What a good girl she is," Carla's mother says.

Carla nods. Though truly Tess is a girl no longer.

They watch Tess go from JAKE'S into the post office. She's glad Tess is the one to reach in the box and find no letter from Rudy, the one whose face Carla's mother will search all the way back across the street. Plus how she hates to go anywhere in Danford since Rudy's arrests. Shame. She knows all the busybodies gossip about those Morlettis who live up on the hill. Say what an unfit mother she's been. And of course some of what they say is true.

Tess emerges from the post office. She's smiling and waving a white envelope.

> Gramma — Don't come to visit — I had to stand up to a couple of thugs and that lost me phone calls and visits for two weeks — the hearing's been put off again until April 27 — I haven't slept since I got here — I'm starting to see things — they're watching my every move — please, I beg you somehow put together the money to bail me out — I did not violate or have drugs on me — I'm not going to make it if I have to stay in here — Also please ask Tess to find out Sunny's address and mail her the private letter that's in with this — Nooley or Mark may know where she is — anybody who writes me has to put a name and return address on the envelope or they won't give it to me Love — Rudolph

▪ ▪ ▪

[ 29 ]

# Whatever they're calling wacky this week.

When he saw Tess's truck move farther and farther down the road until it disappeared, he knew. They didn't get his letter. He can't call them. He can't call Nooley to find out where Sunny is. He can't sleep. He can't stop moving. They're all watching him. Now they've angled the monitor so no matter how he sits or lies on his bunk they see everything he does. He needs a cigarette. If he had a cigarette, maybe he could get his head to slow down. He has got to get out of here. The C.O.'s never mailed his letter. If she'd gotten his letter, she would've bailed him out. He's got to get bailed out. Ten more days before he can call anybody. Ten days. The hearing's postponed again. What if they keep postponing? What if Granley's in on it? He can't stop moving. His legs keep moving. Somebody's trying to tell him something, but they keep jamming the message. He's got to be careful or they're going to find out. If he could only get some kind of sleep aid. If he could sleep. If he tells them he needs something for sleep, they'll know. They'll think he's crazy. He isn't crazy. He needs a cigarette. He needs to get out of here.

He reads the back of *Rules & Regulations* again. How many more times is he going to read this?

If during your incarceration you feel you need to talk

> with someone from Onango County Mental Health, you must submit a request in writing and we will set up an appointment with a liaison counselor.

Liaison him to the whole dorm. Mark him wacko. Only one step above child molester. Really mess with him then.

Focus on this: He. Has. To. Get. Out. Of. Here. There's only one piece of paper left. One envelope. They won't give him any more paper until next week. Who's his best bet? Nooley? Mark? Maybe Sunny if he knew an address. Not John or Prager. Something strange going on there. Who? His only chance. Try her again. See if this letter goes through.

He lines the paper up so it's all around even with the *Rules & Regulations* book. He scrapes the lead of the pencil with his fingernail to get more point. "Gramma, please …"

▪ ▪ ▪

[ 30 ]

# Do you suffer ... ?

Carla sets Willie Jones up with another draft and a shot of Jim Beam. Next she places the Mood Disorder Questionnaire she just got in the mail at a spot on the bar where she can answer the questions and still be able to read her mother's face as she listens to the lawyer on the phone.

Ollie Burke and Ron Luger's glasses are half full and they're deep into NASCAR on the TV. A business-suit type she's never seen before is deep into going through a bottle of scotch with a little chaser on the side. Maybe another hour before the Edgewater gets busy. She's put an "Out of Order" sign on the juke box and temporarily misplaced the remote so she can keep the TV volume low enough for her mother to hear Granley and to give her brain a chance to cool down.

"Carla, you got any chips … those vinegar ones?" She slides two packages, what Ollie always gets, down between the two men who are tracking those cars. Round and round and round, their heads doing little circles. She's given up trying to figure it.

After three Advils and a cup of heavy cream to keep her stomach from screaming, her head's gone back to its normal size. The wattage on the shooting lights behind her eyes is no longer threatening to bust a fuse. She pushes her reading glasses down on her nose so she can eagle-eye her mother and fill in the questionnaire at the same time. At the moment her mother seems to be taking notes on every word so all she can see is the top of her fuzzy head. Main message Carla wants: Do not bail Rudy out. Rudy out in his current state … well, hard to say what kind of trouble he'd get into, but easy to say whatever it is, they'd all be slogging through the black muck that would result. She has dreams where no matter how hard she pulls, she can't lift her foot out to take the next step, and as far ahead as she can look, a sea of tarry gunk.

*Mood Disorder Questionnaire*

> Take this test to see if you might have bipolar disorder symptoms. Then share the test results with your doctor or therapist.

She used to have a therapist, well a counselor, which is basically the same deal. Joy, at Mental Health. Joy, who's really the reason she finally got her GED. She used to tell Joy her black muck dreams, but mostly Joy was a "You can do it, Carla" counselor rather than one of the stretch-out-on-the-couch kind. 'Course that was before the doctor screwed up the carpal tunnel surgery and she got into the pain medication.

Her mother has now turned her back so Carla can't read her face. Carla watches her shoulders and the tilt of her head, but it's harder to interpret the yes or no on bail from this angle. Of course bail is what her mother wants to do. Mortgage her house, sell those puny diamond earrings T.J. and Bobby gave her for Christmas. Good this Granley doesn't charge for phone consultations. They've been going at it, her mother taking notes for … Carla checks the clock … 5:30 … at least ten minutes.

The bipolar test's got twenty yes or no questions. No little slots for "maybe." No way to sit on the fence. You're either crazy or sane. Her experience: there are a lot of half and halfs out there. She's going to try to answer it as if Rudy was putting down the *X*'s. Then add up the score. Use it as evidence that what Rudy needs is to be sent off to one of those treatment places for mentally ill addicts. An alternative instead of Rudy going to jail. Medication part of the deal, something to cool *his* brain down. Get him in one of those long-term places. Eighteen months, two years. With Rudy having to stay because if he drops out he goes back to jail.

Of course all she has is a stubby pencil, but maybe that's best. Put her into more of a frustrated, irritated, pissed-off Rudy mood right from the go.

> Has there ever been a time when you were not your normal self and: (answer yes or no to the following)

But instead of starting with number one, Carla can't resist what she always does on any of this kind of stuff, she looks at the last question first:

> 20. you suffered from abnormal delusions, paranoia, or hallucinations? ___yes ___no

Huh? What kind of question is that? Like some paranoia's normal? She's been waiting for this test for two weeks and already she sees the person who made it up is an incompetent. How's she going to get any kind of valid diagnosis if all the questions are twisted? She goes ahead and puts an *X* by "yes." Then she places a slash through the number so she can keep track of the questions with mistakes. Use it as evidence if she decides to write a letter to this psychiatric place to complain. She goes back to the beginning:

> 1. you felt so good or so hyper that other people thought you were not your normal self or you were so hyper that you got into trouble? ___yes ___no

Carla reads the question again. Thing is, right away there's a problem. It doesn't take into account the other important factor: crack. Should she take the test as though she's Rudy when he's high or Rudy when he's not using? Rudy gets hyper. Rudy gets into trouble when he's hyper. But does he only get into trouble when he's high? Maybe the first question really ought to be "1. What drugs do you use? ___Cocaine ___Crack ___Meth ___Opiates ___Ecstasy. Go to page 2 if it's cocaine and crack, page 3 if it's meth." One page for each kind of high and a "do all the pages if you do all of the above." Or maybe the first question ought to be "1. Do your friends and/or family members think you're crazy?" Though probably it'd have to be politically correct and say "mentally ill."

She checks on everybody's status. The three-piece-suit guy is slowing a little, which is good because if he kept downing the scotches she'd have to ask him if he was driving, and if he was she'd have to shut him off, and he looks like the kind of man who could swell up and get nasty. Of course to the "what drugs" question, she'd have to add alcohol.

Willie's just about ready for another Jim Beam. If she's going to pump him about Sunny, she has to do it on the next round, because after that he'll be incoherent. Any second Ollie is going to say, "Hey, Carla, how about a burger for your favorite customer?" And that'll mean she won't be able to finish filling in the questions to come up with a tentative diagnosis. Plus it'll delay having her mother give her a blow by blow on what the lawyer advises.

> 2. you were so irritable that you shouted at people or started fights or arguments?

Please. Ninety-nine percent of the world is going to say "yes" to that question. Maybe she ought to give this test to everybody in the bar. Set up one of those control-group experiments.

"Carla, how about making a burger for your favorite customer?"

And just then her mother hangs up the phone and turns, her notes all twisted up in both hands which probably means it's a *no* on bail. This makes Carla want to lift up both her arms with a shout of *yes!* Plus if she's going to get the inside story on Sunny, now is *the* moment when Willie is the exact degree of blitzed to spill every single thing he knows.

■ ■ ■

[ 31 ]

# More Than 50 Lbs.

Tess kicks off her shit-boots. Got to be quick. Betty's headed her way. She slings her coveralls over the hook and moves toward the milk house door. Just give a wave and bound for the truck. Ever since Rudy got arrested again, she can't bear to go through the chit-chat with the Daweses. Especially not after today and not knowing what Rudy's done to lose his privileges.

"See you tomorrow," she calls. "Got to pick up my grandmother."

"Hold up," Betty hollers. "I've got some jam to give you."

No way to escape now. Betty's coming on full steam, giving her the "be not anxious" grin. Of course Betty knows what's up.

She touches Tess's sleeve and starts them both toward the house. "Only take a minute. Thing is, strawberries are going to be coming on before you know it and I've got a freezer full of last year's jam."

They both know this is not about strawberries.

Tess stops in the mud room. "I'll wait here. I stink."

Betty looks to the heavens and pulls on Tess's arm.

If she goes in that kitchen, Betty's going to say something real, and if she does, Tess knows she's going to cry. Boohoohoo, they won't let us see my brother and he's going crazy and God knows what's going to happen now.

"Just sit yourself down for two seconds while I get it. You sure you don't have time for a cup of mint tea? You look a little peaked."

"Thanks, but I better get moving." She is going nowhere near how her grandmother's at the Edgewater because she was too sad to go on up to the house.

Betty disappears into the back pantry. Tess leans in to look at the grandkids on Santa's knee, the smiling family portraits. Tommy in his uniform, his wife and brood. The oldest daughter and her bunch. But no picture of Katie. No picture of Katie's kid. Katie was in Sunny's class. She remembers watching them bad-assing around the halls, big deal seniors when she was in ninth grade, getting into her own kind of trouble. Rudy off following the Dead all around the country selling tie-dye T-shirts.

Betty returns hefting a bag of jam jars. "Tess …"

Here it comes. Tess widens her eyes and breathes deep.

"I can't say much … since well, you know, Hoop being the judge and all, and this is strictly coming from me. Hoop never discusses the cases. Never. But I just want you to know I don't believe Pat Keegan's story. Not one bit of it. And I better stop right there. My Katie … well sometimes I think there must have been something in the macaroni and cheese they were serving in the cafeteria those years … my Katie and Sunny Jones, Rudy, Pat … well, you know, the troubles they've seen … And here's another thing I want to clear up. We know there have always been rumors that Rudy might be the father of Katie's son, Billy, but that isn't so. Definitely that isn't so."

And with that, tears, the both of them. Betty puts an arm around Tess and leads her to a chair. She sets a box of Kleenex on the table and turns to put on the kettle. "Just sit for a minute. Where's your grandmother? I could give a call, tell her you'll be along soon."

Tess blows her nose. "No, it's okay. She's visiting with my mother at the Edgewater." She laughs. "Probably listening to some regular's tale of woe."

"Well, main thing, I could see you've been ducking out, avoiding us, and I just wanted you to feel easy again. Believe me, Hoop and I, we know what it is to worry about a child … our Katie … she's cut us off completely. We did that tough-love stuff, and well, no matter how

I try to get through to her now, she won't see me or answer my letters, my calls. That's why we don't have any pictures of her and Billy on the refrigerator, 'cause that would mean every time I reached in for the butter, I'd start bawling. Hoop, too."

Tess touches Betty's arm. "This is why when I start feeling maternal, Queenie and I plan to get a box of kittens from the little boy standing outside of Walmart."

Betty laughs, and they both blow their noses, loud, without any holding back. Betty loads mint leaves into two little silver tea balls, hooks their fragile chains on the edges of the cups, and pours the boiling water in. "Add a generous dollop of honey." She plunks the pot between them. "Well, it soothes … our bees too. But you've got to let it steep."

Tess puts in a big spoonful. She hasn't eaten since breakfast. Of course, if she mentioned that, Betty would be up and making her a platter of something. Sunny. No question Betty may know something. "You mentioned Sunny Jones. Would you have any idea where she is? I'd like to get a letter to her?"

"Rudy?"

Tess nods.

Betty leans back, clearly thinking it over. "Well, I could give you Katie's email. Not her address. She wouldn't want me to give out her address. But my guess is she'll know where Sunny is and she could find out if Sunny even wants a letter from Rudy."

"All right."

Betty takes a pen from the jar and writes the email address on a corner of the napkin. She passes it over. "You do know the sad story of Sunny and Pat Keegan's baby after they ran away to Florida? Must be ten or twelve years ago now. Sunny, only a few years out of high school?"

For a second Tess doesn't respond. She doesn't know and she's not sure she wants to know.

"The thing is, it might help you understand Rudy better. Puts him in a better light."

Rudy in a better light. Lately she's been remembering the better Rudy: his genius at fixing her bikes, her skateboard. The time he and Papo built her the tree house. She'd even been thinking of seeing if they might practice some sets together, do a few gigs — places the probation rules might have allowed. All futile now.

But this story about the baby. She guesses she's going to have to let that in.

Tess rises. "Let me call my grandmother at the Edgewater to tell her I'm going to be late."

Betty hands her the phone.

▪ ▪ ▪

[ 32 ]

# Love Songs

Angela sits a little forward, a sheet of paper held up before her eyes, while Willie Jones pushes the swing back and forth with one foot in time to his low Danny Boy hum. Willie's sad song, the rush of the brook just beyond the edge of the porch, an occasional drunken laugh from inside the bar: if Angela or Willie were to reach over and give the other a comforting pat, the tears would flow. But neither does. Instead Angela tries to once again read her letter to Rudy by the light from the Coors sign each time they glide past, but it's too dim to catch more than a word or two. Even so, she continues to hold the sheet of paper in both hands ready to show to Tess. Tess will arrive. They will drive up the hill. Tomorrow will be another day.

Tess makes the turn onto Main Street. Most of the houses are dark except for the blue lights of TV screens flickering. She wishes she could just give a blast of her horn or there was some way she could signal her grandmother from the window of the Edgewater porch, so she doesn't have to go in, go through the motions of "How are you?" Gramma sounded weary and defeated on the phone. And this story about Sunny certainly does nothing to lighten the load.

Even a block away there's the noise coming from the Edgewater. Then she sees the two heads moving back and forth in the blinking light. As soon as she pulls to the curb, there's her grandmother slowly descending the steps, her arm clutching the elbow of Willie Jones. Hard to say which one is holding the other up.

"Hey," Tess calls to the two of them. She helps her grandmother into the truck. But when she turns to say "Can I give you a lift," Willie's already shambling away, a backward wave of his hand his only response.

"Poor little man," her grandmother says as she reaches over to place a sheet of paper under the St. Christopher statue. "My letter to Rudy for you to mail." With that she closes her eyes, and by the time Tess makes it to Main, her grandmother's asleep, resting against Queenie.

Tess inches the paper down, but all she can catch in the street lights are the words "Dear Dear Rudy" across the top. She turns onto the Back River Road. The paper, with what must be bad news about the bail, flutters against the dash. A black night, not one star, no moon. She hunches close to the wheel, ready for deer that come from nowhere. One hand alert to press against her grandmother if she has to brake suddenly. Queenie sits rigid, ready too. Sunny. Sunny and Pat Keegan's baby. Why should she tell Mamo and Gramma anything? Rudy had nothing to do with it. He wants them to know, let him tell. Her only part of this mission is to get Rudy's letter to Sunny delivered. She feels in her pocket once again for the wad of napkin with Katie's email. If that doesn't work, well, she'll track down Nooley or Mark, somebody who can get that letter on its way. The notice about the internship will come any day. Finish the vet tech degree next June. Then, it's Hawaii or some other land where the sun always shines. "Ehh, Queenie?" she whispers.

It's then that she hears them. Off to the left where the beavers have taken over acres of the back side of the Daweses' lower forty. She rolls the window down all the way and slows to a creep. No question it's them: their ratchet of out-of-synch screech and rasp and plunk, more like a machine than something living. She and Queenie lean out to catch it all.

Her grandmother sits up. "What?" she says. "What's that strange sound?"

Tess reaches across and rolls her grandmother's window all the way down. "Peepers. Little frogs waking up after a winter sleeping deep in the mud."

Her grandmother leans out, cups a hand behind one ear. "What are they saying do you suppose?"

Tess laughs. "It's their love song."

"You mean like," and her grandmother sings in a sweet, soft alto, "'Some enchanted evening …'"

Tess joins in, "'you will hear me calling.'"

She turns off the truck. They sit and listen in the warm dark.

▪ ▪ ▪

[ 33 ]

# Promoting Natural Behavior

Brennan, one of the good C.O.'s, unlocks the cell at the far end of the infirmary. He motions Rudy to step in. "Like I told you, Morletti, week or two down here on your own — good for all concerned. You'll get your privileges back Thursday. No daytime lockdown after that. You can use the phone."

Rudy pushes the clothes bin under the cot. Watches Brennan as he goes down the hall, listens for the click of the infirmary door. While the rest of them were at breakfast, they moved him downstairs. Wannabe gangstas return to the dorm with oatmeal on their chins. Where's Rudy? Gone bye-bye. So, here he is. In the recovery cell block. Only eyes on him now the surveillance camera and an occasional glance from the nurse's office at the far end.

Only other inmate in this section is an old guy in the cell across the way who says nothing, simply sits and stares at the gray floor. Just the sort of companion he needs. Rudy stretches out on the cot. Might be able to actually get some sleep here. His nerves have calmed. Less twitch. How many more days before it's Thursday and he can make a phone call. He thinks and thinks, tries to count back to when he knew where he was in time.

"Any idea what day it is?" he calls to the man. No response, not even a twist of a shoulder. It's like that panther poem from the jail library: Beyond those bars: no world. One good thing: even though the bars are still here, his legs have stopped making him go back and forth, back and forth.

There's a clank and the door opens down the hall. Rudy rises. A rush of adrenaline, but it's only Brennan. "You got two letters, Morletti. Also a message from your lawyer. He's going to meet with you after court tomorrow. Late afternoon." Brennan passes the letters to him. One from Prager which he sets aside. Probably another veiled paranoid warning which even the illiterate C.O.'s can decode about how he better keep his mouth shut if he knows what's good for him. The other one from Gramma DeLuca. Bail news. Opened and inspected. The stamp removed in case she dropped a bit of acid on the back. He studies the carefully written address and decodes that: bad bail news. His hand shakes as he pulls the single sheet out. A little church card drops to the floor: picture of Jesus, looking all wimpy, surrounded by a bunch of lambs. You look like that in here, Jeezo, and they'd fuck you over big time.

Rudy breathes, unfolds the paper:

> Saturday, April 9, 2003
> Dear Dear Rudy,

He lies down and places the letter on his chest. Already he knows what it says: no bail. And he knows why. She wanted to do it, but his lawyer convinced her that it was best for him to stay in jail until the hearing. Mamo, no doubt, dancing a jig about that. He looks at his hands. Good sign he didn't go all bonko over this news. The angel has passed over again and marked him with a "Do not destroy." At least, not this time.

He skims the letter. Word for word what he already thought. Only thing new: must be she told the lawyer about him not sleeping 'cause Granley's advice is to contact mental health which will look good for the hearing. Show he's taking positive steps on his own, buying into the whole "the rest is up to you."

Bottom of the paper in bold print: "P.S. No luck getting your letter to Sunny yet, but I've got some leads. I am totally on it. Love, Tess."

Love, Tess. He smiles. See that: a smile. Must be she's finally forgiven him for locking her in the crawl space with the spiders. He searches in the bin. No paper left. If he hadn't been so wacked, he could've ordered some from the commissary. Have to make do. He removes Granley's note about the postponement from the envelope and inch by inch, loosens all the glued places to open the envelope out into a flat sheet. Then he refolds the creases in the opposite direction and runs his thumbnail along all those edges. He tears off all the flaps with an even pressure until he's left with one clean oblong, only his and Granley's names and addresses on the other side.

He opens the *Rules* book so he can see the section he needs for spelling all the words correctly, then places the paper evenly on the printed lines of the opposite page. See through to keep his writing straight. In his head, he figures exactly how he's going to say it. He's not going to use the word "need."

"Please set up a appointment for me with a Onango County Mental Health liaison counselor."

He looks it over, then goes back and adds the letter *n* to make it "*an* Onango" — *a, e, i, o, u* — he got that. It was the *p*'s and *g*'s that messed him up.

He does a simple signature — no phony flourishes — folds the paper, and places it in the *Rules* book. Let it sit for a while. Talk to Granley. Check all the angles before he hands the request over to Brennan. Maybe, if he has a little chat with some counselor, the session may include a couple of Camels.

He pulls the blanket up, turns away from the bars. He can feel it: sleep. Sweet Jeezo, bring it on.

▪ ▪ ▪

[ 34 ]

# Balance

Carla stops at the top of the stairs and checks the sign on the door straight ahead: "Onango County Mental Health & Chemical Dependency Clinic."

Looks like they've got the druggies and the crazies in together now. Save the county a few bucks. She leans against the wall for a moment to catch her breath. Three flights up: if she'd still been smoking, she'd never have made it. Definitely take the elevator next time if she ends up having to mess around with this whole business again.

Got to convince the powers that be that what Rudy needs is to get mandated to long-term inpatient drug treatment, mandated medication to calm him down. Phoenix House. Daytop. This Granley lawyer guy's dead set against this according to her mother. What does he know? His son's probably president of the student council.

She checks herself over, pulls down on her sweater, and opens the door. New office, but the same ratty furniture. Same interior decorator they've got over at Social Services, but there's no security guard here searching your purse to make sure you don't have a gun.

She goes over to the window with the little opening. Waits for the receptionist to get off the phone. Windows, with little openings, the

M.O. in this part of the world. At least there's no trough for her license. The woman puts down the phone and smiles.

"I'm Carla Morletti. I have an appointment to see …" She hesitates.

"Ben Jacobs. He's with a client right now. Running a little late. There's coffee. Bottled water."

"I was wondering where Joy …"

The phone rings. "Excuse me," the receptionist says.

Joy. That's who she needs to talk to, somebody who knows her story already and doesn't have to go plowing through some case file. But all she got when she called was a 'Sorry, Joy is no longer seeing clients.'

Carla turns to the little table with the coffee maker, the packets of Splenda, the jar of Cremora. Coffee? Best not to do that to her stomach. Not on top of the three Advil. She picks up a bottled water. Bottled water: what yuppie thing is she going to do next? Start buying organic broccoli?

She takes the best chair and settles in. Feels good to sit. Her brain's still banging from her fight with Tess. She removes her wrist braces and tucks them in her purse. She doesn't want to go in there to talk to this Jacobs guy looking disabled. She pulls out the Mood Disorder Questionnaire and spreads the sheets out on her lap. In the margin are all the tallies on the yeses: her answers when she pretended she was Rudy on crack, then Rudy when he wasn't using, and how she, her mother, and the guy who was deep into the scotch answered. If you scored more than five yeses, the instructions advised you to definitely consult your doctor. All of the tallies were way over that, even her mother's: Rudy had fifteen on the best of the two tries she'd filled in for him. She and the scotch drinker ranged between total crazy and borderline nuts. Of course when she tells the counselor the results from the questionnaire, she isn't going to describe the conditions under which she collected the data.

Slick-looking magazine on the wobbly end table: *Recovery Life*. Bold list of articles down the side: "Are You a Credit Junkie?" "Sex Addiction vs. Erotic Intelligence." Quiz for that one would pep up the Edgewater crowd about their third round when they're making the shift from high to grim. She flips through the pages: lot of colorful ads: "Recovery Dating: How great would it be if your soul mate were also in recovery? www.soulmate.com." Opposite page, an expensive hotel ad: a woman getting a massage from a beautiful man. Clearly better to be rich if you've got a bad habit.

Big article on Wynonna and Naomi Judd: how they balanced their brains. Now there's a good trick. Serve that up at the bar: a few mind calisthenics, like extra cheese on your hamburger only one dollar more. She'd like to read how the heck Wynonna recovered her balance. Might help with the migraines. If she was Rudy, when the receptionist looked the other way, she'd stick this copy of *Recovery Life* right in her purse.

"Ms. Morletti?"

Carla drops the magazine as if the skinny guy in the doorway just about caught her shoplifting.

"I'm Ben Jacobs. Sorry to keep you waiting. My office is right back here."

She follows Jacobs down the dim hallway. Guy looks a lot like those Whole Earth artist people Del Merrick used to hang out with. Rimless glasses, baggy corduroy pants — L.L. Bean that had a second life on a Salvation Army rack.

He motions her to take a seat beside his neat desk. Not a thing on the top. Clearly opposite type from the lawyer. Be interesting to meet both their mothers, get their philosophy on having kids make their own beds.

"Coffee?"

Carla raises her bottle of water in answer.

Ben Jacobs sits and there's a moment of quiet. Like he dimmed everything down. "Usually best if you say what's on your mind, why you've come to the clinic. Then we can take it from there."

Carla breathes and clicks into her little speech. "My thirty-five-year-old son Rudolph Morletti is in the Onango County jail right now. He's been charged with a felony: assault. And also possession. This is his third arrest. Rudy is … Rudy has a serious drug problem. And he's been diagnosed bipolar. I'm here to see if there's some way the clinic can help Rudy be mandated to go for treatment at a place like Daytop, rather than going to prison."

"Has your son ever been a client here at the clinic?"

Carla nods her head. "Both Mental Health and Chemical Dependency. I'm sure there are a couple of fat folders in one of your file cabinets."

"And is he interested in going into treatment? Because I'm sure you already know that's the main thing. The willingness to seek treatment is what matters most."

"Well, here's what I'm hoping. That you could go meet with Rudy and help him see that's his best alternative. I was just reading a magazine out there in the waiting room that talks about balancing your brain. That's what Rudy needs: a total rebalance. In fact I wouldn't mind learning how to walk out on that wire myself."

Ben Jacobs smiles. He reaches in his desk drawer and pulls out a DVD. He hands it to her. "It's an interesting idea," he says. "Check it out."

Carla looks it over. In big green letters on the plastic case: *Brain Training: The Unlimited Powers of a Balanced Brain.*

Ben Jacobs leans her way. "I'm one of the counselors assigned to the county jail. I'd be glad to have a talk with Rudy. But first, he has to make a request to see somebody from the clinic. Can you speak to him about that, see if that's what he wants?"

Carla reciprocates the lean. "Thing is, me speaking to him … well, you know … the mother-kiss of death."

Jacobs smiles a smile that says, yeah, he's got a mother. "You say he has a bipolar diagnosis?"

She'd like to take a peek at the questionnaire, but best go with what she's got jammed in her head — her aching head — already. "Some doctor here a few years back said he's bipolar. From what I've been reading, I think that's right on the money: can't sleep, mood swings, paranoia … what a lot of us have, but times ten. You know what I mean?"

"I do," Jacobs says.

"Whatever he's got, it comes and goes."

"If you're up for sitting here while I skim through your son's records, I might be more helpful in terms of what his chances are of getting into long-term treatment. There are fewer programs for people who have both a substance abuse and mental illness …"

"I know — a dual diagnosis. I'm up for sitting. First time I've had a chance to do nothing today."

In a few minutes, Jacobs is back with two folders. And they are fat. It's reassuring that the clinic's neat and tidy on the filing. Jacobs takes a seat, but before he opens the first folder, he gives her a direct look. "Probably you already know …"

"I do," she says, "it's all confidential, so you can't tell me what it says in there."

"Right."

She likes this guy. He appreciates her not making him go through that little speech. She glances at him; he's slowly turning pages, taking a few notes. And really she wouldn't want to read all that stuff anyway. She already knows more than she can bear.

True, she did want to know what was in Rudy's letter to that girl, that woman, Sunny. Tess's refusal to let her look the letter over upped the ache behind her eyes this morning. "P-R-I-V-A-T-E. That's what it says on the back, Mamo. And we're going to respect Rudy's wishes on that." It's not like she wanted to read it out of curiosity. Some big mystery about this Sunny and seems like it might be helpful to know what's going on to help convince the court to go for treatment instead of jail. Willie totally clammed up, actually staggered out when she started to pump him. Tess won't talk. And she hardly wants to call around the town. At least she now knows her name is Sunny with a *u*. Some comfort in that.

Sooner than expected, Jacobs closes both of the folders. "I see your son's got lots of mechanical talent. Lots of employment potential. Definitely one of the most important things for … keeping one's balance. If Rudy puts in a request to see me, I'll go through these more thoroughly. But already I've got a much better idea of some programs, counseling that might be helpful."

"Well …" Carla says, feeling like it's about time to stand. Nothing more to add to her pitch.

They both rise. Jacob leads her to the back exit. He extends a hand. "No matter what Rudy ends up deciding to do with his life, it's important for you to remember: it's good you came in."

No need to tell this guy, more than anything she wants eighteen months of no calls in the night.

▪ ▪ ▪

[ 35 ]

# The Exact Nature of Our Wrongs

Tess brakes and backs up. Nooley's truck: she's sure of it. Nooley's truck in the Presbyterian parking lot. Same rusty fenders, only a little more so. Who else is still going to have not one, but two peeling Grateful Dead stickers on his bumper? "What a long strange trip it's been." She parks in the shade and rolls the windows down for Queenie, who hasn't even bothered to open an eye.

On the seat, Nooley's leather cap. Nooley's truck in the Danford Presbyterian Church parking lot can only mean one thing: a noon meeting. Anonymity be damned. She can wait or she can go in.

What the heck? She opens the door to the basement: the cold and damp of all that dark and stone. Methodists seem to go more for white clapboard: bound to be a bit lighter in spirit. She heads for the smell of strong coffee. She hasn't seen Nooley since Papo's funeral four years ago. He's got to be at least forty by now.

She scans the group from the door. There he is in the first row. Still got the little ponytail, but hair going thin on the top. Nooley: she never did know his real name, but when she was just a little kid, Nooley stayed with them so much, he was like a brother — sometimes a much nicer brother than Rudy. She slips in and takes a chair in back. About a dozen people, mostly men. No one she knows in her current life.

They're on the eighth step. A woman, with one of those bouffant hairdos and a quivering voice, is sunk so far into the little book as she reads that it's hard to hear the words. Tess tries the hand-cupping-the-ear trick. "Made a list of the persons we had harmed, and became willing to make amends to them all."

She'd actually made one of those lists once, but for every name she wrote down, she'd come up with so many reasons for why the person had it coming, she'd ripped it up saying best thing she could do was to relocate, and that's when at seventeen she'd hitched to Austin and started playing keyboard and singing covers with the Texettes. Seedy joints at first, but over the nine years they advanced to better honky-tonks: less fighting and more money.

An old man in the far corner mumbles so that the ninth step is inaudible. Then, as though to make up for that, the next man booms: "Continued to take personal inventory and when we were wrong promptly admitted it."

Definitely she never made it up that far on the ladder. As the man turns to hand the book to the next row, Tess gets a good look at his face. And right at that same moment he sees her, a big grin and a wave. Everybody turns. Rozmer. Mark Merrick's NA sponsor. Rozmer, and so thinned down from his huge former self, it's hard to believe it's the same person. It's only been since October, right after Mark wrecked the car ... only five months ago, but truly it feels like years. Years. Nooley also gives a cool nod of recognition.

It comes to her that she feels faint, and through the closing-in tunnel, she hears that the topic they're going to pass like a hot potato around the room is "secrets: how secrets keep you from healing." She does *not* want to be here. Getting Sunny's address surely does not require that she listen to people's deepest, darkest. Go dredging in her own subconscious. She's going to trilobite right out of here and wait for Nooley on the sidewalks of Danford where all the passersby are keeping their despicable acts to themselves.

Must she give some apology for her sudden exit? Sorry but I forgot to roll down the windows for my dog. She rises, steadies, and without one word, escapes.

She sits on the cold steps of the damp stairwell, her head between her legs, her knees stopping any secrets from entering her ears. When she's sure she isn't going to pass out, she flees. One thing she can definitely say on her personal inventory: she would never ever leave Queenie cooped up without air.

She gives Queenie a quick run around behind the church. Still plenty of time to pick up the mail. Plus the good luck that the P.O. window's closed for lunch. She won't have to respond to Fred Postmaster's command that she have a nice day.

Two envelopes. First one, no return address. The other, "Langley Zoo." More than one sheet inside. She breathes and opens it:

> We are pleased to let you know that you have been awarded the Primate Enrichment Internship which will run from June 1 until August 20. Your hours will be from 10 a.m. until 2 p.m. Wednesdays through Sundays. Enclosed …

Tucked in a fold of the zoo letter, a note written on a section ripped from a paper bag:

> Congrats. Any chance you'd be able to come over to Cornell this next Saturday around noon? I'd like to show you the whole setup at the vet school. Good band playing in Trumansburg that night. Gary gary.simms@cornel.edu 682.542.8844 (cell).

A life. Out in the world — a life. Well, what do you know?

Tess opens the other envelope:

> Send the letter to me and I'll mail it on to Sunny. 411 Bunson Rd. #6, Langley, NY 45321. I count on you not to give my address to ANYONE.

12:55. She sprints for her truck. She does not want to do the "How are you? I'm fine" with Nooley or Rozmer. To talk about Rudy or Mark.

Queenie is sleeping in the driver's seat. "Shove over, girl. We're in a hurry." She parks across from the P.O., watches Fred make his way from JAKE's, a fat book tucked under his arm. She waits until she knows the window's up.

"One stamp and one stamped envelope, please."

She folds back the edges on the envelope for Sunny so it fits in the one she addresses to Katie. On the inside flap, she writes, "I won't tell anyone your address. Thanks, Tess." Just going to have to trust that all these years later if Katie has any getting-even needs, they've burned down to ash. She slides the envelope through the Out of Town slot. At least when Gramma visits Rudy, she can tell him the letter's on its way.

"Have a nice day," she calls to Fred in a cheery voice she's never heard before.

▪ ▪ ▪

[ 36 ]

# Hard to Say

Brennan escorts him to the same room where he has his meetings with Granley. Going to be no Camels.

The man rises and bends toward him across the table. "Ben Jacobs," he says. "From CDC." No handshake.

Guy looks like an old hippie. A lot like Aaron, Aaron Merrick, how he might've looked if he'd reached fifty. Same off-center wire-rim glasses, but without the duct-tape repair. Kind of guy who'd look like Jesus if he went around the bend.

"I got your request to meet with a counselor."

They both sit down. Rudy wills his hands to rest on the table.

This Ben Jacobs sits easy. Looks at him, but not piercing.

Wait for the guy to fill up the space with a bunch of words. Less Rudy has to say, the better. Why the fuck did he turn in that request anyway? Cigarettes? Sleep aids? To please the assistant D.A.? One thing for sure not to bleat on about Sunny, not to rave about how angry he is. Best to keep that boxed.

Okay. He's going to have to go first. Jacobs has the "got all day" down. Better at silence than he is.

"I'm not sure why I ended up filling out a request. Maybe it's because my lawyer said it'd look good for my hearing." *My* lawyer: first time he's thought of him that way.

"Sounds like good advice," Jacobs says.

"Yeah, I'm feeling I may be able to trust this man — Bill Granley. He gets a good rating from the jailhouse lawyers."

They both laugh.

"Or maybe it's because my first few weeks here I couldn't sleep. I was thinking CDC could prescribe some kind of sleep aid."

"Do you often have trouble sleeping?"

"Comes and goes. You know: Which comes first? Is it the speed? Is it the crazy? Is it the crazy 'cause I can't sleep?"

"What do you think?"

"All of the above. I'm sleeping better since they put me down in the infirmary in a cell by myself. Lot less stress. Not having to swell up to discourage the other hooligans."

"Have you considered going into treatment? Maybe long term where they'd help you deal with 'all of the above' — the no sleep and the drug use? Maybe less pressure."

"Been there, been there, been there. Those sit-around-the-circle, spill-your-guts sessions always make me want to bust right out and shoot up."

"What if treatment was a better alternative than going to jail?"

No cigarettes, but for some reason this Jacobs can ask without setting off the alarms. "The lawyer is dead set against that. He seems to think that even if I get jail time, it's going to be short, and it's going to be county-time, but if I take the treatment route and screw up, then it's double-time on the incarceration and likely to be state-time. Elmira-time."

"And you're thinking that the weight is on the 'screw up' side of the scale?"

"Fuck up, fuck up — that's me. Lawyer says do treatment once I get out if I decide that's what I want. Lot less consequences if I mess up then. Maybe only a little county-time for breaking probation. But I'll tell you one thing: it's best if I don't run into the man who hit me in the face and then lied and lied and lied … Hard to say what I'd do if he came up on me again."

▪ ▪ ▪

## [ 37 ]

# We can help you change your life forever. Call today.

Carla's got them right where she wants them: Tess slumped at the table studying and her mother trailing along the edges of the kitchen, watering her tomato plants. The *Brain Training* DVD is already loaded. She sneaks a peek to check that the player light's on. All she has to do is remote the TV when she's ready. But first she's got a few more things on her agenda.

She glances over Tess's shoulder to see what Tess is highlighting in hot pink marker.

"What in the name of … you know who … are you doing?"

Tess doesn't answer, just shrugs and lifts the paper for her to read. "The Mating Habits of Chimpanzees." No kidding, the specifics of how chimps get it on.

Carla flips the calendar on the fridge to April and places a magnet squarely in each corner. She borrows Tess's marker and *X*'s off the first twenty days. Those days are gone and there's nothing further to be done about them. She stands and contemplates the remaining ten blank squares in which nothing has happened yet: no terrible phone calls, no migraines, no bad news — no news at all.

Now's the time to make as much of a plan as they can. Kind of map out the three alternate routes: Rudy goes to long-term treatment; Rudy goes to jail; Rudy gets released, with only probation. Just the thought of this last one — Rudy on the loose — causes a flash of white light behind her left eye.

Yes, before she gets into balancing the family's brains, specifically Rudy's brain, she first wants to do a little contingency planning. Just then, her mother waltzes by with the watering can. Maybe even before the meeting, it's worth trying to give her mother a small dose of reality.

"Who do you think is going to take care of those tomatoes when you go back to California?"

No response. Her mother just gives Carla a calm smile as she rotates each of the plants. It's like living with a couple of mutes. Should she tell her mother that she's laboring under a total delusion if she thinks Rudy will be let off scot-free? Maybe not, but she will say this much: "If Rudy does get out of jail, do you really think he's going to dig holes out there in this rocky ground? Is he going to weed? Pick off the slugs? Then bring the tomatoes in for *me* to put up in jars for next winter?" Her own answer to this is, Huh?

"Carla, Carla," her mother says.

She could fill a book with the meanings for that answer. Instead she taps Tess's paper with the marker. "How about something with a fine point to fill in our schedules for the rest of April."

From nowhere, Tess produces the perfect pen for the job.

"Okay, Rudy's hearing is next Thursday at four p.m." She prints that neatly in the "27" box.

Eight days away. Another white flash.

"Visit Rudy on the 23rd. But how we're going to get there, Mama, is still a problem since Tess is taking herself off to Ithaca for some undisclosed business that day." Does appealing to Tess's sense of guilt get a rustle? It does not.

"And there's the appointment with the lawyer tomorrow at three." She carefully avoids saying "We've got." Instead she tries, "You know, Mama, there's really no need …"

Her mother puts down the can and squares her shoulders. This means, Don't try to keep me from seeing the lawyer; I'm going; that's final.

But it would be so much better if Carla could nose-to-nose with this

Granley person on her own. She's got to convince him that Rudy needs to be mandated to do long-term treatment because not only does he have a serious drug problem, but he has these periodic crazy spells that make it likely he'll violate probation. Her mother's going to be no help on getting the lawyer to agree to that since all she wants is for Rudy to be tucked away safely in his own little bed upstairs. Good luck.

Carla concedes Battle 1: best to move on to setting a positive stage for watching the brain training DVD. Oh, if they were rich, she'd try to get the whole family to go into one of those brain labs, get all their lobes aligned. There's an 800 number you can call for a free consultation.

She measures out the coffee and water and presses the On button, then slips the cinnamon rolls into the toaster oven. 'Course she'll have to talk fast to disarm Tess, to even get her to sit still for the promo.

In no time the kitchen fills up with the smell of hope. She sets the real butter and the Belgian White Chocolate Macadamia Nut Creamer on the table. No shit, that's what it says on the label, but oh it is so worth the hype. The minute the coffee's ready she fills three mugs and leads her mother to a chair.

Tess eyes her suspiciously. "Watch out, Gramma, Mamo is up to something." Even so, Tess puts down her marker and lifts a cinnamon bun, dripping with icing, then loads up her mug with creamer. Her grandmother does the same. The three of them give their full attention to this small feast.

When Carla thinks they're as sugary high as they're going to get, she says in her gravest tones, "Tess, Mama, Ben Jacobs, the counselor at the clinic, gave me this DVD" — she lifts up the plastic case — "that he thinks might help us understand what's going on in Rudy's brain …"

Her mother's eyes widen.

Tess reaches over and takes the case from her fingers. "'Improve, Enhance, Achieve with Brain Conditioning' … Please, Mamo, some more of your voodoo …"

"I know, I know, it sounds … but I'm telling you …" Carla sees Tess is about to bolt. She flicks on the TV and blurts out the first thing that comes to her: "It might even help you understand the brains of ... chimpanzees."

▪ ▪ ▪

[ 38 ]

# Freeze Release

Tess takes another bun and pushes her notes just enough to the side so she can study without her mother noticing. Better if her mother stuck to reading the horoscopes. Easier to tune that out. First thing the DVD shows is a modern building, the interior professional and expensively done up.

"Mamo, don't you see the con. Right away they're trying to make you think this brain stuff is scientifically based when really it's snake oil. Remember that potato peeler you saw demonstrated at the fair …"

Her mother turns the volume up and scoots the chimpanzee notes out of eye-reach.

The next image is of a man with a bunch of electrodes fastened all over his head.

Tess stands up. "That carnival guy convinced you the little gadget was going to peel and dice and slice. But all it did was rip up the potato."

Her grandmother raises her hand and leans closer to the screen. "Let's watch this, Theresa, what can it hurt?"

Tess sits back down. Okay, she'll be good.

Next they have people come on to do testimonials: how in twelve sessions of this neuro-feedback, they're sleeping better or their migraines have stopped, they're no longer drinking.

But then a neurologist begins to talk about how all pathologies are the result of trauma and he talks about the brain with such authority that … well, she sees with surprise that she's eating every bit of it right up. She turns her chimp papers over and starts taking notes.

Tess fast-forwards again to the section of the brain training DVD where the polar bear is running across the ice trying to get away from the threat, which in this case is a helicopter pursuing him to shoot him with a dart to sedate him. Even before he's sedated the bear begins to slow down, and then he falls on his side. In this state of analgesic shock, he continues to move his legs as though he's running, going through the motions of escaping. His belly begins to rise and fall. According to the neurologist narrating the film, the wild animal has gone through a freeze release, meaning that because he imagines he has escaped, his brain has released the incident and therefore the incident has not caused trauma. Read his brain and there's no red explosion on his wires at that point. According to the neurologist, successfully going through the motions of escape makes the animal more resilient, more prepared for the next time he needs to take flight.

But — unlike animals in the wild — zoo, domesticated, and lab animals do not undergo this natural process of freeze release, and as a result threats cause trauma, which leads to all sorts of pathologies. And of course this is true of human animals, the narrator says, who are also trapped in the cages created by their culture.

Tess looks over the diagrams she's made of the brain, especially the section on the amygdala. She checks her notes on the function of this almond-shaped set of nuclei buried deep in the temporal lobe of the brain. "Amygdala: primary role in the processing and memory of emotional reactions." This whole brain balance, neuro-feedback thing, claims the amygdala is the key to training the brain to stop getting triggered until, finally, the corrupted memory no longer leaps up to cause pain or a compulsion to use or panic … Keep the amygdala from getting zapped by the negative whatever and you don't experience the trauma.

What she wants is to go over all of this with Gary Simms. Maybe even express mail the DVD to the zoo today so he can watch it in advance. Is it too farfetched to think that scientists could place electrodes on captive chimpanzees' heads and read their brain waves, then establish protocols to calibrate these readings to encourage all the lobes of their brains to balance? A kind of ritual. High-tech saying of the beads. Hey, maybe she could get plugged in, cure her asthma as well.

■ ■ ■

[ 39 ]

# The Poison Option

The huge chain saw is no longer in evidence in the lawyer's office, but there are still several tall stacks of folders on his desk, so rather than peer at Carla and her mother through the tunnel of these, Granley has made a circle of three chairs, his chair closer to her mother — already it's two against one. Carla can't help checking out Granley's long braid and his hands as he talks: the hands of a tall man, large and sure, that he doesn't wave about. The kind of hands she likes. She's glad he doesn't have the sleeves of his shirt turned back. And it's clear her mother's working on not looking gaga-eyed as well.

One thing she's got to admit: he listened to her entire spiel and now she's going to have to listen to his.

"I understand your concerns about Rudy's drug use and what sounds like manic behavior. Though I can't share with you any of Rudy's conversations with me, it does seem as if he's made a connection with Ben Jacobs. Once Rudy's released, that connection may be key. But as Rudy's lawyer, my job is to look out for his legal rights. My main goal is to get him out of the criminal justice system. If I felt he was going to receive a sentence of more than eighteen months, the length of long-term treatment, then I might advise him to give the treatment some serious consideration, but I'm convinced that's not how it's going to play out. If Rudy gets any more jail time, most likely it's going to be under ninety days, with a third of that already served."

"And if he violates his probation?"

"Oh, Carla …"

Carla gives her mother the look that causes her to stop right there.

"It all depends … No promises, of course, but here's what I think is going to happen. There's a lot in Rudy's favor: no proof of a baseball bat or any assault weapon, the claimant's record of previous false witness, no proof that the packet found in the bushes at the mill is connected to Rudy. My talks with the assistant D.A. and the police, and what I've seen of the records, make me optimistic — at most a few more weeks in jail. Plus three years' probation."

Carla's hands fly up and begin to massage her temples.

Granley pauses. "You okay?"

"No, but go on," Carla says.

"Since he has two prior arrests, the level of counts against him, the felony and misdemeanor charges, are more iffy to predict, but everything's going to get reduced. What would happen if he violates? It depends on the nature of the violation. Rudy's smart. He's going to completely get that."

"He's smart all right."

"Of course, you're going to be anxious."

"Yes," her mother says, her hands in a knot.

"Do what you can to not keep imagining all the scenarios. Rudy will have my office and cell phone numbers. He'll know he can call me. Maybe he's going to know he can call Ben Jacobs …"

"Well, I tell you this, I do not, I do not want him to call *me*."

"Oh, Carla …"

"You want to give him your number in California, feel free," Carla says. With that she slings her bag onto her shoulder.

"Look," Granley says, and rises at the same time she does. "I've got kids. An older one who went out on all the edges. She's doing okay now, but well, this being a parent …" He laughs. "I'd rather take poison than go through that again."

▪ ▪ ▪

[ 40 ]

# Birth Canals

Tess is early. She drives slowly past the three inpatient facilities of the vet school: separate hospitals for equine, farm animals, and "companions." Queenie expresses increased interest, her nose out the window, wags of recognition. The Cornell Veterinary Research Center is even more impressive than what she'd gathered from her virtual tour on the internet. "Look at me," it says at every turn. "I am ranked the best veterinary school in the U.S." Certainly it makes her own little community college, with its one-story vet tech building, look squat and third world.

Probably Gary comes from a family that slides its children straight down the birth canal into such privilege. She has a flash of Gary driving up to the Morletti door on Chicken Farm Road, the Maverick parked in the yard. When my brother gets out of prison, he's hoping to get it down off the blocks, she could tell him.

She pulls into the lot closest to where she's to meet Gary, picks the shade of a huge maple tree since Queenie's going to be stuck in the truck for most of the afternoon. Even the parking lots are privileged: they're flanked by big trees.

"Sorry, girl, but I'm going to have to put you on a leash." Such an indignity, and one that Queenie has only experienced two or three times in her life. She gives Queenie a leisurely tour of the area to mark all those trees.

Then, there he is. They watch Gary's loping stride as he cuts across the lawn from the building marked "Companion Animal Hospital" on a huge brass plaque. Queenie's first look at him ever. Tess's first look at him without his wool hat. His first look at her without her dreads. His hair is even curlier than hers, a regular explosion of blond ringlets which must have made him the recipient of many gushing sweet cherub *oohs* when he was a toddler. Were they to ever have a kid, any attempt to brush the tangle would be labeled abuse. And where did that absurd thought come from? She barely knows this guy.

She breathes and tries to get her stomach to unclinch. Queenie's tense as well. The absurdity of being tethered by a leash and because she feels how off balance Tess is.

Off balance. Tess checks her bag to see that she has the brain diagrams, the list of questions she wants to ask Gary. She does.

"Relax, Queenie," she says. Relax yourself, Queenie's huff replies.

"Hey," Gary says, reaching out a hand to touch Tess, but then he hesitates when he sees Queenie's guard-dog stance. "And you must be Queenie." He extends his fingers toward her nose.

Queenie does not take a sniff. Instead, she sits down and makes eye contact with Gary.

Unlike Luke, Mark Merrick's big chocolate Lab, Queenie has never been pals-at-first-sight with any of Tess's new friends.

"Oh, I see," Gary says. "You're going to decide if you approve." He withdraws his hand and waits, lets Queenie be the dominant dog.

"You're going to get points for that," Tess tells him.

By the time they take Queenie back to the truck, she's granted Gary the right to scratch her neck, pet her head, but really she seems to be rather bored with it all. She curls up on the seat as soon as Tess cranks all the windows down a few inches.

They head back the way they came.

"You said in your email you'd like the grand tour. I thought maybe we could go through the Companion Hospital first. There's an emergency C-section scheduled on a Siberian husky in a few minutes. We can watch that from the observation room, get close-ups on the monitors, if you're up for that."

"All right," she says. Though really she's not sure she *is* up for that. Even the birth of kittens makes her anxious. Will they all be alive? Will they all be normal? Will the mother give the runt the extra attention it needs?

As the doors open automatically, Gary says, "I found the brain-balance DVD fascinating. First view I thought quackery, but the next time through, I started thinking of the various relatives I'd like to get hooked up as soon as possible. I'm hoping we can talk about it under the influence of a few beers before we go to hear the band in Trumansburg. There'll be no chance to talk about anything there. Too loud. But it's great music for dancing. One whole set of bluegrass."

As the doors close behind them, he does take hold of her arm, gives it a friendly squeeze.

From the observation room, they see that the husky has already been sedated, her legs splayed and secured by straps to the four corners of the table. Her huge belly, with its eight swollen teats, has been shaved and is now being draped in sterile cloths that leave only the area for the incision exposed. There's not even a twitch from the husky; clearly she's knocked out to the max. Three men and one woman, all in blue and wearing surgical masks, move tensely around the table. There's no talking.

"The woman's the vet, the rest are second-year vet students, the tall guy's the anesthesia technician," Gary tells her in a whisper, though surely the observation room is soundproof.

With the husky stretched out on the operating table, most of her body now covered by surgical sheets, it's hard to see her as a dog. Tess and Gary are the only observers. Evidently the husky's owners, the people she "companions," have for one reason or another chosen not to witness. Most likely Tess wouldn't be able to watch Queenie going under the knife either. Queenie was spayed before she chose her from all the others at the S.P.C.A.

"I didn't have time to find out why a C-section's necessary," Gary says, still whispering.

The small room has two monitors: one that gives close-ups of the husky's belly, the other that shows the heart and blood pressure readings.

There's the bleep, bleep of the green line declaring the pulse rate.

They begin the intubation.

"Wider," the vet says to the technician, who's opening the husky's jaws. The sound system is very clear.

Tess makes her eyes steady on the monitor: gloved hands holding the husky's mouth open; other gloved hands pushing the plastic device down into the throat to widen the passageway, then inserting a tube, inch by inch, to finally reach the animal's stomach. Gary is still, all his attention directed to the close-up of the procedure.

"I haven't done a C-section yet," he says.

The anesthetic cup is placed over the husky's muzzle, with the tube trailing out the bottom. Tess has stopped breathing, her throat is tight, a pressure building in her chest. The warning signs of an asthma attack. She closes her eyes and works on relaxing, her own heart beating hard. The birth of kittens, calves … she's made it through those and not passed out. What sort of veterinary technician will she be if she can't watch an operation without fainting?

Suddenly the heart bleeps stop, the blood pressure begins to descend with alarming speed. There's a rush of action.

"Epinephrine," the vet says.

A shot given, a change of the valves on the anesthetic machine. Then a pumping and thumping on the husky's chest. The tubes removed, respiration given. Minutes pass. There is still no blood pressure, no heartbeat. Tess sees she's clutching Gary's arm. Minutes more, the team's movements a silent film of speeded-up action. More time passes.

Finally Gary turns to look at her. Gone, he mouths, no sound at all.

The vet leans close to the table. "Prepare for the section," she says. A technician hands her a scalpel.

"They'll try to save the puppies," Gary whispers, his hand over hers.

The vet pinches the flesh along the husky's midsection. Then, without hesitation, she makes a long slit. The layers part. There's very little blood.

"I can't," Tess says.

Somehow she finds her way outside, to a bench across from the entry. By the time Gary sits beside her, her cries fill the courtyard. An eruption of wails she can no longer contain.

He holds her. He finds tissues in her purse. He places one hand on her cheek. He does not offer up words to still her. Words aren't what she needs.

After a long time, she stops. They sit shoulder to shoulder, look out across the campus, students rushing along the walks in the distance, the world going on.

"The puppies?"

"Stillborn. Probably even before the section began."

Gary takes hold of her hand, turns her palm up, traces her life line, and then folds her fingers into a fist.

"You want to go to my place? Have coffee, eat something? Whatever you want," he says.

They walk to where she's parked. She gives him her keys. He drives slowly out to the main road. Queenie curls between them. The constriction in Tess's chest has eased.

Gary unlocks the door. Tess and Queenie follow him down a dim hall. Past orderly rooms. Lots of anatomical charts on the walls — of dogs and cats and cows. "Pete, Gavin," he calls. No response. "Probably have labs," he says.

In the middle of the kitchen table, there's a violin case. Old and well cared for.

"Oh," she says, "Yours?"

Gary nods.

"You didn't tell me."

"We hadn't gotten to that yet."

"May I?"

Gary reaches over and unlatches the case. "It was my grandfather's. Scottish."

She touches the steel strings lightly. "How I love a fiddle."

"Go ahead," he tells her.

She rests it under her chin. But does not lift the bow.

She gives him a long look and then lowers the fiddle. "I was in a band in Texas. Keyboards. Left home when I was seventeen. I was there off and on for nine years. The Austin area. Three other women. Girls when we started. Mostly covers. Roadside bars. Saturday night sinners; Sunday redemptors. I miss it."

She hands him his fiddle. "Play," she tells him.

He raises the bow and does a few phrases.

"The Dixie Chicks. How did you know?"

"Texas. I knew you had to do that one." He plays some more.

Tess sings softly: "If you ever want to find me I can still be found. Takin' the long way, takin' the long way, takin' the long way 'round." She stops and sits down.

"Ahh." He sets the fiddle back in the case, "Nice. So here's another thing we'll have to do."

"I don't have a keyboard right now. No access to a piano. It's been almost a year since I've done anything."

"I know someone we can hook up with who's got a keyboard, a piano."

"I'd like that," Tess says. "My brother plays. Guitar. Some banjo."

"I didn't know you had a brother."

"Yes, I have a brother. An older brother."

And when she doesn't say anything more, Gary gets down cups, begins to measure out the coffee. While it drips into the carafe, he gives Queenie water. He sits next to Tess and slowly peels away the thick rind of an orange. They breathe in that gust of citrus as he pulls the sections apart to form a circle on the table.

Tess places a slice in her mouth. It's one of those perfect oranges: juicy and sweet.

She looks at him head on. "My brother's in jail," she says. "He's charged with assault for beating up a man. Probably about a woman named Sunny. And she's gone off without letting him know how to reach her."

Gary returns that look. Listens.

"All part of such a sad story. Maybe a story everybody in the town knew but us. And I only know because the woman I work for, Betty, just told me yesterday."

Tess takes another slice of orange. Caught in that moment of stopping there or going on.

"About thirteen years ago in Florida, when Sunny was nineteen, she and the man my brother beat up had a baby. When the baby was one month old, she died. Found in her crib. Sunny came home from work and found the baby in her crib. Crib death, they said."

She closes her eyes, but then she opens them again. She does not want to see that crib.

"There are rumors. Talk that the father was knocking the baby out by putting morphine in her bottles. When she cried, he put morphine in her bottle." Tess looks away again, watches the poplar branches shimmer silver as the wind blows through them.

Gary reaches across and takes her shaking hand.

Her voice is low. "Could Sunny have known this was going on all along?" So low, she's not sure she really said this out loud.

Queenie rests her head on Tess's knee.

Again she looks at Gary. "Why am I telling you this? Something I haven't even told my mother or grandmother? Something my brother has never mentioned to any of us?"

Gary continues to look at her. He cups both her hands between his.

"Strangers on a train," he says. "I've told them all my secrets. Every single one."

▪ ▪ ▪

[ 41 ]

# It is now up to you.

Rudy laces his boots, zips his sweatshirt. Real clothes. This is it: the day for his hearing. Brennan takes him down to sign-out. Two troopers. Neither looks familiar. This is good: he doesn't have to start off with a fist of rage choking him. Neutral. Aim for that.

"I'm Officer Daniels. This is Officer McClusky," the taller cop says. "We have to cuff you. Extend your arms."

He nods to each of them and slowly stretches his hands out, his hands shaking and his heart banging in his ears.

Daniels slips the cuffs on and tests to make sure they're locked. They're cold, but they don't cut into his wrists. Cuffed hands forward rather than with his arms twisted behind his back. He's their prisoner, but, like everything else, it's all a matter of degrees. He's less imprisoned if he doesn't have to go to court with his arms feeling like they're being pulled from the sockets. He won't have to stand before the judge with his body bent in an ape-man hunch.

They step out into the world beyond the razor wire. The world's still there. Across the way, hills in the distance, the maples just beginning to bud. All that hardwood ready to be harvested for lumber.

Daniels opens the back door of the patrol car and gestures for him to get in, and then both policemen get in front.

The radio crackles. McClusky drives by the front entrance, then pulls onto the road. He lifts the receiver: "Car 104. We're leaving Onango County Jail, on our way to Danford Court."

Danford Court. Here we go. He breathes. What he wouldn't give for a cigarette, but at least he's been sleeping. The quiet of the infirmary.

Rudy studies his scratched reflection in the Plexiglas that separates the front and back seats. His good clothes, which were delivered to him this morning, not the mill jeans and grubby T-shirt he'd had on when he was arrested. Instead his grandmother's sent the "try to get a job" outfit she bought him: the gray hoodie, the navy Dickie shirt, black combat pants. Real laces, a real belt. He can hang himself twice if it turns out he's going to get sent to Elmira.

No chit chat. Only occasional radio static. These troopers — very professional, like they took the "Avoid Riling the Bad Ass" training seriously. Rudy leans his head back, closes his eyes, scans for the calm of oblivion.

His hearing — even though he told them not to come, probably Tess will be there. His grandmother, giving off high-voltage anxiety, will be in the back row quietly fingering her beads. But not likely Mamo. Too pissed? Too fearful she'd scream and charge forward to throttle or try to save him? Sunny? He wouldn't want her there, but he would like to know if she got his letter. Big question is, Will Pat Keegan be there? No way to stay neutral if he walks in and finds Keegan sitting in that courtroom. Keegan up there lying. No way he can listen to that.

He opens his eyes, feels the miss of the engine when they start up the hill. Car needs a tuneup, check the spark plugs. There's a hum, left rear. Wheel bearing needs a grease.

■ ■ ■

[ 42 ]

# Even Incredulous Souls

3:30. Angela appears at the door of the kitchen, wearing her Sunday best. Tess closes her book and gets up from the table. Queenie goes to sit by the door. Carla is scrubbing something at the sink, her whole body bent, her hand moving fiercely back and forth. On the drain board are the blackened parts from the gas stove burners. Tess, Angela, and Queenie watch her. Tess takes her own jacket and her grandmother's coat off the hooks by the refrigerator. Then she plants her feet and yanks on the door.

"Carla …" Angela says.

Carla opens the oven and pulls the top rack out.

"Carla …"

Carla bangs the rack against the edge of the sink. "I … am … not … going." Each word punched hard. "I already told you that." She doesn't stop scrubbing.

Tess takes her grandmother's arm. They make a detour around the Maverick. She helps Angela into the front and lets Queenie settle in back. She puts the key in the ignition, but she does not start the engine. Instead she rolls her window down and watches the kitchen door. In a few minutes, the knob begins to turn, the glass vibrates, giving off glints of light. Thuds and a muffled scream. Then the door is thrown back with a crash and Carla starts toward the truck. She smacks the Maverick's hood on her way by.

They move slowly down Chicken Farm, make the turn onto Cobb's Road, and pass the collapsed barn on the corner of Grat's Bend. They watch the smoke rising from the Merricks' stone house across the brook. When they reach Route 8, Tess yields to a milk tanker. The muddy water of Onango Creek has spread into the fields along the highway. They drive the two and a half miles into Danford. The truck turns up the back way to the town sheds, navigating around the deep ruts left by the plows. The town courtroom is housed in the back corner of the big gray building. Tess pulls in beside the trooper patrol car and puts the truck in park.

"Here we are," she says.

The three women enter and move quietly down the dark corridor, a lighted doorway in the distance. The only sound up ahead, something being scraped across the floor. Tess takes her grandmother's hand and they step into the back of the courtroom. Both blink in the fluorescence. Carla hesitates, but then she follows. They steer toward the middle of the back row and sink silently into the metal chairs.

Rudy is seated in front on the left. He is wearing his sweatshirt even though the room is over-warm. His lawyer sits beside him in a suit, long braid neatly tied by a thin black band, briefcase open on the small table. Two troopers sit directly behind them. The judge's high bench is empty. On the right, across the narrow aisle from Granley, seated behind a matching table, is a man in a turquoise pullover, pilled by many washings, and a pair of rumpled khaki chinos. A mess of papers is spread out before him. This must be the assistant district attorney. And this is reassuring because he seems so outmatched by the professional uprightness of Rudy's defender.

There are no other people in the room. Must be that Rudolph Morletti is the only case before the court on this April afternoon. They wait, the stillness interrupted only by the hiss of a radiator.

Finally there's a rustle and a door on the side opens. Judge Dawes, huge in his black robes, enters. The lawyers, Rudy, the troopers rise. Tess pulls her grandmother up and gestures to Carla. Once the judge is seated above them, they settle in again.

Judge Dawes surveys the court and then there's a low squeal of feedback as he switches on the recorder. "April 27th, 2003. Four p.m. Town of Danford Court. Onango County. Judge Dawes presiding. Case … ," he turns and lifts a folder, puts on his reading glasses, "4658. Rudolph Morletti, thirty-five, a resident of 374 Chicken Farm Road." He then raps his gavel twice and says, "Court is in session."

The two lawyers exchange looks and rise. "Your honor," the assistant district attorney says, "may we approach the bench?"

"You may."

The two men move forward. "We'd like to confer with you in chambers," the man in the rumpled chinos and sweater with static cling says.

And with that Rudy's lawyer, the assistant D.A., and the judge exit.

Tess, Carla, and Angela look at each other. Rudy does not turn. No one moves. It is hot in the room. They wait. They wait for a long time. Finally the taller trooper rises and opens one of the windows. He moves to the back and turns a switch. The ceiling fan begins to rotate, giving off a rough murmur. The trooper looks at the three women, one by one. "It won't be long now," he says.

And the trooper is right. Within minutes, the three men return and are once again seated. Judge Dawes notes the fan and the open window. He looks around the court, and when the tall trooper nods, says, "Thank you. Now how about shutting the radiator off. Don't want to hear about how I'm blowing taxpayer money out into the great beyond."

There's the screech of metal on metal as the trooper turns the knob. Judge Dawes taps, taps, the tape-recorder mike and looks at the courtroom clock. "5:35. Continuing the Rudolph Morletti hearing. Attorney William Granley and Assistant District Attorney James Murphy and I have reached an agreement. Rudolph Morletti, please step to the bench."

Tess, Carla, and Angela stop breathing. Rudy and his lawyer move forward. Rudy stands directly before Judge Dawes, his shoulders back, his head raised.

"Rudolph Morletti, you have been found guilty of one Class A Misdemeanor for harassment. Thirty days have already been served at the Onango County Jail. No further jail time required. Though, should you violate your probation, it's likely you will find yourself once again sitting in a cell. The order of protection will remain in effect for one year, to end on April 27th, 2004. Until such time, you will not in any way make contact with Patrick Keegan. Your lawyer will give you a list of all the Danford streets where you will not be permitted. You will be placed on probation for three years. The terms of probation will be explained to you by your probation officer when you meet with him next week. You may be picked up from the Onango County Jail later this evening as soon as they've completed all the release paperwork."

There's a muffled sound of someone weeping in the back.

Judge Dawes leans forward. "Rudolph Morletti, I hope you know how fortunate you are to have a family that's still willing to back you up. Seems to me you'd walk out of here with a promise in your heart, and you know what that promise is."

▪ ▪ ▪

[ 43 ]

# Inhabitants

Tess pulls the truck in by the fence with the razor wire. She leaves the engine running and keeps her low beams on. That way Rudy will be able to see the truck the minute he steps out of the jail. She removes the "Zoo Intern Information" sheets from beneath the St. Christopher statue and switches on the inside light. Goal: to stop being in the present for the duration, until she and Queenie are on the beach, the waves sucking at their ankles. She twists toward the overhead and holds the paper only a few inches from her nose.

Taking the Animal's Perspective

> To fully appreciate enrichment (or lack thereof) it is important to consider the environment from the animal's perspective. Let's imagine two hypothetical exhibits.

Rudy: keeping his perspective set on the promise that's supposed to be in his heart, or "Rudy on the loose?" At least Mamo and her grandmother did not choose to be part of this next act in the drama—the plucking up of

Rudy from the maws of incarceration. She only has to deal with her own revving motor while she waits, doesn't have to breathe in the tension of them on the edge, ready to read Rudy's pulse, the clues of his every gesture, beginning with the velocity of the jail doors as he pushes them open.

> Your initial impression of the first exhibit is that it is drab and messy. Everything is a shade of brown or gray. The available perching consists of unpainted metal poles and PVC piping, often making it difficult to see the inhabitants.

She reaches back and yanks her duffle over the seat. Queenie opens one eye: What now? Tess places the notes in her teeth and rummages. She knows it's in there somewhere: the pack of Camels her grandmother slipped her on the sly when she dropped them back at the house. Heaven only knows how long she's had them tucked away with her hopes that Rudy was going to be freed after his hearing. Finally, Tess's fingers fish the pack out and she sets it on the dashboard squarely in front of the passenger seat. Queenie rises and gives it a tentative sniff. Then she circles a few times and settles back down with her nose tucked between her paws.

Then there it is: the glint of the jail entrance doors as they swing open. She stuffs the zoo papers back in her bag and tosses it over her shoulder. Then she snatches the cigarettes off the dashboard and puts them in her pocket. Of course she'll give them to him if he asks, *but* she is not going to start right off in the roll-over posture, appeasing and tiptoeing around Rudy's every mood and move. She has a life and she's going to get on with it. She doesn't urge Queenie to hop in back so the seat's ready. This way when he opens the door, there Queenie will sit to deflect his first waves, whatever those may be.

Low beams over by the fence and an engine running, the light on in the cab. He steps out onto the road and squints. Last thing he needs is for Prager and his associates to have gotten wind of his release, to have decided they'd like to have a little friendly chat. Recent read-between-the-lines threatening notes from Prager indicate that the guy's mental health has reached an all-time low. Afraid Rudy's agreed to wear a wire, inform on their operation in exchange for a get-out-of-jail-free.

Only one head visible in the truck, but he can't tell for sure if it's Tess. If it is her, at least this means she's come alone. The static in his brain stills. He turns his face up to the sky. Stars. Jupiter and a ring around the moon. Been a long time since he's been out in the night. He moves cautiously toward the lights. Then he sees a small dark form rise and press against the glass.

He speeds up and opens the door. "Queenie. Tess. I'm glad it's you, just the two of you," he says.

He lifts Queenie and slides in, puts the brown bag with his belongings on the floor.

Tess hands him the pack of Camels. "From Gramma."

"Gramma DeLuca," he says. "What a pistol."

"Your angel."

They sit for a few long minutes and say nothing. Then he turns. It feels as right as it's going to get. "Tess … Tess, I need to find Sunny. My best chance, maybe my only chance, is for you to tell me who's been getting my letters to her."

Silence.

"I called Mark and Nooley. They didn't even know she was gone."

More silence.

Finally Tess speaks. "Rudy, I'll keep sending your letters on. Maybe they aren't even being forwarded. But I promised not to tell who or how. And I'm going to keep that promise."

Sitting in the darkness beside this woman, his once-baby sister, is there any way he can make her tell him? No there isn't, Rudy, there isn't.

Soon the jail is far behind. The truck's high beams the only lights on the long road that stretches before them.

▪ ▪ ▪

*Doing Time Outside*

[44]

# Discharge Planning

Rudy once again slides most of the big flattened piece of cardboard under the Maverick. Then he hefts the new used transmission from the back of Tess's truck and sets it down on the edge of the cardboard. Next he backs her truck onto the road. On a rare day off, that she's been willing to leave her keys in the ignition for this maneuver is indeed a vote of trust. Hard to believe, but by doing something called googling on a computer, Tess actually found a used 1974 Maverick transmission at a salvage yard in Roscoe.

He checks the sky: black, and the air's heavy with the smell of rain. Well, at least he'll be under the car when it lets loose. If after all this, the Maverick still doesn't shift, he's going to push it down to the back field and torch the goddamned thing. Maybe he could take the car not working if he'd get some word about Sunny. Just to know she's okay. Like Tess said, maybe she hasn't even gotten his letters, his promises of reform.

He rechecks the bag of tools Tess borrowed from Dawes and pushes them in by the drive shaft. He knows without looking that Gramma DeLuca is watching him, ready to run out, rain or no, if she sees him slithering out from under the car to get something he forgot.

It's taken him since noon to replace the clutch disk and remove the old transmission, and it's going to take him until dark to put this replacement in. And even if he does get this clunker running, chances are probation won't let him apply to Motor V for a special license to go back and forth to a job. If he can get a job. One small piece of luck, the key to the ignition was under the seat.

He spreads the greasy page he's ripped from the auto repair manual out on the hood and places his oily finger on the "Transmission, Replace" section, then laughs at the instructions:

> Reverse procedure to install.

He sticks the instructions back in his shirt pocket, gives his Gramma a thumbs up, and shimmies under.

▪ ▪ ▪

[45]

# Swinging from Branch to Branch

It'll be dark soon. Angela sits in a chair by the window watching Rudy, whose entire upper body is draped across the Maverick's oily innards, his legs propped up on a rickety table, the hood rocking above him every time he shifts his weight. Runnels of rain cascade off the hood to stream down the fenders. He's been out there for hours, but his last signal to her — both black thumbs raised as he emerged from beneath the car and jacked it back to the ground — must mean that he's almost done. She begins another round on her rosary and concentrates on praying that the hood doesn't suddenly come slamming down.

Carla slips her reading glasses on and removes the cap from the Day-Glo marker. She flips the refrigerator calendar page to May. "April's gone. Let there never be another month like that. Now, we got to figure how we're all going to get to where we've got to go. Rudy to probation on Wednesday."

She Day-Glo's that appointment in. "Pray to God they're going to mandate he goes to mental health, CDC, and AA."

She puts an *R* for Rudy at the bottom of the calendar and four pink strike marks like she's keeping score. Then she replaces the cap on the marker so it won't dry out. "Okay, that's Rudy. Plus there's Tess who's got to get to school and work, you to the doctor. I'm counting on Dirk for some rides to the Edgewater and back. The Lord only knows how we're going to manage."

Maybe it's the mention of the Almighty that finally breaks Angela's focus on the bouncing Maverick hood. For the first time in hours, she puts meaning to the steady stream of words that are forever coming from Carla's mouth. "But we'll have two vehicles," Angela says, and immediately returns her gaze to the car.

"You really believe Rudy's going to get that piece of junk running again? And even if he does, all the prayers in the world won't get it to pass inspection. Plus Rudy's got no license and no way are they going to let him get one. Which is a good thing. Rudy with a car. Please."

Carla steps into the hall and hollers up the stairs, "Tess, I need your class and work schedule *now.*" When there's no response, she shouts again, and this time there's the sound of something heavy dropping to the floor.

"Up there reading about apes."

Suddenly the hood's shaking increases. Angela reaches into the closet and brings out Tess's old red high tops.

"And what may I ask in the names of all the saints are you going to do with those?"

Angela quickly laces the sneakers up, puts her raincoat on, sticks the flashlight in the pocket, and places both hands on the doorknob. She gives it all she's got. The door doesn't budge.

Tess comes in, still wearing pajamas, and hands Carla a paper. "Gramma," she says, "why are you going out in the pouring rain?"

"I want to take Rudy the flashlight. I want to keep the hood from falling."

"Don't help her with that door. That's all we need, for you, Mama, to get pneumonia and have to go to the hospital."

Tess extends her hand. "Here. I'll take him the light, and if he feels like the hood's a problem, I'll hold it up." She turns to get her jacket.

Angela shakes her head. "I want to do it."

"If we had an umbrella, I could ..."

Angela shakes her head again. Tess nods and gives the door a yank.

"I'm going to hold you responsible if she catches her death," Carla says, and begins to enter the dates from Tess's schedule on the calendar.

Tess watches her grandmother make her way to the Maverick. She sees Rudy scramble down and usher her into the passenger seat. Then he sets the container marked "transmission fluid" on the ground and lowers the hood. He gets in the car. She hears the engine fire up. The lights go on. Slowly the Maverick backs out of the yard onto Chicken Farm Road. Rudy gives the horn three blasts and the car speeds away.

▪ ▪ ▪

[ 46 ]

# Have mercy on us.

Tess manages to make the turn just as the light changes to red. Rudy squeezes his eyes shut when the white-and-blue statue of Mary looms up down the block. Already people going in. Bells ringing. Stoned it wouldn't be so bad. Xanaxed. Even if he could suck a little nicotine down, but no smoking's allowed in the truck.

Tess slows. "I'm going to let you and Rudy out here, Gramma, then park around the corner. Got to study for my finals." She pulls into the "No Parking" square in front of the church.

Big letters inside the welcome box: "Jesus said, 'Come unto me.'"

Rudy gets a flash of the Jeezo-shit-eating smile that would accompany such a message. His own mouth is dry and his hands wet.

Right away, Be-Not-Afraid Gramma DeLuca opens the truck door.

"Wait," Tess says, starting to step out to go around to assist.

He wants to grab Tess by the back of the neck and cry out, "Don't leave me."

"Not necessary," his grandmother tells Tess, and slides down out of the cab, one hand on the door, the other clutching the back of the seat.

As soon as she lands, Rudy wipes his palms on his pants and pushes the seat forward to angle out. Last time he felt like this was when Papo dropped him off for his first day of kindergarten.

Once on the sidewalk, he turns back to Tess. "You sure you don't want to join us? Since I'm going to have the job interview with the priest after, it'll be a long time to sit in the truck."

A squeal of laughter from this person he locked in the crawl space. "You're no lamb to the slaughter," she says, and shifts into drive.

Just as he closes the door, she yells, "Meet Gramma and me at the Edgewater when you get done."

"Best I not be seen in such a den," he says. "Make it the coffee shop."

Gramma DeLuca waits halfway up the walk, smiles at the people going in. People who look a lot like her. When he gets to her side, she reaches up and dusts off the front of his hoodie. "I'm proud of you, Rudy, for keeping your word about going to Mass with me."

He doesn't remind her that it was a one-time-only deal.

She takes his arm and they start up the steps.

"Are you sure your parents never ever took you to church?"

"Never."

"Have you ever *been* in a church?"

"Once." For Aaron Merrick's memorial service, but Jesus, he doesn't want to think about that now. And he better stop using the *J* word. In this place he might get a "Yes," which would definitely send him around the bend.

He opens the door for her. There's the sound of a piano and singing, a choir dressed like angels off to the side of what looks like the main event. There are already dozens of people seated. It's not a big room, but it's still got that cold-cave feel because of the stone. It's dim, even with all the stained glass. The ceiling's high, and of course there in front, his hands and feet nailed to a huge cross, Jeezo. Rudy winces and looks away. If possible he wants to steer them toward a seat where that whole scene is on the periphery. No matter whether you believe this life-after-death stuff or not, that has got to be a terrible way to go.

His grandmother stands on tiptoe and says in his ear, "Only do what you feel comfortable doing, but like I told you, you won't be allowed to join in Holy Communion."

Though he's only got a vague idea what that is, he doesn't mind not being invited to the party.

A woman, a pretty woman with one of those lacy black things on her head, steps forward and hands them programs. Sweet Mary on the front, surely painted before she got the bad news. The program lady looks familiar. He'd forgotten there might be people here he went to school with; though not likely any of his druggie compadres will be in the crowd on a Saturday evening.

Gramma DeLuca dips her fingers in a sort of bird bath full of water. Then she touches her forehead — going to do what he knows is the sign of the cross. He's seen her make this sign often. And number one in the many things that he will not be comfortable doing.

She starts down the aisle. Unfortunately the only empty seats near the ends of the rows are in front. He follows her. He wishes she'd let him keep his hoodie up, but she'd told him before they left that would be disrespectful. She does another sign and a little bob up and down, a little curtsey, before she takes a seat, the cross only a stone's throw away.

He sits beside her and she hands him a book. "For the hymns and the readings," she whispers. Then she reaches over, opens his program for him, and runs her finger down the print to signal that these are the stage directions. Immediate message from here to the Earth as he knows it: whatever they are going to be doing, it's got a zillion parts.

A voice begins to sing. Hard to say where it's coming from. Clean, with no effort on the high notes, probably a young boy before all the shit starts to go down. His "How Great Thou Art" stills the room like the passing over of a cool wind. Rudy settles back and breathes. No question about it, these Catholics are right on pitch for the start of the set.

A man enters from a side door wearing a long green robe with what looks sort of like bulls eyes running down the back, with lacy skirts swaying beneath. Most likely this is the priest. Alberto Rios. Good Guinea name, which may make his Morletti-DeLuca genealogy a plus for once. Father Rios, as Rudy's been instructed to call him, is followed by a young boy, maybe twelve, dressed in a costume as well. The main thing Rudy wants during this church business is to check this guy out, get a feel for how to play it before he goes in to try to get this part-time maintenance-cleaning job, something probation is likely to approve.

On some signal he misses, everyone rises. He gets up a beat or two late. It appears that they're all supposed to stand during the bold-type sections of the program, which means there's going to be a lot of up-

and-downing.

The priest says, "In the name of the Father, and of the Son, and of the Holy Spirit."

Rudy jumps when everybody answers, "Amen."

Next the priest says, "The Lord be with you."

The audience answers, "And also with you."

He feels his grandmother glance at him when he doesn't join in, but joining in is number two of what he's not going to do. Hard to get a read on this Alberto Rios, the man, since he's so hidden under all those layers.

His grandmother points to her program, then to half a page of bold print. And the whole group is off and away. *"I confess ..."* It's probably good that he's standing; all this joint chanting makes him suddenly drowsy. *"that I have sinned through my own fault."* Well, yeah, he can relate to that. *"And I ask blessed Mary, ever virgin ..."* Ever virgin? Now there's a truly hot topic for debate. Given that Jeezo is her son, he'd love to hear the hustle on that one.

And then there's a lot of back-and-forthings of *"You have redeemed the world."* Redeemed? Be good to get an explanation on that as well. Much of the world's going down for the third time, and though off camera, coffins coming home regularly from Iraq. Seems like "redeemed" is a real stretch.

There's a rustle of pages and then they all begin to sing: "Glory to God in the Highest." His grandmother points to the page in her hymnal, but he smiles and touches his finger to his ear. He's just going to listen. And he does listen. He likes the tune and even feels a swell in his chest. It's called the Gloria, and he can see why. He leans a little closer to Gramma DeLuca. She has a mellow alto. Have to get her to join in with him and Tess on a jam. "We Are Fam-i-ly." Oh, she'll laugh at that one.

In a kind of daze now, he gets up when they get up and sits down when they sit down. A woman in regular clothes stands in front and says, "The word of the Lord." She reads from what he knows must be the Bible. A man gets up and reads. Then they all stand for an incredibly long bunch of words which ends with "We look for the resurrection of the dead, and the life of the world to come. Amen." Now in *his* world, the answer to this resurrection jazz, from the usual suspects, would be, "You must be smoking some powerful stuff, man."

And at last they all get to sit down.

His grandmother moves closer. "Communion," she whispers.

She's so mysterious about it, he's actually curious.

Now the priest and the kid begin a sort of dance behind the long table. It's clear that everything is memorized: the big book is moved, a silver goblet is made much of, things are covered and uncovered, folded and unfolded, opened and closed. And always the drone of their words. But when it comes to making a movie, there's way too much repetition. Too much jumbo-mumbo.

He lost the swell in his chest way back there. He's getting muzzy and he definitely doesn't want to fall asleep. Just his luck the one time Father Rios finally gives him the eyeball, his head'll be on his chest. Nodding off. He smiles at the thought of this kind of nod as opposed to the nod that would have been part of his former M.O.

When Rios places a white disk in his mouth and says, "The Body of Christ," Rudy blinks to full attention. The body of Christ? "Amen," the crowd says. Then the priest drinks from the goblet, "The Blood of Christ." Blood? Next the priest does the body-and-blood thing with the kid.

After that Father Rios lifts his arms and says, "This is the Lamb of God who takes away the sins of the world."

Rudy hears his grandmother's clear reply: "Lord, I am not worthy to receive you." Rudy leans into her a little. If Gramma DeLuca's not worthy, well, his own chances would be truly hopeless.

At this point Father Rios and the boy move up to a railing that runs along the front of the church, and as they do, a line of people come forward and kneel. The priest and the boy go slowly down the line. The priest places a small white disk on the person's tongue while the boy holds a plate with a handle on it under the person's chin. The priest says, "The Body of Christ." That's it. No goblet. Evidently the people don't get the blood. Which might be okay in Rome, but seems like it would cause a stir here.

For this first line of people, Rudy really tries to grok it all. The Body of Christ, the Body of Christ. No question these Catholics are on a weird trip. If he didn't know better, he'd suspect they were *on* something. Well, in a way they *are* on something, a kind of trance induced by all this over and over and over. And maybe that's not a bad thing. Whatever gets you through the night. Maybe if he'd been brought up on this "hallowed be thy name, Lamb of God" stuff when he was that kid's age — but well, what he'd like right now is to be out there in the sunshine having a cigarette.

Finally, finally, he hears what he knows has got to be THE END: "Go in peace to love and serve the Lord."

"Thanks be to God!" they all say, and he could join right in on that one.

▪ ▪ ▪

[ 47 ]

# Fire Power

The Bible-reading woman told Rudy to meet Father Rios in the church office in fifteen minutes. Fortunately that allowed him to duck out and fortify himself with a couple of Camels. But now the party's over. Grill time. He goes down the dark hallway following the arrow that says "Office."

Before he reaches the open door, he stops to stare at a huge painting of Jesus on the back wall. In some chilling way it seems to be beckoning to him. Jesus, with his shirt open and on his chest, a bloody heart with a sword sticking out of it, fire leaping up from behind. Then he hears someone swear in Italian.

Rudy knocks on the frame of the door. The priest, in black with a white collar, has a vintage fan turned upside down on the desk, and he's going at it with a screwdriver. He looks smaller out of the green outfit.

"Father Rios? I'm Rudolph Morletti."

The priest waves the screwdriver in a gesture for him to come in. "Rudolph. But I'm betting you're called Rudy. Only my grandmother called me Alberto. To everybody else I was Al or something worse. Now it's Father Al or something worse around here if I've stepped on somebody's toes. Have a seat. Just let me fiddle with this another minute.

So hot in here, but I'm afraid this piece of junk is kaput."

Rudy steps up a little closer. "Probably be a good idea for you to unplug it while you do that," he says. "Want me to take a look?"

Father Al laughs, reaches over and pulls the plug from the wall. He hands the screwdriver to Rudy. Rudy finishes taking off the bottom plate. "It is something of an antique. But see here, it's just a loose wire." He reconnects the wire and screws the plate back on. "Give it a try."

Father Al sets the fan by the open window and plugs it in. A small breeze stirs up the papers on his desk. "Ahhh," he says, leaning into that gust. "I'd say that's about all the interview we need. You want the job, we've got a riding mower you can work on next. It's only minimum wage. No benefits. Have a seat."

"The thing is, I have to first get approval from probation. I think my grandmother told you about all that. I meet with probation Wednesday. Then I'm guessing my probation officer will call you to check things out."

Father Al laughs again. Definitely this man's a laugher. "Doing maintenance and cleaning for a small Catholic parish. I can't think you can get much more legitimate than that."

"Right," Rudy says. "Definitely a few notches above some of my former sources of income. But the other thing is, probation has to also allow me to get a special driver's license to go back and forth to work."

"Fine. Have the probation department call me. And then keep me posted on how it goes. In addition to the mower, there's some heavy-duty cleaning way up on a ladder that needs to be done. Do you do high up?"

"High up? Yeah, my father was a commercial painter. He was fearless when it came to heights. I seem to have inherited his balance."

Father Al riffles through his top drawer. "I know it's in here somewhere, a brochure on the church you could give to the officer."

Meanwhile Rudy feels Jesus looking at him again. Both of Jesus' wounded hands are pointing to the blood-dripping mass.

Father Al looks up to see Rudy leaning toward the painting. "The Sacred Heart," he says. "Your grandmother said you weren't raised a Catholic. My guess is you're thinking we're a strange lot. This painting especially."

"True, as an outsider, it's like landing on a different planet. I do have some questions."

"Well, I'd be glad to try to answer them once you start working here. Not that I don't have doubts myself from time to time. It's often a little tricky to turn my back on that." He points to the painting. "And you'd never guess what some of our devout young people actually do with that image, the Sacred Heart …"

Rudy raises his hand to signal for the priest to give him a chance to guess, to give the answer that flashes up from that mysterious beyond: "They get it tattooed on their chests."

▪ ▪ ▪

[ 48 ]

# The Mango of Knowledge

Tess sets all the bags on the Daweses' huge kitchen counter. "I really appreciate you helping me with this, Betty."

"This way, " Betty says, unloading the cans of Hawaiian Punch, "I can find out what wild thing you're up to now with those chimpanzees."

Tess takes off her coat and turns the last bag on its side. "We've only got about an hour. I have to take Rudy for his first probation meeting this afternoon."

"How's Rudy doing?" Betty says. "Hoop tells me the first weeks out are the hardest."

"So far, so good." This is a bit of an exaggeration. Rudy's edgy, and he's getting coded machine messages from Larry Prager that translate to threatening. She hopes Betty doesn't ask if Rudy's heard from Sunny. Though, from time to time, she has wanted to ask Betty how she's so sure Rudy isn't the father of Katie's son. More proof if she ever decides to present any of this to Mamo. But really what she needs to do is distance from this whole tangle.

Betty hands Tess two five-gallon buckets. "I only used water to wash these. Any hint of Clorox might've made the chimps suspicious, thrown off your whole project — your project with that nice vet student."

"Good thinking," Tess says. She plays deaf on Betty's ploy to find out more about Gary … her and Gary. Not that there's all that much to find out. They are taking it slow. One lesson she's learned: fast brought her nothing but trouble. Exhibit A: Mark Merrick.

Betty slips an apron over Tess's head. "Every time I think about how I'm helping to make a bunch of chimps less bored, I laugh. It even made Budd smile when I told him about it at breakfast."

Tess pushes the ten large cans down the counter as Betty slaps the first one on the new electric opener her children gave her for her sixtieth birthday. As promised, it's silent and lets go with one firm tug.

"Yep, Budd perked right up and gave us a full sentence. He said, 'If this juice ball works, people should try it on their kids.' Too late for my grandchildren. The only thing they can use their opposable thumbs for is to kill everybody on those whatdoyacallits. And I don't want to know what you *do* call it."

"Should I chop these on this board?" Betty nods. Tess rolls a dozen ripe mangoes out of the bag and chooses what looks like the best knife for the job.

"'Course I've also got a fancy chopper you could use. My kids keep giving me all these wonders because they figure having to learn to operate them will stave off *my* boredom. I'd like to tell them what I want is a big recliner so I can put my feet up and never slice or dice or mash another thing for the rest of my earthly days."

Tess begins trying to cut the first mango into inch-size pieces, but the knife keeps hitting the hard pit at the mango's core. "No way you could chop. This is going to be more of a whittling process."

Betty holds a mango up to the sunlight. "You know, I've never tasted one of these."

"Me either," Tess says. She slides the knife into a soft rosy side and cuts a wedge for each of them.

They both take a large bite.

"Oh my, so sweet," Betty says. She wipes the back of her arm with the corner of her apron. "And so juicy. Why I'd have to take my clothes off and get into the tub if I wanted to eat a whole one of these. If Eve had handed Adam a mango, we'd have ended up somewhere else entirely."

Tess cuts two more wedges.

Betty glances toward the barn. "Do not give Hoop any of these." She begins to pour the Hawaiian Punch into the buckets. "But won't these chimp experiments be expensive?"

"Gary was able to get a grant from Cornell for all the foraging supplies."

"Gary. Not sure why, I *do* like that name. Should I go to about two inches from the top? That way they won't slosh when we carry the buckets to the freezer."

"That'll be good," Tess says, "and it'll give Gary and me a bit more space when we go to shimmy the frozen hunk out."

"How're you going set this all up for the chimps anyway?"

"We'll stick one of the frozen buckets in the zoo freezer as soon as I get there. I figure the mixture will thaw just enough on the drive over so we can dump the other one out to hang from a tree in the chimp enclosure. Then I'm going to watch the chimps for four hours and take notes on everything the six of them do. Down the line, if these fruit balls work, we're going to have the kids in children's programs also do observations."

Tess scoops up a bunch of the mango chunks to drop into the bucket that's full of juice.

"Hold off on that," Betty says. "I'll put the fruit in once the juice starts to thicken in the freezer. Otherwise the mangoes are going to all be at the bottom." She pushes the chunks into a pile. "I don't get it: What are you hoping the chimps will do?"

"Well, see, a lot of zoos give out food in a sort of room-service way. They just dump the feed in a trough. We think it'll keep the chimps healthier — now don't laugh, but better balanced in their minds and bodies — if they have to work for their food. Be challenged. Gary's got a vet intern at another zoo who's going to observe chimps who aren't required to forage, a kind of control group. Plus we're doing research on chimp foraging behavior in their natural habitats. Other zoos all over the country are doing these same kinds of experiments."

Betty laughs. "Oh, Budd's going to love this."

Tess gives Betty a look and wags a finger at her.

"Honestly, Tess, I'm laughing because I think the whole thing is so wonderfully wild. But, yeah, because I'm imagining Budd's reaction. Making the chimps work for their food … it's so anti-welfare. He's liable to call it in to one of those crazy right-wing programs he listens to. So what kinds of things are you looking for while you watch the chimps?"

Tess hesitates. If Betty thinks this is funny, she'd really get a kick out the idea of having the chimps watch a computer with electrodes on their heads.

"I'm truly interested," Betty goes on, "but I'm laughing also. One doesn't exclude the other." She slides the first mound of fruit into a plastic bag and sticks it in the refrigerator.

Now Tess laughs too and keeps on chopping. "Okay, but I'm glad I'm not going to be at lunch when you present this as standup comedy to Budd and Hoop. We're looking for things like do the chimps use sticks to dig out the fruit, how long does it hold their attention, is there any difference between the adults' and the adolescents' responses. Gary's going to do the same kinds of observations three days later."

Tess checks the clock. There's still time.

"We plan to hide food in all sorts of ways that make their foraging more natural, all the while observing their behavior to see if overall they seem happier, fight less, lose less hair, et cetera. We're even going to construct something that looks like a termite mound. They'll have to use sticks to reach in to get the food out of it. Then we'll collaborate on writing up the results."

"The two of you will separately watch these chimpanzees for hours and write down everything they do?"

"Yes," Tess says.

Betty slips another piece of mango into her mouth and smiles. "Well, it's not like going to the drive-in, but it's something."

▪ ▪ ▪

[ 49 ]

# A Law-Abiding Life

The probation office is in the same building as the Marwick lockup and the fire station. A bunch of firemen are standing around outside rednecking it up. Last thing he needs is to have to report to probation once a week in front of these assholes.

"Drop me around the corner," Rudy tells Tess. Even though he can't see Gramma DeLuca in the front seat, he knows she's gone all anxious. Every move he makes gets metered by these three women, a needle always bouncing back and forth between Okay and Heading for Fuck Up.

Tess lets him out her side. "From the papers they sent me, it looks like I'll be a while." A needs assessment, a plan, a drug test — jerk him every which way but loose. "Swing by this corner when you get done at Motor V. If I'm not here, then just hang out at the diner until I get there." He should give his grandmother some "don't worry" gesture, but he doesn't.

The clock by the bank says 1:50. He's got time for a cigarette, time to calm down. He doesn't want to go in there all damp and shaky. He looks toward the hills. Just the thought of it, all the bullshit he's about to step into, makes him want to run. What the papers call "abscond."

Going to have to fit that word into a song. Bond, johned, beyond. Wave his wand to abscond and he's outta here.

Probation is on the second floor. Lucky at least he doesn't have to go all the way to the Onango County office. And he's back in familiar territory: the metal detector, the bulletproof glass, the blank-faced receptionist, the trough for his identification.

"Rudy Morletti. I've got an appointment at two to meet with my probation officer."

"Have you filled out the forms we sent you?"

"Yes."

The receptionist taps the trough. He folds the papers and passes them through. These fill-in-the-blanks he first did on scrap paper for Tess to check over.

"Take a seat. Your probation officer will be with you shortly."

"Officer Drake," the man says. He's young, pale, and tense. Not at all what Rudy expected. No eye contact. Drake doesn't rise, simply gestures to the chair in front of his desk and then begins to go through the papers and Rudy's file.

Rudy sits and waits. The office is in one of those small cubicles set up so he can't see any of the other probationers. He wills himself to stay still. Then he waits some more. The only read he's got on this guy is that he's new and nervous which means he's going to be by the book and that Rudy needs to be careful. Careful careful.

"All right," Officer Drake finally says. "Based on your record and the judge and D.A.'s recommendations, you're going to be classified Level I Supervision. This means you're going to be required to meet with me four times a month, once a week."

He passes a pencil and two stapled sheets across the desk. They're calendar pages for May and June 2003. Drake then looks his desk calendar over. "Mark in Wednesday, 2 p.m., for the 18th, the 25th, and June 1st. Plus I'm going to visit your place of residence unannounced at least once a month or maybe more. Do you still reside at 374 Chicken Farm Road, town of Danford? Is your phone number still 456-246-8772?"

"Yes."

"Should you decide to change your address, you are to contact me first. Is everything clear so far?"

Rudy nods. For the first time Drake looks directly at him. "Yes," Rudy says.

"All right. Your own needs assessment says the first thing you need to do is get a job and then you hope to get a limited license so you can drive back and forth to that job. Of course any employment you get has to be approved by the probation department, by me. How likely are you to be able to get this maintenance job at the Catholic Church in Stanton?"

"If I can get a limited license, I'll be able to work there twenty hours a week."

"Okay, I see you've got the priest's name and number, the address. I'm going to need to talk to him. Then if this job sounds like it will bring about improvement in your conduct and general attitude toward society …"

Rudy leans forward a little to see of Drake is reading this stuff from some manual, but no, he's got it all in his mouth — no visual aids.

"Well, then we move on to deciding on the limited license. Is that all clear?"

"It is." He feels like if he grunts "yes" one more time, it's going to reflect negatively on his attitude toward society.

Drake passes him a sheet titled "Probationer Rehabilitation Guidelines." "All right. I need to read you the ones that apply, and you should put a question mark next to the ones where you need clarification."

Drake eyes the pencil on the edge of the desk. On this cue, Rudy picks it up and poises it above the sheet. Careful, careful is what's required with this man, who reminds him of an alien who's just landed with instructions to pass as an earthling.

"Ready?"

"I'm ready." Is that submissive little yelp his? Clearly his brain has already started to be snatched. If this Drake had said, "Repeat after me" no doubt that little voice would have said, "Yes, sir."

Officer Drake squints at the sheet and turns up his volume. "A. Avoid injurious and vicious habits."

Delicious, suspicious, maybe alowishious.

"B. Refrain from frequenting unlawful or disreputable places or consorting with disreputable persons."

Consorting: the possibilities for jailhouse comedy material abound.

Rudy pushes the pencil lead into his palm just enough to zap him back into careful, careful.

"C. Adhere to Specified Conditions of Conduct set forth in an Order of Protection."

Actually Rudy does have a question about that, but just as he goes to put a mark, Drake passes him another paper.

"Here are the streets in Danford you must avoid for the next year. All right, now you can see the next two guidelines state that you must undergo available medical and psychiatric treatment and you need to participate in a substance-abuse program. This means you're expected to call to make appointments with Onango Mental Health and Chemical Dependency Clinic this week. Then you need to contact me to let me know you've taken care of that." He hands Rudy yet another sheet with the numbers for the clinic.

Rudy takes out an appointment card and passes it to Drake. "I'm all set to meet with Ben Jacobs at CDC next Tuesday. And I've lined up a sponsor to begin going to NA meetings." Rudy watches Officer Drake's face to see if he gives any "What a good boy" muscle-twitches, but all the man does is pass the card back and make a note of the date on Rudy's needs assessment.

"Since you're Level I Supervision, I'm required to contact these collateral people — specifically the priest and Jacobs — at least six times a quarter. Only other thing to remind you of is that you are not allowed to leave Onango County without permission and you have a curfew of 10 p.m. for the next three years unless a further evaluation indicates some revision on that."

Three years. Once he gets a better understanding for who's really inside this android, he'll put out some feelers on the possibilities of trading drug information for a shorter probation. Even consider wearing a wire. Him, living in this Supervision I box for 150-plus weeks without smashing one of the windows ... well, the odds aren't good.

Drake rises. "Last order of business is the drug test. Please step into the bathroom. I'm required to go in with you to stand beside you at the urinal to be sure that it's your urine that is placed in the test cup."

Rudy pushes himself up and follows Drake to the men's room. He goes in. Drake takes a pouch from the shelf, breaks the seal. "Once you provide a specimen, I'll replace the cap and attach the security seal over the cap. I'll then peel the label off this multi-drug test card and set that timer. Then within five minutes we'll have the results. Two red lines will appear if it's negative. If you test dirty, that is positive, there will only be one line."

Drake stands on Rudy's right side. "As I said, I'm required to keep a direct line of sight on the cup during the collection."

Drake is by the book, by the fucking book. Rudy feels sweat run down his back. He hasn't used anything since he smoked a joint at the mill moments before his arrest thirty-seven days ago, but Cannabis stays in the body longer than any other drug. Weeks. He should have reminded Drake about the joint, the number of days ago. His hands are trembling so much it's difficult to unzip. Drake hands him the cup, which almost slips from his fingers.

For what feels like forever, he can't relax enough to go. He should've told Gramma DeLuca to pray especially for a negative on the piss test. Finally the shaking cup begins to fill.

Please, please, Jeezo, let me pee clean.

▪ ▪ ▪

[ 50 ]

# No two chimps have the same call.

Rita sidles up to the juice ball with her son Mac riding on her back. It's still surprising to Tess how long mother chimps continue to transport their children. At three, though Mac does some knuckle-walking, he still mostly travels holding on to Rita. Jo, who as usual is cradling her Troll doll, moves to the other side of the tree, signaling she's going to allow Rita to approach. Rita hands Mac a stick and then stands close enough so he can poke away at what's left of the frozen chunk. Next he reaches in and pulls out a piece of mango. Rita claps and appears to grin. Tess smiles too and notes this all on the observation sheet.

Five more minutes to go and the first four-hour observation will be up. Tess stretches out her legs slowly so as not to distract the chimps. Even though they know her now, if she moves a lot, some of them, definitely Jo, will come to the fence to talk and want to hold hands, even give her a kiss. Smart of Gary to get permission to close the chimp exhibit to visitors during the observations. And lucky that even on this eighty-degree day, the juice ball is still only half gone.

She should have listened to Gary when he suggested sunscreen and his Yankee baseball cap. Gary. In a few minutes she's going to meet him for lunch in the employee lounge. Right off there are two definite things she can show him: the fruit ball interested all six chimps, and though no big surprise, they took turns in social order, with the alpha male, Bach, in control.

Her next observation sessions, she's going to watch the chimps at the fruit ball through the one-way window inside their indoor enclosure in case her presence where they can see her beyond the fence is somehow affecting their behavior.

Too soon to draw this conclusion, but compared with her previous time with the chimps, they seemed to be smiling more, making calls that sounded like laughter. None of them went inside to bump against the wall with a vacant look in their eyes. She'll have to tell Betty the juice ball results, so she can rev up Budd a little more.

The lounge is empty. No Gary, though the computer's on, his notes open on the table — the data from his vet friend on the chimps that get their feed delivered.

She pulls her Smurfette lunch box from the lounge fridge — no kidding, a little blue Smurf girl on both sides, though severely disfigured from the time she took a nail and scratched off most of Smurfette's long blond tresses. It'll give Gary a laugh. She's going to tell him how she carried this box to school every day when she was in fourth grade. Except of course the times when she'd run away from Danford Elementary in a rage which eventually led to her being classified as a PINS, a Person In Need of Supervision. Or as her mother says, Parents In Need of Supervision, since she and Mamo and Papo all had to go to court with threats of putting her in foster care if she didn't shape up. Maybe she won't tell Gary that part. Not yet anyway.

She opens the box — speaking of having your food delivered, Gramma Deluca has packed her a secret lunch. She can share it with Gary. And where *is* Gary? She makes a tour around the room checking for his bobbing blond head out all the windows.

Then there he is and looking not at all like himself. He's hunched over, his face ashen, one hand pressed to his abdomen. Jesus, an appendicitis or something. She opens the door for him.

"My God, Gary, what is it?" She grabs his arm and leads him to a chair.

"I get these attacks."

"Attacks? Should I drive you to Emergency?"

"Wait awhile. See how it goes. It's already subsided some. Main thing is I have to stay close to a john." And with that he ducks into the lounge bathroom.

She stands just outside. She's reluctant to put her ear to the door. Such an invasion of privacy. But she calls, "Gary?"

Right away he answers, "It's okay. I didn't pass out or die."

At last he emerges, his face a little less white and standing straight as he comes toward her. He stops by the table and picks up the lunch box.

"Of course," he says, "this is yours." He manages a laugh. "You didn't eat yet?"

"No, I was waiting for you. You want some of it? Gramma DeLuca's specialties."

"Food's the last thing I want right now."

"Gary, tell me what these attacks are? That is if you want to."

"Eat first. It's not a topic suitable for mealtime conversation."

Tess pushes the lunch aside. "Maybe later."

Gary lifts the box and runs his fingers over the deep scratches around Smurfette's head. "Perhaps you'd like to tell me the story behind these."

"You first," Tess says.

"Well, it's not like we're strangers on a train."

Gary settles in at the computer and pulls a chair over close for Tess. He types Crohn's Disease in the Google slot and then clicks on the Wikipedia entry. He reads it out loud to her:

> Crohn's disease, also known as regional enteritis, is an inflammatory disease of the intestines. It primarily causes abdominal pain, diarrhea (which may be bloody if inflammation is at its worst), vomiting, or weight loss...

He breaks off and turns toward her. "It's not a pretty story."

Once again, she places her hand on his arm. "How are you feeling right now?"

"Much better."

"Truly?"

"Truly. It's one of those conditions that comes and goes. Though I don't want to minimize the whole deal. It's progressive. Fortunately I got an early diagnosis. I'm careful with what I eat. I don't smoke or do drugs other than an occasional beer ... The thing is, aside from this," he points to the screen, "Crohn's also has a genetic component. Both my sisters have it. In other words it can be passed on to one's children through either parent. It's important that I tell you this."

She squeezes Gary's arm even harder and works to suppress a laugh. "Sorry. It's certainly not funny, but when it comes to predispositions, the Morlettis and DeLucas win the bad-genes contest hands down."

"Now for something a little lighter," Gary says, and turns to the computer. He brings up the zoo's website, then clicks on Chimpanzees. Amazing headshots of all six of the chimps appear on the screen: Bach, Jazz, Jo, Tillie, Rita, Mac.

"Surprise," he says. "I've been constructing this special chimp web section for the last week and I just posted it online this morning. Pick a chimp."

Tess moves the cursor to Jo's picture and her profile appears:

- Jo
- Born 1979 in captivity
- Jo is very curious and watchful, and is careful and deliberate in her movements. She can take a little while to warm up to new people, but is quite playful once she has decided to trust a person. Of her chimpanzee family, she spends the most time with Tillie. She and Tillie can often be found quietly grooming each other. Prior to her life here at the zoo, Jo had five babies during her years in biomedical research, including a set of twins. All of her children were taken away from her when they were very young — sometimes just days old. Jo adopted a doll to care for here at the zoo — a Troll doll with bright pink hair.
- Click on the asterisk * if you'd like to be one of Jo's pals.
- Jo's current pals are:

Tess moves the cursor and clicks. When the Pal sign-up slot appears, she types in "Theresa Morletti."

▪ ▪ ▪

[ 51 ]

# Frequently Asked Questions

He's expecting Ben Jacobs, but what he gets is this frozen fish: Ida Butler, P.A.

"I usually do the evaluations for the medications," she says as she looks through his folder. His thick folder. "I see you were prescribed lithium in the past. Did that seem to keep the manic episodes in check?"

"I'd prefer not to be placed on medication. I'm sleeping. I'm keeping my life simple to cut down on stress. I'm not using drugs or alcohol. I'm going to be doing a lot of work up on a scaffold, so I need to be completely alert." He's amazed how this little speech turns on without any previous rehearsal. Not how he would have played it with Jacobs.

"The contact with your probation officer indicated that you were to enter into mental health treatment. Given the many instances of psychosis described on these evaluations, medication for your bipolar disorder is clearly indicated."

Straight out of the freezer. Okay, so he gets the meds, but he flushes them down the toilet. It's tempting to try to work this Butler robot around to giving him a scrip for Xanax, just a small number of hits for when he does get schitzy. Suck up a little by telling her he's meeting with his NA sponsor right after this appointment. But no, for sure in big red letters, front and center in his file, it says "NO ANTI-ANXIETY MEDS," since last time he was able to deal those for morphine.

"It looks like the probation department is working on getting you set up for Medicaid. Until that's in place, I'm going to prescribe lithium. See how that goes. Of course that means you'll have to get your blood checked once a month."

Butler glances at her watch. Then she writes out the prescription and hands it to him. "Have the receptionist set you up for an appointment in three weeks. You can contact Ben Jacobs if you have any concerns. Looks like he's going to be your chemical dependency counselor."

Concerns? Concerns?

She opens the door, gestures he should exit first, and exit he does.

Rozmer's truck is already idling at the curb outside Mental Health. No time for a cigarette. And last thing he wants at this moment is to go through the drill with Rozmer. Their only contact so far was on the phone and over the wire has been about as much of a connection as he's felt ready for. All those years of hearing about Rozmer from Mark Merrick keep giving him the I've-been-here-before whammies. He steals up and swings into the truck.

"Hey, Buddy," Rozmer says.

Rudy resists slamming the door. Luckily Tess has warned him ahead that Rozmer's whittled himself down considerably.

Rozmer pulls out. "I'd say you look good and pissed."

"I'd say you look like the thin man."

"Yep, I'm off the Whoppers. Want to go to a meeting?"

Rudy breathes and shoves his shaking hands in his pockets. "Be better for me if we just go get coffee." He readies himself for Rozmer to lay on some wisdom about how taking his anger to a meeting would be the best thing right now.

Instead Rozmer pulls in beside Duke's Diner. "I know the main thing on your mind is sucking up one of those cancer sticks," he says. "I'll go ahead in and get us a booth and order myself a fat-free salad."

▪ ▪ ▪

[ 52 ]

# Cryptography

The minute Jonathan Manchester steps into the Edgewater, Carla sets Willie up with another draft and smacks a vinegar chips bag down next to Ollie and Ron, so none of them will interrupt her plan. Then she pours Jonathan a Cutty Sark, with a side of water. Jonathan Manchester. Jonathan. This guy's got aristocrat written all over him: a snooty long nose, perfect teeth, and expensive suits. She even considered him tentatively, but blue blood granted, he's a drunk, and she needs no astrological reading to know that Cutty Sark would be way ahead of Carla on his alphabet of interests.

Sometimes Jonathan is chatty: books and politics and the nature of paranoia. Other times he just sits at the bar and reads weighty volumes. But he always drinks. That never varies. Then when any normal person would have long ago fallen off the stool, he rises and departs without a stumble. He lives in a big Victorian house just up the road. No driving. Otherwise she would have to shut him down about three scotches from now.

Unfortunately, right when she wants to pump him for info, today he's already got his book open before she sets his drink down. "Much obliged," he says without looking up from what appears to be an antique

— a water-stained leather cover and bound by rawhide ties.

Carla looks over the questions she wants to ask and places them on top of the pages Tess printed out for her. While she washes glasses, she keeps a close eye on Manchester's drink. About halfway through his second one is when she plans to approach. She lowers the sound on NASCAR to create the best conditions. Ollie and Ron don't notice.

Hard to believe, but this man who's got such a love of scotch is some sort of lapsed psychiatrist. And even if today's a silent-reading one, before he gets too removed, she's going to get him to give her a free consultation regarding the best medications for Rudy. No doubt right at this moment Mental Health is prescribing some magic potion for him. But from the stuff Tess found on the computer, some of these concoctions sound dangerous. Side effects up the wazoo. She wants Rudy subdued, but she doesn't want him to become a diabetic.

Antipsychotics: Zyprexa, Abilify, Risperidone, Clozapine

Hard enough that they've got all these outer-space names, but they've all got generic names as well. Antipsychotics: those are for when Rudy starts looking out all the windows every five minutes and sleeping with a tire iron under his pillow.

Mood Stabilizers: Depakote, Tegretol, Lamictal

But the weird thing is that it says these are really "anticonvulsant medications" for people who have seizures. Rudy does a lot of crazy things, but fits aren't one of them. Asking about this is one of the questions she has for Manchester.

But here's the one she wants to really find out about because she knows it's a medication that Rudy used to take:

Lithium. Side effects: blackouts, pounding heart, hallucinations . . .

Manchester is halfway through his second drink. She lifts up the sheets and stands directly across from him. "I wonder if I might have a few moments of your time?"

He stops reading and glances up. He doesn't close his book, but he does smile slightly. "Yes," he says.

"My son has a diagnosis of bipolar disorder. Right now he's at the Onango Mental Health Clinic. I think they're going to prescribe some medications to keep him from having manic episodes and to just make him more balanced. I wondered if you have any recommendations about what are the best drugs to accomplish that?" She opens the folder.

Manchester does close his book. He cocks his head to the side and really looks at her. Then he reaches over and closes the folder. He takes a long drink. Then he tips the glass in her direction. "Carla, if you wanted to know what scotch does to the human brain, the heart, the liver, why I could tell you exactly, but these bipolar cocktails that modern scientists are beakering up, what all those compounds do to the brain … A crapshoot in the dark."

"But …," she says.

He turns the book and pushes it toward her. "Humans," he says. "I think you'll find this much closer to the truth about human behavior."

The title is written in a kind of language she's never seen before.

Jonathan Manchester touches her arm and hands her his glass, "Why don't you join me for one of these?"

▪ ▪ ▪

*Doing Time Outside*

[ 53 ]

# Maker of All That Is Seen and Unseen

His first job is to clean a bunch of plaster pictures, raised up sort of like sculptures, that line the side walls of the church just below the stained-glass windows. Father Al says they may look gray, but really they're supposed to be ivory, and they haven't been cleaned in the twenty years he's been here.

What the church has is not scaffolding, but the tallest — at least seventeen feet — and heaviest wooden stepladder Rudy has ever seen, probably purchased the same year as that fan. Even on its side beneath the stairs it's a monster to maneuver. It'll be best to drag it, rather than trying to lift and swing it around all the statues and fonts and candles and baskets of plastic flowers — what he thinks of as Catholic paraphernalia.

So as not to scrape the flagstone floor, he places a couple of the heavy cleaning rags under the base and drags the ladder to lean against the wall by the first sculpture. Now for his next trick: to get this mother set up without having it crash into the Peter window. That managed, he locks the braces, gathers the rags, the spray cleaner, and ascends. If someone asks what he did all morning, he can say he put up a ladder.

The first sculpture panel takes him an hour to get completely clean: a bunch of long-haired guys in robes bullying the girly-looking man in the center, who's got both wrists shackled. His own wrists twinge in sympathy. He jockeys the ladder over to the next sculpture. By the time he finishes that one — five men struggling to place a cross on the guy's back — it's clear who this story's about and he already knows the ending. But, Rudy, his grandmother would say, that isn't the ending because three days later Christ went up to sit at the right hand of God. Gramma, Gramma, you believe that, you'll believe anything.

When he finishes the third one, where Christ has fallen to the ground under the weight of the cross, which seems a little early in terms of building to the climax, Rudy backs his way to the center aisle to get the full effect. Again that swell in his chest. The three sculptures actually glow in the light from the windows. Whoever made the original molds was the real thing. Looking at a lot of this ivory connivery, well, he can see how all these people got hooked.

Okay, eleven more to clean. He should be able to finish by early next week. Got be on the road soon since his special license says the Maverick's going to turn into a pumpkin if he isn't home by twelve. He pushes the ladder over to the fourth sculpture. Almost time to leave, but he might as well begin on this next one. Through the grime, he sees that Christ is back on his feet, a woman close by his side. A woman? The plot thickens. He shakes the spray can. Going to have to get more cleaner at the market and have a cigarette break at the same time. Convenient that it's just across the street. Rudy's been cleared to put cleaning supplies on the church tab, but he imagines when he goes to check out with five aerosol spray cans, Dara Moore's mother is going to be sure he's sniffing them to get high.

He pulls on his hoodie and lights up as soon as the door closes behind him, and then he stops and steps back into the corner of the entryway, his body charged by a blast of adrenaline. Pat Keegan's just setting a big bag in the trunk of his car. Rudy waits. Keegan pulls out. Rudy gets in the Maverick and backs onto the road. He does not tailgate. He stays just close enough so that eventually Keegan's going to see the Maverick in his rearview, Rudy at the wheel.

Rudy, go home. When you get to Danford take a right on Fyler Hill. Do you want to go back to jail?

Keegan turns onto Route 12; Rudy follows.

■ ■ ■

[ 54 ]

# Heaven

Angela adjusts the plastic square that magnifies the newsprint on the "Religion" column. "Carla, did you read the 'Letters to Billy Graham' in today's *Sun*? Some woman wants to know, 'Is it wrong to wish for heaven now?'"

Carla doesn't answer. She's deep in the problem of how to fit everybody's schedules onto the one-by-one-inch spaces of May. "Rudy's probation meetings, NA, mental health, his job at the church. Then there's Tess's exams, barn chores, her crazy experiments at the zoo, me getting to the Edgewater, your eye appointment. It's like I'm some goddamned traffic control person trying to get everybody cleared for takeoff in the two vehicles we've got on the runway."

"Well, at least now the Maverick's registered, inspected, insured, and Rudy's been granted a work license. It's all going to be a lot easier," Angela says.

"Rudy being able to drive the Maverick on his own … well, that scares the bejesus out of me."

"Scares the dickens," Angela says, though mostly she's given up on trying to make Carla less blasphemous. "I know you aren't going to believe this, but I think Rudy's starting to hear … well, I think going to

Mass with me last Saturday, working in the church today, he's starting to be filled …"

"You're right; I don't believe you."

"Okay, but here's what he said when he got back from work: 'I was about to do something really crazy and then something took hold of me and turned me the other way.'"

"Maybe the lithium has kicked in, or maybe Jiminy Cricket."

"Oh, Carla, I know you're not nearly as tough as you pretend to be."

Angela places the magnifying square back on the Billy Graham column. "Here's what the woman says: 'The Bible tells us we won't have any more pain or sorrow. But if that's true, why doesn't God take us to heaven right now?' Did you ever feel like that, Carla?"

There's the crash of something heavy above them. Carla looks up at the ceiling expecting the plaster to drop a few chunks on the table. Next they hear Rudy's guitar and the sound of his voice, then footsteps and the sound of Tess joining in.

"One of their father's favorites," Carla says. She raises her arms like she's going to fly and sings low and sweet, "There's a slow, slow train coming round the bend."

"What?" Angela says.

Carla takes a chair across from her mother. "As much of a doubter as I am, I'm going to risk saying that being here in this house tonight … Tess and Rudy upstairs, everybody safe … well, it's like a normal family. The Waltons. Like when we turn off the lights, through the darkness, voices are going to call, 'Night, Mamo. Night, Gramma.'"

Angela wipes an eye with the back of her hand.

And right then there's the sound of steps on the porch.

Carla looks at the clock. 10:30. "Who in God's name … ?"

There's a hard knock and then within seconds the sound of Rudy pounding down the stairs. Tess right behind him.

"Probation," he says as he yanks open the door as wide as it will go and steps back with a sweep of his arm to invite them in.

The two men enter the kitchen. One in a sheriff's uniform and wearing a gun.

"Officer Drake, I'd like you to meet my mother, my grandmother, and my sister, Tess."

▪ ▪ ▪

[ 55 ]

# Early Separation

When Tess makes the turn into the Daweses' driveway, Betty's over by the heifer barn waving for her to hurry up. Some emergency that needs four hands. Hoop's truck is gone. She steers onto the grass and runs.

Betty yells when she gets halfway there, "Change your clothes. One of the heifers has been in labor way too long. Hoop won't be back until evening milking and I haven't been able to roust a vet."

Coveralls, boots, hat. Her heart is pounding in her ears. She's watched the natural birth of lots of calves, but never assisted when there was trouble. The image of the husky being cut open flashes up.

As soon as Tess closes the gate, Betty hands her a rag and a bucket of water and motions toward the cow who's nosing the fence nervously in the far corner of the paddock. "Gabby's been at it for seven hours. Even for a first calf that's way too long." Betty pulls on rubber gloves and begins to grease her arms. "Her water bag broke about an hour ago. We're going to have to help her."

Tess doesn't know Gabby; she seldom deals with the heifers; but she knows enough to be wary of a kick. She holds Gabby's tail off to the side and begins to wash around the vulva, which is an angry scarlet and many times its normal size. The water-bag membrane pushes out farther with each contraction. Giving teenage girls this job for an hour would be way better than telling them to just say no.

"Good," Betty says. "Now pull her tail off hard to the right and be ready to jump away if she rears up." Betty slowly begins to insert her right arm, all the while saying, "There, there."

The cow's only reaction is to nose more completely into the corner.

"The calf's alive. It moves when I pinch it, but just as I feared, it's facing rearward. Get those birthing cords on the fence. Once we see a hoof, we're going to have to hurry."

Tess knows that's because the umbilical cord will then be pinched closed or ruptured. If the head was forward, the calf would be forced to breathe, but rearward it'll soon smother.

"Okay, here's the contraction." A hoof appears. "Reach in there and take hold of that leg with both hands, Tess. I've got hold of the other one. Now with the next contraction, we'll pull together. Maybe we won't need the cords."

While she continues to hold onto one of the calf's back legs, Betty skins the rubber glove off her right hand by running her arm hard across Tess's back. "Better traction," she says and places that hand back inside the cow.

"Just pray to God the contractions keep coming. Sometimes a cow will stop and rest once the calf's feet are out. We're lucky she's still standing. Right about now a lot of cows lie down."

Lucky, hard to think there's anything lucky about any of this. Tess would like to wipe the sweat that's dripping off her nose, but she doesn't dare remove even one of her hands.

"Okay, this is it," Betty says. "Pull slow and even, slow and even, keep pulling."

Both women have their feet planted and they are hip to hip. Suddenly the calf whooshes out. They both fall backward on their rears. After a couple of deep breaths, Betty toes the calf with her boot and when it moves and breathes, they both raise their arms and laugh.

"Way to go, Gabrielle. Way to go us," Betty says. "I'm getting too old for this."

"Me, too," Tess says, and skims her hands along the grass to clean off some of the gunk, then wipes her face on her sleeve.

Betty stretches and gently toes the calf again. "Want to see if it's a heifer. Yep, another milker. Hoop will be pleased about that."

"Pretty amazing," Tess says.

"Yes. Let's just rest here. See if Gabby expels the afterbirth and attends to the calf."

They scoot back across the paddock grass to lean against the far fence. They watch Gabby's sides. After a few powerful contractions, the placenta is expelled. The cow glances rearward and steps away a little. Then she turns and begins to nose the wet mess at her feet. Slowly, steadily, she licks the calf clean.

"How can she know to do that?" Tess says.

"Just another miracle." Betty pulls off the other glove and begins to wipe her arms on her pants legs.

They sit and watch and say nothing for a while. The calf begins to twitch and push its front legs under its body.

"Now for the next miracle," Betty says.

The calf staggers up. Then all four legs splay out as it crashes back to the ground. Gabby nudges it with her nose. After a few minutes, the calf staggers up again and wobbles forward a few steps. Its mother turns and pushes the calf toward her bag. After a few false starts and failed attempts, the calf begins to suckle.

"If Hoop was here, he'd already be milking Gabby for the colostrum. He'd have me separating her and her firstborn within the hour. Feeding that calf with a bottle till it got that first couple of quarts it needs for the antibodies. It hurts me every time we do that. Hoop, I always say, at least let them be together for twenty-four hours. He always pats me tenderly and goes ahead and moves the calf to its pen."

"But why can't the calf stay with its mother? Surely they'd both be happier in the long run."

"Oh, Tess, once Hoop gave in to me. Let the dame and its calf stay together for forty-eight hours. When we took the calf away, that mother bellowed for her lost child for days, day and night. I couldn't stand it. This way, if we separate them early, Gabby will nose around a little, but she will not bawl for her loss over and over. She'll appear to have no memory of it at all."

▪ ▪ ▪

*Doing Time Outside*

[ 56 ]

# Others to Eat Fire

There's a tap, tap, tapping.

Rudy pushes up from the dark of some huge weight pressing on his chest, choking him. Another night of almost no sleep with a motorcycle roaring him awake when he finally did drop off. Prager. These roar-bys are getting to be night-torture regulars. And there are frequent gunned drive-bys when he's at the church. As risky as it is for his probation rules, he may have to confront Prager in some way that doesn't escalate the situation.

Another tap, then a hushed, "Rudy, it's 7:45. Rudy ..." Gramma hovering outside his door.

"Yeah." He does not add "Leave me alone." Somehow he's got to get away from these three women, their constant surveillance. He puts his feet on the floor and tips the shade open enough to see it's raining. Then he pulls on his pants. Even if he speeds, he's going to be late for work.

His mother and Tess's doors are still closed. One shred of luck. Just as he gets downstairs, the phone rings. He motions for his grandmother not to pick up. Every time it rings the fiery scrape on his nerves ups the burn. Finally the machine comes on: "We know what you're up to. This is our last friendly warning." He doesn't recognize the voice. He walks to the machine and presses *Delete.* He doesn't look at his grandmother. Her panicked expression is the last thing he needs. "Please don't mention that," he says, the machine message still echoing in the kitchen, "to them." He points to the ceiling, to the bang of irritation from his mother's room.

Just as he steps onto the porch, his grandmother calls, "Don't you want some breakfast?"

He doesn't answer.

Rudy takes the corner at Grat's Bend so fast the Maverick skids onto the shoulder. If he didn't have this fucking order of protection he could go through town, but no, he has to take the long way. Has to take the long way on all of it. Three years more of this shit: the curfew, Officer By-the-Book, Rozmer and the NA meetings, the home hover, the hassle from Iceberg Ida. The lithium. He's got to find out if they'll know he isn't taking it when they blood-test him. To say nothing of the paranoid drama coming from Prager & Co.

As he approaches Stanton, he slows down a little. If he's late, he's late. Rios won't be on him about that. Rios seems to get it. He turns at the light, being sure to keep it at thirty, and pulls into the parking space in back of the church. As he does every morning, he scans the state land that rises up behind the firehouse. Only a mile or so over that hill to the sawmill. It wouldn't surprise him to see Prager up on the crest, binoculars, or something more lethal, pointed his way.

Rudy steps into the dim of the sanctuary. At least he has this job, money to buy his own cigarettes. And only two more sculptures to clean. If it stops raining, he may even be able to start on the mower. If, if, if he doesn't totally schitz out.

He's tempted to throw a little holy water on his face since he didn't get to wash up. From the center aisle he takes in the glow of what's he's done so far, the ivory connivery set off by the stained-glass blues and reds and greens even on this dark day. Stations of the Cross they call them. Stations. Choo, choo. Just the thought of it loosens his chest. These Catholics are singing a strange song for sure, but it's got a calming tune.

That's it: numbers thirteen and fourteen finished. He steps back to check that there are no smudges left on any of the surfaces of these last two sculptures: Jesus down from the cross, his body stretched over what must be his mother's lap. Then he's placed in the tomb. End of story: a "That's it, Buddy," from us infidels.

Just as Rudy's struggling to push the heavy ladder back under the stairs, he feels someone lurking in the dim. He turns his anxious "Who's there" into a neutral "Hello," which bounces back from the stone.

"Just me … Father Al."

Rudy gives one final shove and moves past the baptismal font back into the sanctuary. Father Rios is turning slowly toward one wall and then toward the other. He does this several times and touches his heart.

Rudy's about to suggest he better stop rotating or he's going to get the whirly-gigs.

"Glory. Glory," Rios says. "They are … well, they're magnificent. You've done such a fine job, Rudy. I can't wait to feel the joy that's going to lift us up when people take these in for the first time at Saturday evening Mass. Thank you." With these words, Father Al makes a few tentative movements in Rudy's direction.

Rudy backs up. "You're welcome."

"I don't suppose you'd consider coming to Mass Saturday, so the congregation could thank you in person."

Rudy ducks his head, and when he looks up Father Al has somehow glided within back-patting range.

Then the priest laughs, a big laugh that ricochets back. "I didn't think so. But I'm going to thank you in absentia anyway if that's okay with you."

Is it okay with him to have his name broadcast out there? Who knows who might be in the audience? Some sister or brother or girlfriend or mother of one of his enemies? "You better not. Best if I lay low."

"Well, you know I'm right in there, my back to that scary painting, if you want to stop by, if you ever want to talk about anything …"

What he wants to say is this: "There's a woman named Sunny. What can I do to earn her forgiveness?"

But what he says instead is, "Guess I'll go have a look at that mower."

▪ ▪ ▪

[ 57 ]

# Sinners shall find an infinite ocean of ________.

Carla watches her mother dithering over by the payphone while she loads another twelve-pack in the cooler. A pain shoots to her elbow every time she shoves another bottle in the ice. Three p.m. and still no word. Is she never to have any peace?

Then her mother scoops all the change back into her hand and pulls on her coat.

"Now what are you doing?"

"I'm going to talk to Father Rios before I call the lawyer."

Carla glances down the bar to see who's listening, but Luger, Manchester, even Willie, are absorbed by the thousandth rerun of the President with the "Mission Accomplished" banner flapping above his head. Flip it to NASCAR, it'd be the same story: bullshit going round and round.

Carla motions for her mother to come closer. "I'm telling you; don't alert anybody, especially Granley. Maybe there's some rule a lawyer's got to report it if somebody on probation runs off. Besides, like I told you, Rudy not getting back with the Maverick on time may mean nothing. Maybe his probation meeting was switched to Tuesday or he got permission to drive to a clinic appointment …"

Her mother sighs. "His appointment isn't until tomorrow. Anyway he would've told us about that so we wouldn't worry."

The answer that wants to pop right out of Carla's mouth: Maybe not. Rudy's that sick of our tailgating concern. But instead she says, "You already left a message for him to call us here. That phone's going to ring any minute, him with a logical explanation. Sit down and I'll make you a Shirley Temple."

Her mother takes off her coat, but she doesn't sit down. Instead she goes back toward the Edgewater kitchen. "I'm going to clean out the refrigerator," she says.

Maybe when Tess gets back from chores at the Daweses', Carla will have her go out and nose around. Drive by Rozmer's, Nooley's. See if Mark Merrick's moved back into the stone house yet. Rudy's had that crazy look flashing off and on the last few days. Maybe he's back into the crack. Banging around in his room half the night, and every morning he looks like he's been run over by a truck. But surely he wouldn't be nuts enough to just take off.

She swallows two Advils with a glass of milk. Right about now she'd like to join Jonathan for a scotch. A couple of shots of tequila is mighty tempting.

Things are slow. Good day to wash the big pickle jar and dust off the cheery little bar signs: "You don't have to go home, but you can't stay here." Just as she scoots the big bottle off the back counter, the door in the pool room slams open and her heart does a jackknife into her throat. Her mother appears in the kitchen entry, both hands cradling her head.

Ollie Burke bursts into the bar, his mouth going. Carla holds onto the counter to keep herself upright.

"Big bust. Big drug bust out at the sawmill on Route 12. Dozens of cop cars. State troopers, the sheriff patrol. People say they've uncovered a big drug ring. Tons of heroin and cocaine. Arresting people left and right. They got warrants out. Traffic's backed up for half a mile with rubberneckers."

Carla sits down on the cooler.

Her mother puts on her coat. "Father Rios," she says, and goes out the door.

The phone rings. Carla somehow manages to get around the bar to pick it up by its third scream.

"Mamo," Tess says. "have you heard about the sawmill?"

"Yes."

"Do you know if Rudy's back at the house yet?"

"No."

"I'm leaving Dawes's right now to go there. I'll call you as soon as I get home."

▪ ▪ ▪

[ 58 ]

# Refuge

Rudy's car is still not parked behind the church. It isn't anywhere nearby. Angela even walks far enough to see if it might be parked at the lawyer's. Granley's car isn't there either. A fine mist of rain, already her head and face are wet. Rudy was right: she does need a hoodie.

Angela steps into the church vestibule. She's not going to tell Father about the sawmill. Worse, she still didn't tell Carla about the threatening phone message. Lies of omission. Angela knows she's going to pay for them. She wants to kneel and pray, light a candle, but she doesn't.

"Father Rios," she calls into the darkness, and when there's no answer, she goes down the hall, the flaming heart of Jesus lighting the way. She begins to whisper the eleven graces: "I will give peace to their families. I will console them in all their troubles. I will be their refuge in life and especially in death …"

Father Rios's voice gives a "Hello" and then he's there in the doorway. As soon as he sees her face, he comes to her, "Angela … child, what is it?"

Tears. For a minute she can't speak. Father Rios leads her to a seat and brings his chair close, gives her a tissue.

"It's Rudy. It's Rudy, Father. He didn't come home at noon. He still wasn't there when his mother and I left for the Edgewater at two. No one answers when we call. Something's happened."

"Let us pray," the priest says, and takes both of Angela's hands. "Merciful God, take care of Rudy. Let no harm come to him. In Jesus' name we ask you. Amen."

"Amen," Angela says.

They sit in silence for a few minutes as though they are waiting for an answer.

"Rudy was here all morning, at least until eleven. I spoke with him for a few minutes out in the sanctuary to thank him for the job he did on cleaning the Stations of the Cross. He looked tired, but he seemed all right — though I could tell something was on his mind. Then he went out to work on the mower." Father Rios pauses to think. "Now I remember: I heard the mower motor try to turn over and then stall. I assumed he left at his usual time, but I don't know that."

Angela leans back in the chair and closes her eyes as though she too is going back through the last moments of seeing Rudy. "He's been irritable. He hasn't been sleeping. I had to wake him up this morning because it was getting late. I have a feeling he isn't taking that medicine they've given him at the clinic."

She rises. "I should get back to the Edgewater. Maybe he's called."

"Would you like me to get in touch with anyone?"

"Oh no, don't do that. We don't want to cause any trouble for him with the probation department."

"Do you want to call him from here? Or better still, would you like me to take you to the house to see if he's there? Perhaps he isn't answering the phone."

"I wouldn't want him to see me with you. He'd be angry that I've interfered."

"Isn't there a way we could see the house from a distance, see if the car's there. If it is, I'd drive you back to the Edgewater. If the car isn't there, well … you could decide then what you want to do next. But first come. Come and see the job Rudy's done."

They stop to dip the holy water and make the sign of the cross. Father Rios leads her to the center of the sanctuary. He holds her shoulders and turns her toward the first seven stations, then after a few minutes he turns her the other way. "Through all that grime of years, we could hardly even see the story. In only a few days Rudy did this."

"There's so much about Rudy that's good, Father."

He squeezes her arm. "I know." He leads her to the door. "My car's in the garage."

It's raining hard now. Father Rios goes back to get his umbrella. When he and Angela step away from the church, the wind is so strong, it feels as if it may turn the umbrella inside out. Just as they round the corner, they come to a full stop: barring their way, parked halfway across the walk, the riding mower, the engine cover up, its battery on the blacktop. Four screws scattered nearby.

"Mother of God," Angela says.

Father Rios steers her toward his car. "Go ahead and get out of the rain."

Then he lowers the hood of the mower, shifts it into neutral, and pushes it into the shed. He places the screws, one at a time, on its seat.

▪ ▪ ▪

[ 59 ]

# ( X ) My Soul

When she makes the turn onto Chicken Farm Road, Tess leans forward and prepares herself for whatever's coming next. Queenie rises and looks alert. Tess's chest is so tight, she feels an attack coming on. If Rudy's car is parked in front of the house, well, their world will drop back into its fragile spin. If it's just that he had some special permission to use the car, some changed appointment, well, she's going to walk in there and kill him for not letting Mamo or Gramma know. A deliberate, cruel, passive-aggressive omission.

But if the car isn't there, if Rudy isn't there, if he doesn't show up soon … Every scenario she can think of is so troubling she has to pull over to dig the inhaler out of her duffle. Her mind veers off every time it approaches the sawmill business. Is there a connection? Oh, if she could only bypass *her* amygdala, her small brain chamber that records panic, if she could fall on her side like the polar bear, imagine she's escaping as all this trauma pursues her. Or even better, if she could just go on the run like maybe fucking Rudy has, catch a plane to anywhere but here, disembark as a total amnesiac, every trace of memory expelled from her brain.

"But know this, world," she says to the rain banging on the windshield.

"My zoo internship starts in a few days, and nothing, nothing is going to keep me from signing in on time." Gary? No need to tell him about any of this. Not yet.

She pulls back onto the road. Queenie gives her a lean of support. One more blind curve, then whatever's coming is going to smack her in the head ... and there's nothing she can do to stop it.

All the possible spaces where a car might be are empty. The Maverick is not there. It's 4:30: four and a half hours of whereabouts unknown. Poor Gramma, poor all of them. She parks a little away from the house and slowly walks along the road to see if there are any fresh tire tracks. She goes around the corner to their falling-down barn to see if Rudy might have pulled the car in there. Hiding out from the sawmill gang. No Maverick.

She turns the knob and heaves one hip against the kitchen door. Even on this May afternoon, the kitchen's cold. No dirty coffee cup, no smell of cigarettes, no hoodie on the hook. One red flash on the machine. She presses *Play:* "Rudy, please call us at the Edgewater when you get home." Gramma. According to the calendar on the fridge, Rudy's got probation and mental health appointments tomorrow. No show on those and the jig is up.

She climbs the stairs to Rudy's room. His guitar case is in the corner. His Dickie shirt and black pants on a chair. He has almost nothing, but of that nothing, nothing seems to be missing. A few crumpled sheets of paper by the bed. She unwads the first one: "Dear Sunny" is all it says. Then she flattens the other one out:

Plenty of time to come up with a rhyme
for DOWN
36 months
1095 days
23,760 hours

She wads the papers back up to their original size and places them where they were. Then she sees, on the floor just under the edge of the bed, three books and a neat stack of envelopes held by a rubber band, "Sunny Jones" printed on each one, but of course with no address. If Rudy doesn't return soon, it may be necessary to open these to see if there's some hint of what's happened, but certainly not yet, not yet. She replaces the letters and slides the books out. A beat-up Webster's dictionary, with the front cover torn off; a thesaurus; and most surprising of all: a Gideon Bible. Folded inside the Bible, a lavender oblong, bordered with a repeated floral design. She carefully opens it up: twenty by twelve, maybe, with a rather amateurish colored pencil drawing of Jesus' face, his long hair, his head all covered with … what must be thorns. His eyes are closed. One tear on his cheek. All of this in light purple. In gold, a few inches below his beard, "Church Prayer Rug." And at the very bottom:

> Look into Jesus' eyes you will see they are closed. But as you continue to look you will see his eyes opening and looking back into your eyes. Then go and be alone and kneel on this Rug of Faith. Then put an *X* by your prayer needs on our letter of faith to you.

Christ, it's true. As Tess focuses on the picture, Jesus' eyes open right up and stare at her. Optical illusion or not, it creeps her right out. Quickly she folds this thing and places it back in the Bible. Where on earth did Rudy get it? Rudy up here in his room praying on this sheet of paper, this "rug"? Rudy becoming a religious rapper? Rudy in some sort of messianic delusional state? For now she'll mention this to no one.

Tess realizes too late she didn't pay attention to the exact page marked by the prayer paper. She places the books back on the floor in the same order. But Rudy's so paranoid, even with care, he's going to know someone's been here. Probably has something rigged to the door — a hair or a thread — that will let him know his space has been invaded.

There's the sound of an engine, a car with a hole in its muffler. Not the Maverick. She steps into the hall and pulls the shade back a little. A balding man in black scurries around the car to open the passenger door. With his help, an old woman emerges, looking like Tess feels. The priest and Gramma. Diagnosis: high voltage struck *her* amygdala.

Tess wrenches the kitchen door open for them. She hugs her grandmother and leads her to a chair, which she crumples into. "Dear, dear Gramma" is what Rudy's note to her should say. Tess puts both hands on her grandmother's shoulders. "Rudy hasn't been here. No clues of any kind. Your message was still blinking on the machine. We need to let Mamo know."

"Father Rios, this is my granddaughter, Theresa."

"Tess," she says, and reaches out to shake the hand he extends toward her. A warm hand, a good grip for pulling people out of going down.

"Father Al," he says. He sits. Queenie nuzzles his leg, leans her head on his knee. He scratches behind her ear.

"I'll call the Edgewater. Gramma, maybe you should go lie down."

Her grandmother looks near collapse.

"Yes," Father Rios says.

Her grandmother lifts her chin, her shoulders, as if she's about to head into a strong wind. "A cup of tea is what we need. Go ahead and call your mother. Tell her you and I are going to drive around a little. You'll know where, Tess."

"Would you like me to help look as well?" Father Rios offers.

"You've been so kind, Father. Your praise of Rudy at the church, bringing me here. But now, I hope you'll go back and pray for us."

"All right."

Her grandmother reaches out her hand. "I have this premonition that Rudy might show up there to tell you what he couldn't say this morning. Anyway, it better just be Tess and me if we're able to find him."

Tess turns up the kettle and gets out the tea bags and honey, the white chocolate creamer. Then she dials. Her mother picks up on the first ring, which means she must be practically sitting on the payphone.

"No sign of Rudy. Gramma's here with the priest. She and I are going to drive around to look for the car: Nooley's, Rozmer's, the stone house …"

"Tess, Rudy's run off. I just know it."

"Mamo, please keep your voice down. We don't want anyone to know Rudy's gone. Not yet."

"They're saying there's a warrant out for Larry Prager. He escaped through the woods when the police pulled in … They've got the dogs out, roadblocks. He and Rudy …"

"Mamo, unless there's something you know for sure and we have to hear it right now, don't say any more. We're on overload as it is."

"Rudy just took that car and …"

"I'll call you as soon as I get back to the house."

The kettle is screaming. Father Al lifts it and turns off the burner.

▪ ▪ ▪

[ 60 ]

# Selling Postcards at the Hanging

Six o'clock. Why hasn't Tess called? Surely they've checked out most of the possible places, driven the back roads. If Jonathan hadn't given her a Valium, she would have lost it by now.

When the payphone rings, Carla practically breaks her neck to get there, but it's only Ron Luger's wife, and Luger's at the end of the bar doing a "not here" dance.

"I don't see him," she tells Ron's wife. Not quite as much of a lie.

Carla sets another pitcher of beer on the table in the corner. Four men she's never seen before. Every stool is taken. There are three guys playing pool in the front room. All are afire with the excitement of the drug raid, the arrest of two men. Larry Prager still on the loose. She's given up on trying to reach Dirk to tell him she's ill. Maybe it's better for her to stay right here until closing to sort through the gossip for any clues.

"Hey, Carla, how about a burger for a hungry man?"

She gives Ollie a nod and pulls the meat from the fridge. If Ollie, if any of them, have put two and two together to remember that her son used to work at the sawmill, they aren't saying anything about it unless it's very off to the side.

Just as she flips the hamburger over, the noise in the bar goes up a notch, and then it becomes quiet except for one voice. She steps to the door. Sam Tabor, the volunteer fire chief, center stage: "I tell you I heard it from somebody reliable. When they searched Prager's girlfriend's, his gun was gone. Since his motorcycle's still at the mill and he hasn't got a vehicle, they think he's holed up some place local. Maybe got a gun on somebody to keep them from calling the police. They're going house to house right now."

Carla turns the burger off. Jesus. Her mother and Tess traipsing around the back roads, going to Nooley's, which is within a mile of the mill … She dials their house even though she knows they aren't there. She drops the fifty cents in the slot. After a thousand rings, the outer-space voice of their machine comes on. At the tone, she says softly into the silence: "Rudy, dear God, Rudy, if you're there, pick up."

▪ ▪ ▪

[61]

# Soft-Bodied

6:30. After they check Rozmer's and Nooley's, she'll call the Edgewater. The drive all around Marwick — to look for the Maverick parked near the probation office, the mental health clinic, St. Anne's for an NA meeting — well, that was a total waste of time, but she'd been so hoping to find Rudy doing something within the rules, something sane. Must be that, unlike Mamo, she's still got Rudy over in the *Innocent* column.

Once again she reviews the note she left for him, sees it there on the kitchen table in her mind:

> There's been a drug bust at the sawmill. Prager got away. Gramma and I are out looking for you now. Call Mamo PLEASE.

She'd wanted to add, "Put the car in the barn. Be careful." But of course Rudy'd know all that and it would just piss him off. She should have left the note in a less obvious place. Folded it up small, pasted it near the secret shred hidden in his doorway where Rudy would find it. If the police come busting in their house, they'll see her incriminating message right there by the salt shaker.

Christ, being around Rudy so much is making her as crazy as he is.

She slows for the railroad tracks, goes over the bridge, and turns left at the Mobil station.

"Rozmer's place is only a few blocks from here. If his truck isn't there, we'll swing by the halfway house where he works. Are you okay, Gramma? You're very quiet."

"There are two things I have to tell you."

Tess wants to say, "Please don't tell me anything more," but instead she breathes, gets ready, and says, "I'm listening."

"Someone left a threatening message on the machine around 8:30 this morning, right before Rudy left for work. The person said they knew what he was up to and this was their last friendly warning. Rudy erased it and told me not to tell you. It wasn't that man we saw at the jail, that Prager. I'd never forget that voice. I should've told you and your mother, but I hated to go against Rudy's wishes."

Tess grips the wheel tighter at this ominous news. "Rudy's got us so anxious, we aren't doing what we'd normally do. It's all right, but it's good you told me now." She's not going to remind her grandmother about the second thing. She needs some time to find the breath to think about how this call might connect to Rudy's disappearance.

"And the other thing makes me feel something awful happened." Her grandmother stops and knots both her hands together. "Rudy left the church lawnmower out in the rain."

Tess gets hold of a good breath on that one, information she can handle. "Gramma, lawnmowers can be left out."

"He left the lawnmower out in the rain, with the thing that covers the engine up and the battery sitting out in the rain too. A bunch of screws thrown on the ground."

Tess pulls into the Quickway. She squeezes her grandmother's hand. She sits to figure things out for a minute. "I'm going to call Mamo, just to let her know why we've been so long and that we're on our way to talk to Rozmer. We'll wait to tell her about the mower and the message until I pick her up when the Edgewater closes. Wait until she gets home. Otherwise she'll get hysterical right there in the bar."

She dials the number. The phone's busy. She tries it again. Waits a couple of minutes. Still busy. She goes back to the truck. Try once more after she sees Rozmer and Nooley. Maybe she'll have some encouraging news by then. See if they know anything, even tell them the whole thing. What's best to do now for Rudy, for all of them?

▪ ▪ ▪

*Doing Time Outside*

[ 62 ]

# Deliver us from evil.

Rozmer's truck is in front of his house, but no Maverick. The rain's so heavy it blurs the world beyond the windshield.

"We've got no umbrella, of course."

"I'll wait here. I'll be fine. Queenie'll keep me warm."

As Tess gets out, Queenie jumps into the front. When Tess looks back, she sees her grandmother's lips are moving, her eyes are closed.

Even from the porch, through the downpour, Tess can hear the pounding of drums by someone who's better at loud than skilled. She rings the bell, and when the drums don't stop, she raps on the window.

Gabe, Rozmer's nine-year-old son, opens the door, a couple of beat-up drumsticks in his hand and taller than she remembers.

"Hey, Gabe, is your … is Rozmer around?" Gabe and Rozmer don't do the "dad" thing.

Gabe steps aside to let her in. "He's downstairs doing something with the electric."

Tess follows Gabe through the kitchen, past a sink full of dishes, which he points to. "I got to do those before Mom gets home from teaching night school, but I figure I better first practice the drum rolls Mark assigned me."

The mention of Mark Merrick means he must be doing okay or he wouldn't be working with Gabe. Somehow this reassures her about Rudy, counterbalances the dark fear that people never get well.

Gabe calls down the basement stairs, "Tess Morletti's here."

Soon Rozmer appears at the bottom, smiling, a big screwdriver in his hand. Once again Tess is startled by how much thinner Rozmer is than when the two of them were heading up to the stone house to confront Mark about his return to using only nine months ago, a few weeks before Mark went to rehab.

"Come on down. I've got to get the dryer hooked back up before Lynn gets home."

When Tess reaches the basement, Rozmer indicates a stool by a workbench covered with electrical gizmos. He looks at her, then continues removing screws from one of the parts.

"I know something must be up with Rudy or you wouldn't be here."

Tess settles herself on the stool and gathers air for the full launch. "Rudy didn't come back with the car at noon like he was supposed to, and there are clues he left work in a big rush. Around the same time Rudy disappeared, the police raided the sawmill and made some arrests, but Larry Prager's still on the run."

"Prager," Rozmer says, like that says it all.

Tess takes hold of the bench with both hands. The weight Rozmer gives to Prager finally comes down on her hard.

Rozmer takes a step toward her. "You okay?"

She smiles. She'd hoped Rozmer was going to take on some of the weight, but it isn't going to happen.

"My grandmother and I are out driving the back roads looking for Rudy. Definitely we're not okay. Maybe you already know, Rudy's been getting threatening messages from Prager for a while." She breathes, tries to loosen her chest. "He got another message this morning from a voice my grandmother didn't recognize."

Rozmer puts the screwdriver down, gives her his full attention like he knows exactly what she's going to say, and so she says it. "What do you think we — me, my mother, my grandmother — what should we do now?"

No hesitation, Rozmer answers, "Tess, you know what you need to do." He goes back to working on the switch. He doesn't give off any signs of alarm. Somehow this is reassuring.

"I do?"

"You've got to contact the police and the probation department. If Rudy's mixed up in this, well, he needs to be picked up. If he isn't involved, then the police need to be looking out for his safety."

All the way up the stairs, all the way out to the truck, Tess pushes down hard on Rozmer's answer: "You've got to call the police, you've got to call the police ..."

Queenie squeezes over when she opens the door. "Rozmer doesn't know anything about why Rudy hasn't come home. Let's head for Nooley's. Give me a minute to think and then we can talk about what Rozmer said."

She takes the first left. By going the back way, she won't have to pass the sawmill. Though the rain has stopped, the ditches are full to the top with the rush of muddy water, some of it even running over, cutting trenches across the dirt road. The truck slides on the curve. Her grandmother clutches Queenie. Tess slows and finally turns the squeaking wipers off.

The thing is, if she calls the police and this leads to Rudy going back to jail, she'll want to become a "whereabouts unknown" herself. Rudy's never raised a hand against her, but if she's responsible for him getting picked up ... well, he'll never forgive her. What if Rudy simply took off, nothing at all to do with Prager, and by tomorrow at two p.m., he'll be on his way across the country, on his way to starting a new life?

Tess looks over at her grandmother, with Queenie now stretched out on her lap. Gramma, pale and tired, her head turning at every driveway and side road in case the Maverick might be there.

Gramma. There will be no way to convince her that calling the police is the right thing to do. Never. Besides, if Rudy has absconded, when he doesn't show up for probation tomorrow the cops will come banging on their door to pick him up for violating anyway. If she decides it's best not to call the police or that probation officer, maybe she doesn't even need to tell Gramma or Mamo what Rozmer said.

When they're only about a mile from Nooley's, Tess says, "Okay here's what Rozmer thinks we should do ..." Right then she sees the trooper car blocking the road. She pumps the brakes. Two troopers motion for her to stop. What the hell else could she do? Queenie jumps to the back and sticks her muzzle over Tess's shoulder.

"Gramma, don't say anything more than you have to. Reach in the glove compartment and get my registration. And Queenie, for godsake, do not bite the hand of the cop who reaches in for my license."

She rolls her window down.

■ ■ ■

[ 63 ]

# Slow Train Comin'

It's late. The three women sit at the kitchen table with only the range light on. It's a warm May night. The rain has stopped and there's the smell of lilacs in the room even though the windows are all closed and locked. A dark night. If one of them went to the window and looked up at the sky, she'd see there's no moon. No stars. But none of them gets up from the table. They do know it's late, way past midnight, for that's when Tess and Angela picked Carla up at the Edgewater, sitting there waiting outside on the porch, the Coors sign no longer blinking. And so it must be very late, for they have been here at this table, in this dim kitchen, for hours.

Over and over each of them retells what she knows and they again try to piece it together: Rudy's wild looks the last few days, his irritation, his sleepless nights, the unopened bottle of lithium, the wad of paper that counts out the hours left in his three years of probation, the roars of a motorcycle night after night, the threatening messages, the lawnmower left out in the rain with its engine cover up. And the one Angela keeps saying over and over until, if she wasn't her mother, Carla would reach across the table and place her hand over her mouth: "The screws were thrown on the ground, not set down carefully one at a time so Rudy could place them back where they belonged. No, thrown, like some evil power had grabbed hold of Rudy's hand and forced him to do something he'd never usually do."

And yes, the way Larry Prager acted that day they saw him at the jail, saying Rudy better call him. His "or else" tone. Plus, of course, the drug raid, the gun, the house-to-house search — if that really happened. The roadblock proves that as of seven o'clock, Prager was still at large. At large. Now she really knows what that means. And the biggest unknown of all: Does the sawmill raid have anything to do with Rudy's disappearance?

So little to go on.

Carla's verdict: "Somehow Rudy heard that the police were about to raid the sawmill and he went totally paranoid. He panicked and made a run for it." She does not voice her darker theory: that Rudy's back on the crack and he knew the cops would find something at the sawmill that would implicate him. Though it's true a complete search of his room turned up no signs of drug use, only a bunch of song lyrics in his guitar case and the bottle of lithium. A few books, the packet of letters to Sunny, which Angela has spirited away, saying she'll steam them open if it comes to that.

Beyond the screws, all Angela will finally say is this: "Something terrible happened." Each time she says this, she does another silent round on her rosary.

What happened? Rudy was standing talking to the priest at eleven, out starting up the mower, and then he was gone. Tess is all over the map on the possible causes. The answer she wants most to believe is this: Sleep-deprived and in a deep depression, hating having to live under the constant watchfulness of the three of them, Rudy simply could not face the 23,763 hours ahead. No word from Sunny. No word from Sunny. Maybe he just turned the key in the ignition and headed out to try to track Sunny down.

But there's no point in their sitting here going over all of it again. They can't put it off any longer. They must decide what they're going to do. Tess reaches across the table and takes her mother's and her grandmother's hands. Both women look at her in wary surprise, for they know she is not about to say a blessing.

"We need to go to bed and try to get some sleep, but before we do, we must finally decide. Really we only have two options: Should we call the police and report Rudy as missing because he may be in some danger or may even have had a psychotic break? Or should we wait, and when Rudy doesn't show up for his probation meeting at two p.m., just let whatever's going to happen as a result of that take its natural course?"

■ ■ ■

[ 64 ]

# Iron Vests

Tess wakes to the smell of coffee. The sun is long up. It must be after nine. She pulls on clean clothes, even combs her hair, brushes her teeth, washes her face. She does not look in the mirror. It's not a face she wants to see, the truth of just how scared she is of what the day may bring. A fist of ice squeezes her chest.

Somehow she's got to keep herself together to do her barn chores at four and even to work on collecting the materials for the termite-mound construction for the chimp project. How much does she need to tell the Daweses? At least there's this: no more classes until September. She's got the 4.0 behind her, the internship ahead next week.

Rudy's door is open. Gramma has made his bed. Folded his Dickie shirt and black pants and placed them on his chair. Queenie waits for Tess at the top of the stairs. "Okay, girl," Tess tells her, "this is it." And they go down.

When they get to the kitchen, she sees that her mother and grandmother are both combed and dressed as well. Her mother is scrambling eggs. Her grandmother is watering the tomato plants. No doubt she's already called Father Al to fill him in.

"First, we're going to have some breakfast, a cup of coffee," her mother says. "Tess, butter the toast and get out that strawberry jam."

Some of the tightness in Tess's chest eases: Mamo has assumed command. Her mother sets their plates on the table and slides the pan into the soapy water.

"Both of you sit, eat this while it's hot."

She does not say "to keep your strength up," but that's clearly what they are about here.

They sit and chew and take it slow. They do not talk. They are talked out. The time for talk is over. Queenie goes from chair to chair and nudges each of them.

Mamo stands. "All right." She puts on her reading glasses and pulls a chair to the phone. She takes the sheet of paper from her pocket and tilts it toward the light.

Tess encloses her grandmother's hands in both of her own.

Her mother dials the number. In only a few seconds, when the Onango County Sheriff's dispatcher answers, she says, "I want to report a missing person. My son, Rudolph Morletti, disappeared yesterday sometime between eleven and twelve, and we fear he's in danger."

The dispatcher says he'll pass the family's concern on to an investigator, but first he needs some preliminary information. One, two, three … Carla answers, leaning close to the list they had compiled all spelled out in Tess's neat, large printing on the sheet that now rests on her lap: full name; birth date; physical description, clothing; social security number; location of last place seen, date and time; make of the car and license plate number. To the question "What makes you think he may be in danger?" Carla keeps her answer simple, just as they agreed: the threatening phone calls from Larry Prager, the special work license rules about being home by noon, the fact that Rudy left the job in a rush. Best at this point to let the Sheriff's Department fill in the next set of blanks.

Before going to bed, they had also agreed they must answer honestly any questions put to them. Since they don't know of anything illegal, anything in violation of the probation rules, this wasn't difficult. It did take some pressure from Angela and Tess, in their final round of dead-of-night discussions, to get Carla to promise not to offer up any theories beyond the basic facts as they know them.

Finally Carla hangs up the phone. "The dispatcher said an investigator will get back to us within the hour. What I wouldn't give for a fistful of Valium. Okay, now for the lawyer. Get his advice about contacting probation."

Tess and her grandmother remain completely still, suspended, as though by not moving they can direct all of their energy toward helping Carla dial and stay on track.

▪ ▪ ▪

*Doing Time Outside*

# Bares Its Teeth

Tess leaves the fifty cents for the *Morning Sun* in the cup and avoids eye contact with anyone in JAKE'S. She keeps feeling everybody else knows more about what's going on than they do. She pulls the truck around the corner and parks in front of the fire station before she unfolds the newspaper.

Major Drug Raid Yields Heroin and Cocaine Worth $450,000

Marwick — Two men have been arrested and charged in the town of Stanton: John Bergen, 38, owner of Onango Sawmill and Lumber, and Burton Stokes, 41, of Queens. Lawrence Prager, 46, of Stanton, who is also alleged to be involved in the drug ring, escaped on foot through state land that borders the mill. A warrant for his arrest has been issued. Prager is believed to be armed and dangerous.

The raid is the result of several months of ongoing investigation. Bergen and Stokes are being held at Onango County Corrections. Anyone having information

> should call the Onango County Sheriff's Department at (456) 489-6677.

"Armed and dangerous." Somehow seeing that in print ups the current. "Ongoing." Perhaps that means they're still looking for more people. But in this game of seek, there's nothing in the article that makes her feel like it's saying 'hot' and heading for Rudy. Burton Stokes? No one she's ever heard of.

Tess makes herself drive around the block so she can check the post office. What if, at long last, Sunny has finally written Rudy a letter, a letter that might have changed the course of everything if it had come two days earlier?

The post office door is propped open. She makes a dash for it. With any luck Fred Postmaster will be so busy, he won't be able to smack her with some cheery greeting.

Nope. His hail and hearty grin's dialed directly her way.

"Top of the morning to you, and what a beautiful day it is."

"Yes," she says, and fakes a smile. Best to stay on this man's good side.

No letter for Rudy. Just a copy of the notice from the New York State Department of Health sent to the zoo verifying that Theresa Morletti has never been charged with child abuse. For a second she's amazed to see that Langley Zoo is that careful about the treatment of the chimps, but then she realizes the abuse check is because she'll be conducting workshops with kids as part of her internship.

Just as she makes the turn onto Cobb's Road, she sees a man jogging in the distance. No, not jogging, running, the graceful lope of a serious, practiced runner. A tall, lean man. And even though he's still quite a way up hill, she knows it's Mark Merrick. Mark, whom she has not seen since that morning last October when she gave him a ride to rehab, right after she picked her mother up at the hospital, Mamo's leg cast stretched across Tess's lap because it was the only way they could fit her in the front seat and close the door.

Tess swings out a little and pulls alongside. Mark doesn't break his stride, doesn't turn his head to see her. He simply motions for the truck to keep on going, indicating that he does not want any interruptions. When she continues to match her speed to his run, he does look long enough to see it's her. With a look of wary resignation, he lopes behind the truck and comes up to her open window, still not breaking his rhythm. She could easily reach out and grab him by his bushy graying hair, and for a second she feels the urge to do just that.

"Can't stop. Can't talk. I'm getting ready for the marathon. Doing the first timed twenty-six today."

"I just want to ask ..."

Mark, his eyes straight ahead, his breathing measured, cuts her off. "Rozmer told me about Rudy. I've no clues. Haven't seen him since he threatened to Molotov-cocktail you and me at the stone house last summer. Can't get involved. Got to keep it simple."

Or she could reach out and grab him by the throat. How lovely for him that he can so easily detour around all this shit.

"Suggest you talk to his counselor, Jacobs. Hear he's got a good lawyer. Jacobs, Rozmer, the lawyer. Doesn't get any better than that. "

With this he gives her a grin and returns to the side of the road.

Tess does not burn out so that a cloud of dust fills Mark Merrick's eyes and lungs. She does not turn the wheel the fraction of a turn that would run him off the road into the blackberry canes. And when she glances in her rearview mirror to see him raise his hand to give her the peace sign, she does not give him the finger.

▪ ▪ ▪

## [ 66 ]

# The wheel of karma comes around fast.

Carla leans forward and gently, but firmly, grips Tess's shoulder. "I still think it'd be better for just me to go in to talk to Jacobs. If the three of us go bursting into the Chemical Dependency Clinic saying we'd like to jump in to take Rudy's appointment, that little receptionist is liable to go all rules and regulations."

Her mother turns, gives her a tearful look, and goes back to her beads.

Tess makes no reply whatsoever. Instead she pulls into the Daweses' driveway so fast, Carla slams her foot down on the floor of the truck.

"I'll only be a minute," Tess says. "Just want to let them know I probably won't be able to work this evening since the investigator's coming to the house right about then. You stay, Queenie." With that she sprints for the barn.

"What a good girl she is," her grandmother says

Carla sighs. "Woman. One thing at least, she's gotten rid of that terrible tangle of hair." She touches her own head, is once again surprised by how frizzy it's become now that she's gone all gray. And no wonder she's gone all gray, given that crisis is the one-a-day pill she takes every morning. She reaches forward and pats her mother's hair, which has grown back in all soft, no bristles.

Her mother smiles for the first time all day.

They watch Tess head back toward them. She gets in, swings the truck around the drive, makes the turn onto the Back River Road.

Carla holds her tongue, hoping that for once Tess is going to volunteer what Hoop Dawes had to say about the consequences for Rudy if he's gone on the run. But, as usual, Tess makes no goodwill offers of information, and she's liable to get all huffy if Carla isn't careful.

Just as she opens her mouth in search of a neutral question, Tess says, "Hoop wasn't there, so I only had to talk to Betty. The police already called Hoop, but she has no idea what they said. Not that she could tell us even if she did. But one thing she did say was that Hoop looked sad instead of angry."

"Sad instead of angry," Carla repeats this, and though she has no idea what it might mean, she finds it comforting.

For a while they drive in silence. For Carla it'd be better if they kept talking, but her mother and Tess seem to be of the less-said-the-better school. This keeping everything on mute makes her want to turn the sound on full. It urges her to cause trouble, which is what will happen if she gives voice to her next thought. So she does.

"I wish we had one of those cell phones in case that investigator's trying to reach us with some news," Carla says. "My guess is as soon as I told that dispatcher about the Prager threats, the usual missing-person procedure took a sharp turn."

"What are you thinking?" her mother says, her face tightening up with fear.

Tess shoots her a dirty look. "Mamo, I thought we agreed no guesses, no coming up with scenarios that just make us more anxious."

"What, Carla?" her mother asks. "Best she goes on with it now, Tess." She swivels around in the seat so she can read Carla's face.

"I mean it feels to me that instead of looking for Rudy as a missing person, they're looking for a running person. Like they've put out an all-states bulletin for the Maverick with two men sitting in the front seat."

"Oh, Carla," her mother says. She puts her hands over her ears and turns completely away.

Tess's eyes in the rearview are on fire. "These leaps over the edge into catastrophe are exactly why Gramma and I are going in with you to talk to Ben Jacobs."

"Sorry," Carla says, "but I can't help what I'm thinking."

Tess stops at the light in Stanton. Even from here Carla sees the back and forth of the swing on the Edgewater porch. Willie Jones waiting for the bar to open up. No question, on top of everything else, she's going to lose her job if Dirk has to keep filling in for her.

"Anyway," Tess says, "if you were right, I think the police would've swooped down on the house and made a search."

"See," Carla says, "I'm not the only one thinking."

"Mamo, please."

"All right, no more guessing out loud. How about passing me the paper." Something to fill her mind, something to do with her hands now that she's no longer smoking.

She doesn't look at the front page. She definitely doesn't want to read that headline again, the part about Prager at large. One good thing, Rudy's name isn't in there, doesn't even feel like it's between the lines. 'Course the article was written before she called to report Rudy gone. And there's another good thing: Granley sounded sad rather than angry as well. He made it clear that no matter what happens, he's still Rudy's lawyer. And he'll do his best for him. And yeah, the third good thing, by way of counting her blessings: when she called the probation officer, she got his machine instead of him. This is Carla Morletti. Rudolph Morletti will not be able to keep his appointment today. We called the Sheriff's Department at ten this morning to report him missing since noon yesterday. She read it off her notes and click, hung up the phone. Definitely sad was not the tone she was going to get from that guy.

Her eyes fall on the horoscope for today, May 25th, 2003. Though she has given up all that, she can't resist glancing at Aquarius, Rudy's sign:

> Not often do you get a chance to help someone who is precious to you. The wheel of karma comes around fast, and be assured no good deed goes unnoticed.

Carla closes the newspaper. You hear that, Rudy — call your grandmother today to let her know you're all right.

"Just let me give Ben Jacobs a call to let him know you're here," is what the receptionist says when Tess tells her that the three of them would like to take Rudy's appointment slot since Rudy's not able to be there.

Before they even take a seat to wait, Jacobs appears in the door. His look of concern, rather than alarm, helps them begin to take normal in-and-out breaths. The total blankness of his desk, the complete order of his space, the way he pulls their chairs out for them are soothing. Already, before they even begin, some of the anxiety lifts.

Ben Jacobs sits across from them, both hands open on his empty desk. "What's happened?" he says.

Tess briefly summarizes all of it, beginning with how troubled Rudy has seemed all week; the drug bust; the screws thrown on the ground; that they're expecting the investigator, a Mr. Harold Riley, to come to the house to question them early this evening. That the lawyer has advised them to simply tell the truth and to keep it brief, no speculations. On that one Tess gives Carla a long look.

At that point Angela speaks. "Mr. Jacobs, we know you can't tell us anything specific, anything that was confidential. We're here because we hope there is something you *can* tell us that will help us get closer to what has most likely happened to our dear Rudy."

Jacobs gives them what is definitely a sad smile. "Though I can't, as you say, share any of my conversations with Rudy, I can say it's my belief that as of my last meeting with him, April 28th, he had remained clean and sober. And though this is strictly speculation, I do not believe that Rudy has joined with Larry Prager. If he has decided to make a run for it, I think he's done it on his own."

■ ■ ■

[ 67 ]

# Friendly Submission

"Carla, do you think it's really necessary to have this calendar taped to the refrigerator with all these bright-pink announcements of our comings and goings?"

Tess knows what her grandmother means, of course. All of Rudy's appointments, sure proof of his previous misconduct. One hour before the investigator is scheduled to arrive, and Grammy, with her good-luck red bandana around her head, is in a dither of concealing as much of their dysfunction as possible. Currently she's busy feather-dusting the window sills. Though where she could have gotten such a high-class cleaning implement in this house Tess can't imagine.

"Tess, could you locate the Windex? We can't do anything about this door that neither opens or closes, but at least we can do something about Queenie's nose prints?"

Queenie perks up her ears.

"And, Tess, wouldn't it be better not to have all those ape pictures around your dresser mirror? It's bound to give this Mr. Riley a wrong impression."

Tess and Carla both burst out on that one. The first good laugh they've had in, well, a very long time.

Tess kisses the top of her grandmother's head and applies some vinegar and water to the kitchen-door glass.

"Go ahead and make fun, but I believe it's best if the investigator sees that we're respectable people who keep a clean house and that we believe Rudy … Rudolph Morletti … has turned over a completely new leaf."

Tess has to give the ceiling a roll of the eyes on any number of those assumptions and she's sure Mamo's doing the same. But oh what would they have done without the faith and steady love of dear Gramma?

One thing for sure, it's definitely a plus that the little plants growing in the window boxes are three varieties of tomatoes rather than the startup of the family marijuana crop that filled those planters in years past.

▪ ▪ ▪

[ 68 ]

# Learning Complex Tasks

The investigator, Harold Riley, looks like an insurance salesman — nondescript suit, tie, haircut, and nose — which is maybe good if he does undercover or decides to hold up a bank. The three women respond as one cooperative unit. Each introduces herself: I'm Rudy's mother, Carla Morletti. I'm Rudy's sister, Tess. I'm Rudy's grandmother, Angela DeLuca. They gesture toward the kitchen table, and all four of them sit down. No thank you, he does not want coffee. They give him almost the same word-for-word facts as they know them that they have given to Rozmer, the dispatcher, the lawyer, Ben Jacobs, but with all emotional undertones deleted. Each one takes a turn at telling when the prior teller hesitates.

The investigator has a clipboard and a pen at the ready, but he doesn't write anything down, he doesn't probe. What the heck kind of investigator is he anyway?

When he asks if they have any recent photos of Rudy, all Carla can think of is Rudy's 1986 yearbook picture. All three have a flash of that on a *Wanted* poster in the P.O. Rudy, all young and beautiful. How could someone with that sweet face have gone so wrong?

Then the investigator says, "I'd like to look over Rudolph Morletti's things."

The three of them rise as though they all plan to guide him, but then Tess and Angela sit back down. They can't all three go up to Rudy's room. Certainly none of them says, "Do you have a search warrant?"

Carla takes the investigator upstairs. Tess and Angela go softly into the hall so they can hear what goes on up there, though they know this looks odd, even a bit suspicious.

They hear some sounds of things being opened and closed, the scrape of a chair. Surely he'll look in Rudy's guitar case.

"We went through everything to see if there were any clues that might help us understand what happened, why he didn't come home."

They're relieved; they can hear what's going on.

"His grandmother made his bed and folded these clothes."

She must then be pointing at his black pants and Dickey shirt.

"His sister opened these two wadded pieces of paper and read them."

The "Dear Sunny" beginning of a letter, the counting of the hours and days,

"And these three books were on the floor by his bed."

The dictionary, thesaurus, and Bible. There's a minute of silence while Riley must be looking all these over. They're glad about the books, especially the Bible. The books rattle the Rudy-as-thug stereotype. But they're a little nervous too.

"Have you removed anything from the room?"

They both tense up over that question but relax a little when they hear Carla's "No," answered in a steady voice like she's telling the total truth.

If Carla was given a polygraph test, she'd flunk because of the Sunny letters, which when skimmed by Angela contained no clues about Rudy's disappearance. Carla knows nothing about the prayer rug that is no longer in the Bible, no longer in Rudy's room. The morning of the dispatch call Tess looked for it, and when she found it no longer tucked in the Bible, she knew what had happened. Did her grandmother kneel on it to pray for Rudy? She didn't ask.

"And this bottle of pills?"

"I took that out of the guitar case. Lithium. The Onango Mental Health Clinic prescribed it as medication for a bipolar disorder."

Maybe it would have been better if she hadn't been so specific. Maybe that's going beyond simple.

"Do you know for certain that's what's in this bottle?"

"No."

"I'd like to take this if I may."

Must be she nods yes and hands it to him.

"And what are these?"

"Lyrics for songs that Rudy must have been writing that I also found in with his guitar. And lists of rhymes."

"I'd like to take those as well."

The lyrics, the columns of rhyming words, dozens of lists. Just more proof of how down Rudy was, but no specific clues to any plans. Except maybe the words of that Jeezo song. Tess spirited those lyrics away to hide in her bottom drawer, thinking Rudy's little private talk with Jesus was nothing the cops needed to hear.

"You'll have to sign a release for these items," the investigator says. "They'll be returned to you when we conclude the investigation."

Conclude the investigation. This is so ominous Tess and Angela take hold of each other, but they don't whisper. And when they hear footsteps, they fade back into the kitchen, lift their chairs quietly, and sit down.

Carla and the investigator return. Carla says, "Are you sure you don't want coffee?"

"I'm sure," he says.

Carla sits, assuming Harold Riley is going to continue his questions. Instead of joining them, he turns toward the table, looms above them.

"What do you think has happened to your grandson, Mrs. DeLuca?"

No speculations.

"I don't believe that Rudy ran away."

"What do you believe happened instead?

A flicker of hesitation. "I don't know."

"What do think happened, Mrs. Morletti?"

Angela and Tess resist giving Carla warning looks.

"I don't know what to think."

The investigator lets that response sit there, waiting for further words to come from Carla's mouth. When none do, he turns toward Tess. "And you? What do you think happened to your brother?"

Angela's eyes plead.

"I don't believe my brother ran away either."

Again there's a long pause.

"All right. I'll give you a call just as soon as I have any news. I appreciate your cooperation."

The investigator places his hand on the door. They prepare to see him struggle to open it. None of them makes even a twitch to assist. But before he turns the knob, he looks at each of them again.

"I do wonder," he says, "given all your concerns for his safety and your belief that Rudolph did not flee, why you waited twenty-two hours before you called the police."

They look down and say nothing.

The investigator opens the door with no effort at all.

▪ ▪ ▪

[ 69 ]

# Using Tools in the Wild

May 26: Danford Man Missing

> Rudolph Morletti, age 35, of Chicken Farm Road, town of Danford, has been missing since around noon on May 24th. He was last seen at Our Lady of Sorrows Parish, where he works as a part-time custodian. Anyone having any information, please call the Onango County Sheriff's Department at (456) 489-6677.

The *Morning Sun* photograph above the article is definitely not of a beautiful high school boy. Is it his special license picture taken from the Motor V computer, or is it a mug shot from the Onango County Jail file? Whichever it is, if the man in that photo stepped up on your porch to ask if he could use your phone to call for a tow because his car broke down, you wouldn't let him in. A woman home alone wouldn't even open the door.

His mother, his grandmother, his sister give that photo one flinching glance. Then they turn the newspaper face down on the end of kitchen table. Face down. And every time they have to pass that way, they give that paper a wide berth. They take out the 1986 yearbook. Rudy at nineteen, a beautiful dark-haired boy, his head cocked to the side to say, "Here I come." The three of them agree that's closer to the Rudy they remember.

At least there's nothing in the newspaper that connects Rudy with the drug bust. If the name Larry Prager manages to bang its way into their minds, they slam it back to the dark. In fact, there have been no further articles in the paper about the drug-ring investigation since that first morning, which now feels like months ago even though it's only been … ? They stand before the refrigerator calendar. Today is May 27th. They count back. Surely it's more than four days.

The only news from the investigator is that there is no news. The Sheriff's Department patrol cars have checked every back road in the county and adjacent counties. The all-states bulletin has yielded no information. The Maverick has not been seen. The three women are doing what they can to keep at least the appearance of semi-sanity in the free fall through all this gray nothingness.

Who can believe it, but Carla is actually out there right now spading up a patch in the sunniest place in back of the house, so her mother can put her tomato plants in. It's the quiet labor she's after. It sets her up to face Willie and all the rest of the men who line the bar. They ask her no questions. They clear the tables themselves, call for no burgers once the kitchen's closed, leave her bigger tips. Her mouth is freezing into a permanent fake smile.

As she turns over the earth and breaks it up, she throws the rocks that surface into one of Steve's big empty five-gallon paint cans, a can that's still kicking around even though Steve's been gone from this house … what … ? Fifteen years and dead now for at least four. Steve. He would have been relentless. One way or another he would've tracked Rudy down, gotten to the bottom of what happened.

Every time she fills the bucket, she half drags, half hefts it to dump over the steep bank that leads to the brook. After she's done that for a while, she takes a couple of Advil. A few more mornings of digging and hauling and there'll be a square big enough for the eight tomato plants to spread out. Maybe even a little leaf lettuce, but no zucchini. She draws the line on that freak plant's overproduction.

Carla looks across the valley. All the trees have finally leafed out. All that green. Oh, there have been times, there have been times when she loved this place, when she was happy here.

The last two mornings Father Rios picks Angela up at ten. They say a prayer together for Rudy. Let him be safe. Watch over him. Amen. When they get to the church, Angela spends the first hour doing small incidental cleaning jobs. No pay, absolutely not. She's offered to mow since they haven't hired someone to take Rudy's place. She's sure she could get the knack of it, but Father Rios says one of the men has already volunteered to take care of the grounds using a hand mower for now.

The next hour Angela spends in quiet prayer: she lights candles, says her rosary, slowly walks the Stations of the Cross. Then she sits in the park by the firehouse and eats the lunch she brought.

At four, Angela walks over to the Edgewater to sit in the swing with Willie. They count on Carla coming along soon to open up.

Angela waits.

From: Gary Simms (gsimms@cornell.edu)
Sent: Wednesday, May 27, 2003 7:26 AM
To: Morletti, Tess (tmorletti@marwickcc.edu)
Subject: only an hour away

Of course I'm thinking of you and your family. Please let me know if I can do anything. Call me at 453.622.8817 if you want to talk or you'd like me to come to Danford.

The first children's chimp-observation program is Friday. I'm sorry you can't be part of that.

But I'm glad to hear that you plan to begin your zoo internship this next Monday as scheduled. Have no concern about the gruel for the PVC tubes. I can mix that up when the time comes. I've gotten all the materials for constructing the termite mound, which you can help with or not depending on what you want to do.

We miss you: the chimps and me.

Love,

G.

From: Morletti, Tess (tmorletti@marwickcc.edu)
Sent: Wednesday, May 27, 2003 11 AM

To: Gary Simms (gsimms@cornell.edu)
Subject: Thanks for the thoughts

Thanks for the offers to talk, come here … but at this point I am talked out. Maybe when I see you next week when my internship begins. Who knows, I might just drive over to assist you before that … escape the weight of Danford for a few hours.

I'm using the Daweses' computer right now. Betty's going to help me with the chimp gruel. She happens to have most of the ingredients, including their own honey. She says it'll be good therapy for her. Her son is in Iraq and she and Hoop haven't gotten any emails or calls for two weeks. We pretend to be brave together while we do the barn chores.

My mother and grandmother manage to keep going while we wait for news. I want to hear and I don't want to hear. On mornings when I'm driving to the Daweses' in the dark, I make up a good news story. I set the scene and fill it with just the right amount of sun and rain. Upbeat characters saying upbeat things. No dramatic tension. This happy-ending story gets me through the morning.

The truth is that if the news is bad, I'd rather never hear it. I figure I can learn to live with the waiting, that over time the ache in my heart might dull down to a 2 like when they ask you to rate your current pain at the doctor's.

Love,
Tess

Basically the good news story she imagines is always the same one. It's a small-town garage in the Southwest where the sun shines just about every day, with a cooling rain that blows through early afternoons, and the sky is often that pink sort of blue that declares for sure that gods did or do live somewhere beyond that butte. The owner of the garage is such a good mechanic that he never lacks for business. He's got a nice apartment right upstairs, and he's on his way to paying off the mortgage. Finally his life is going so well, he thinks it's safe to get in touch with his family back home. Not by mail or phone. That's too risky. Some way that will let them know he's alive and doing fine. Maybe something through Father Rios. Some coded reference to a little job he did at the church that only he and Father Al know about. Enough of an anonymous hint mailed from some nearby state that the priest will contact his grandmother to signal all's well. No return address of course.

■ ■ ■

*Doing Time Outside*

[ 70 ]

# Common Descent

Gary almost drops the rope and halter that holds the frozen fruit ball he's hanging in the tree when he sees her. "Tess, am I glad to see you."

She steadies the ladder and reaches up. "Here, toss down the rope. I'll pull it taut until you swing around to the other side to do the final knot."

Between the two of them, they manage to get the ball suspended from the tree at the right height for the adult chimps to dig out the mangoes.

"You're just in time to help with the children's program if you feel up for that."

"I don't know how I got here. Instead of the truck turning onto the Back River Road after chores, I found myself on I-88 headed for the zoo. Automatic pilot. The need not to think, not to talk about our troubles for a few hours, I guess."

"Well, the chimps and I are thrilled. We've got about twenty minutes to show time. First help me shove the observation benches closer to the fence."

Once that's done, they jockey the sign into place: "Chimpanzee Area closed between 3 and 5 for Educational Program."

"Mostly I just need you to keep an eye on the children while I do the presentation. Quell any unrest before it spreads. You okay with that?"

"Yeah. I'm only a little tense over dealing with a bunch of kids in a classroom situation based on my previous life as a child."

Gary squeezes the back of her neck. "Well, it's only a half hour of captivity. I'm pretty sure watching the chimps forage for food outside is going to hold their attention."

They head across the enclosure. Gary looks at his watch. "Let's check the chimps before we go in to set up."

They approach the observation window in slow motion and stay off to the side. Rita and her son, Mac, are hunting for food in one of the tire swings. Toward the far wall, Jo is rocking her Troll doll, while Tillie grooms her. Bach and Jazz swing from platform to platform, giving calls of goodwill. If they notice Tess and Gary, they'll start to act out like children who've been good at day care until their parents arrive.

"The real unknown is that the chimps may be more interested in the humans lined up on the benches than they are in the fruit ball. We've got to remind the kids not to do anything provocative. Though they'd probably get a real kick out of Jo performing one of her displays."

When they reach the presentation room, Gary hands Tess the participant list so she can place the right number of clipboards on the chairs while he loads the video and pushes the big TV screen into position.

"How many kids today, and what's the age range?"

Tess looks over the sheet. "Twelve children between the ages of eight and eleven. No names. They're from right here in Langley, the Meadowdale After School Program. None of them have been to the chimp exhibit before. One counselor and one parent."

"Eight through eleven. My favorite ages. Eager and without a mad rush of hormones. My favorite personal age as well. I spent those years out in the woods with my dog, Gommer. That's when I decided to become a vet, I think."

"Me? That was the age of my Smurf Girl lunch box. I was busy running away from school. That's when I decided to become a juvenile delinquent."

Gary gives her one of those "I get it" looks, but really she can't take too much sympathy. Not if she wants to stay in trilobite mode.

And as though Gary gets that too, he steps back a little. "It's time," he says. "How about you cast a calm spell on the room while I go get them."

In a few minutes, the children troop in, get seated. Four boys; eight girls, many of them taller than the boys. All on the younger side, except for one dark-haired boy who's already muscling up. Tess relaxes. Though at this point all she can see are the backs of their heads, she feels as if the vibes in the room are on low. Nobody's antsy yet. While the video plays — one she's watched so many times she could probably do the script from memory if the audio suddenly went mute — she busies herself putting together the zoo packets the kids will take with them when they go: stickers, chimp info, schedules of future programs.

When the video's over, Gary looks at all the children with a confident smile. "Any questions?"

The kids squirm and duck their heads with the familiar body language of "Don't call on me."

Gary passes out the observation sheets and the pencils, tries to connect with each child as he moves down the row. "Now the first thing I want you to do is write your name on the top line so if we end up publishing the results of this study, we can give all of you credit."

The children bend to the task. This is a good sign.

Gary continues once the heads come up again. "In a few minutes we're going to go outside so you can sit on the benches by the fence to observe the zoo's chimps while they search for food. Each chimp is wearing a T-shirt with his or her name. These sheets are so you can help us with an important experiment my assistant Tess and I are conducting."

A few of the girls turn to look at her. Noting the increased movement in the room, Tess tries to signal Gary to speed up, but he's lost in his enthusiasm for the project.

He lifts a clipboard and points to the sheet. "This is how scientists test their theories. Your observations are going to help improve the lives of all chimpanzees living in zoos, because when chimps have to go hunting for their food as opposed to having their food delivered, they are more challenged and therefore healthier and happier. Just like you wouldn't want to lie around all day, watching cartoons and having your mothers serve you candy and Pepsi."

Definitely there is no "ha ha" response to this big laugh line.

Just then Tess registers that a boy in the second row on the end is starting to poke the girl next to him. The older dark-haired kid she'd noticed before. A boy with a long reach. She can't see his face, but she knows he's no longer on his best behavior. She tries to signal the counselor, but without crossing to the other side and causing a distraction herself, she can't catch the woman's eye.

Instead she goes up to stand close to the boy. Just close enough so he'll know she's there, but not enough to provoke him into bravado. She doesn't put her hand on his shoulder. Already she knows that would be a mistake with this kid. Just as she reaches his side, he turns to look at her full on. Her throat seizes up, her chest tightens so she can't breathe, her heart bangs. She's looking into the face of Rudy. She says nothing. She simply steps back and works on taking in air.

And something about her shock seems to hit the boy. He's gone completely still. She wishes she'd thought to put her inhaler in her pocket. Her chest continues to tighten.

Meanwhile Gary is winding up his explanation of how to mark the sheets.

"All right, now I'd like you to line up quietly. Once you're seated outside, Tess will open the door for the six chimps to enter the enclosure. It's very important for this experiment that you remain as quiet as possible, so the chimps will hardly notice you're watching them. Try not to do anything that will distract them. Especially don't call out or mimic."

While the children form a line, Tess feels her chest loosening. She doesn't look at the boy as she goes to open the door that will allow the chimps to enter the enclosure. Once outside, she waits until she sees that the children are all seated on the benches, with their clipboards ready. All six chimps quickly knuckle-walk their way into the hot summer day. She slides the door closed, but instead of going to join Gary and the children, she enters the inside area.

There's the rank smell of urine and feces mixed with rotting fruit. For a moment she looks toward the thick Plexiglas that runs from ceiling to floor and wall to wall at the front of the enclosure. Usually a bunch of people would be standing there looking in. Fortunately, the area is closed for the workshop. What behaviors might they note on their sheets if they were observing her: *Homo sapiens,* female, age between twenty-five and thirty, weight 140 lbs., coloring and features often associated with Italians, clearly in some sort of distress. If one of the onlookers started to mock her gestures, wouldn't she be tempted to run at the glass, to beat on the spot closest to the person aping her anxiety?

She moves slowly along the wall toward the observation window that looks directly out on the fruit ball and beyond the fence to the benches. Gary stands with his own clipboard. His face rapt. Surely the same look he had when he and Gommer tracked their woods.

The twelve children are watchful, waiting; each time one of the chimps does something, their heads go down and their pencils record. And there on the end, the closest boy to her, is Rudy. Rudy, age eleven, his dark curls so much like her own, his large mouth and eyes that could flare from joy to black rage in a flash.

She studies the boy's face. When Mac drops off his mother's back and knuckle-walks up to the enclosure fence directly in front of the boy, the kid laughs and Mac laughs back.

Rudy at eleven; Tess at four. Not the Rudy who locked her some years later in the crawl space. This is the Rudy who took her and their beagle, Lola, to the brook to help him heave rocks from all around the submerged roots of the big sycamore. They waded in the rushing brook up over her knees to reach below the cold water to wrestle stones free from the muddy bottom. When she tried to climb out because her feet and ankles were freezing, he'd say, "Oh don't be a quitter. If we can just keep digging out rocks, we're going to have a pool deep enough to swim in." "But I can't swim," she'd say. "Well, if you keep on working, when the pool gets big enough, I'm going to teach you to dog paddle. I'll even teach you to float on your back." But by the time they got the hole about big enough, hot summer came on and soon the brook was dry.

No matter what Betty has told her, no matter what Betty believes, Tess knows that the name on the top of this boy's sheet will say "Billy."

▪ ▪ ▪

*Doing Time Outside*

[ 71 ]

# Welcome to Oregon

The traffic's starting to pick up. Rudy passes two semi's. Always there's the hope Prager might be careless enough that in this just-dawning light a trucker will spot the gun and call the highway patrol.

"Look: I got three years probation — weekly piss tests, beddy-bye at ten for the next one thousand nights, NA meetings, mandatory chitchat with the kook doctor ... Does that sound like payment for doing the cops favors? Besides, no way I'm ever going back east to do that dance now that you've given me this transcontinental opportunity to make a run for it."

"What a speech. You've always had the golden gift of bullshit. Even back when we worked together at the mill. Before you turned snitch." Prager moves just enough for Rudy to see the revolver's shiny muzzle peering at him from beneath the road atlas on Prager's lap.

"I'm telling you, Prager ..."

"True, you've been a good boy so far. 'Course that may be 'cause my little friend here has been giving you the eye all the way. Still, I am twenty percent beginning to believe you didn't tip the narcos off. You keep minding your manners, and I may just let you go when we get to Portland. You and this piece of shit car."

Rudy knows to stop what's reached the level of begging, knows not to say anything more to press his case. Especially since he's been singing variations of this same song the last two thousand-plus miles from any lick he can pluck. Though he would like to mention in passing that the Maverick, which must have at least two hundred thousand miles on it, has brought them across the country with a minimum of fuss: one flat tire and quarts of oil and transmission fluid every five hundred miles or so. The sputter of the engine in Salt Lake just requiring a blow-out of the gas filter. However, since he figures Prager has only kept from shooting him and dumping his body in some river because he needs a resident Maverick doctor for the road, he doesn't want to venture into how fit the car is.

"It's getting light. Go off 84 at the next exit. We need gas anyway."

This will no doubt mean that he's going to once again be locked in the trunk — always Prager's paranoid routine a few miles before they stop to fuel up and get food or when Prager has to conk for a few hours. And really this is not delusional for indeed Rudy is alert to any chance to grab the Ruger that Prager keeps at the ready. That is, except when Rudy's curled in a ball in the trunk trying not to waste any oxygen by hyperventilating. In fact, that gun has been their constant companion ever since Prager stuck it in Rudy's back while he was bent over the mower behind the church. "Get in the fucking car and drive or I'm going to blow your brains out." Cop-show clichéd as this sounded, Rudy knows Prager's crazy enough to do just that. Especially now that Rudy's heard line by line the whole drug-bust saga, the likely consequences if Prager gets arrested.

"Slow down. Don't start doing shit to attract the troopers. Don't make my finger nervous, Rudy."

He gives Prager a sideways glance. Just enough to see that the muzzle is now aimed directly at his head. And he's sure that finger's also ready should Prager hear anything suspicious like Rudy trying to jimmy out of the trunk. Who would have thought Prager's crank-addled brain could have had such powers of focus? Even showed up at the church with New York State license plates and had Rudy do the changeover before they got to Elmira. But one thing Prager was a bit careless on: a sloppy frisk. He doesn't know Rudy's got the screwdriver he was using on the lawnmower stashed in his boot, with the hope of making use of it before Prager comes to the right bridge for his disposal.

Sun's finally up. Exit 25. Bellmount. Rudy signals. Nights they take the interstates, days the back roads since the Maverick is so easy to identify. He's surprised Prager didn't steal another car along the way. Portland's 557 miles straight ahead on I-84. If he's going to make a move, he'll have to make it soon. The closer they get to the Portland connection, the closer he is to Prager finishing him off.

"Okay, pull into the car wash up ahead."

Car washes when no other cars are in any of the bays are Prager's favorite places for stashing Rudy in the trunk.

"Go in the first one."

Rudy does as directed.

"Now give me the keys."

Prager moves around the car to the driver's side, the gun on Rudy. Rudy gets out. Prager unlocks the trunk. They've done this so many times, every move is choreographed. There's just one position that works, since the Maverick trunk, even with the spare thrown in the back seat, is only about five by four, with Rudy always curling his body toward the opening: more air. Plus this is the only position that allows him to continue to work on one of the escape plans he's come up with so far.

"After we get gas, I'm going to drive for a while. It's a cool morning, you can have yourself a nice little nap in there."

"Prager ... " This is a new twist on the usual arrangements. So far Rudy's done all the driving.

"Take a piss." Rudy does. "Now get in. No fucking around."

Prager slams the trunk. Rudy relaxes his chest, stills the panic, the claustrophobia he always feels in those first few minutes of dark entrapment. At the same time, he always has a flash of Tess at seven locked in the crawl space the time he forgot her all day. Karma, Tess, karma.

The car turns back onto the road. He twists enough to pull the screwdriver from his boot so that when Prager stops he can use the time Prager's in by the cash register to do a bit more work on the brake-light cover panel. The car slows, turns, backs up, comes to a stop. The Maverick's become an extension of Rudy's body, he's so tuned to its every move and sound. Life-and-death decisions depend on reading those sounds right.

The cap turns, the nozzle clanks into the hole. There's the rush of gas, the stink of fumes. He holds his nose and takes careful breaths through his mouth. Oh the luck that the Maverick's exhaust pipes have no rust-outs, otherwise the carbon monoxide would save Prager the trouble of shooting him.

The gas cap screws back in. Now Prager'll have to go in to pay, get some food, go to the can. As soon as he's sure Prager's gone, he begins loosening the final screws on the brake-light plate. One good thing: he already had the Maverick's trunk interior stripped down from when he rewired the lights.

In the next hour or so, he's going to have to make up his mind. Should he rush Prager and get the gun as soon as Prager lets him out of the trunk, grab the keys, and take off in the car? What are the chances of such a Hollywood maneuver? Or, the next time they pass a noisy truck or a beater without a muffler, should he shove the brake-light panel out and stick his hand through the opening to frantically wave in the hopes that someone behind the Maverick will call 911 and the police will come to his rescue? Or there'll be a high speed chase, the Maverick will crash, and he'll burn. One thing at least if that happens, Gramma Deluca will know, since he was in the trunk, that he didn't run: he was abducted.

Oh, Gramma, say a prayer for me.

The creak of the driver's door. Rudy freezes, readies to push the screwdriver back in his boot if Prager decides to check the trunk. Next there's a slight sinking as Prager's weight settles. The slam of the door, the roar of the engine — way too heavy on the gas. Though if the car broke down from Prager-abuse, it might offer new options for escape. In a few seconds they begin to move. Rudy brings his breathing back to regular. He's got to calm down, calm down and think step by step the best way to keep from dying.

"Morletti," Prager shouts, "hope you're back there copping Z's."

Rudy stops breathing. Prager's words are so clear, he could be his bedfellow.

"I figure you're too smart to plot some derring-do."

Derring-do. Definitely he's underrated Prager's poetical mind-fucking talent.

After a long stretch of quiet, he once again stills enough to think. To plot. To replay again the movie frame by frame of Prager's moves whenever he lets him out of the trunk: Prager unlocks the trunk and releases the catch. He then moves back a few feet and leaves it for Rudy to push up the door and step out. Always the Ruger's aimed. Prager's never within lunge distance. Then there's the hands-up march to the driver's side, the door already open for the slide in. Prager's backward walk around to the passenger side, the gun always aimed at Rudy's head. Then the slide back in with the gun pointed. Where in each of those moves is there a space where Rudy can grab the Ruger? Nowhere.

And he does not, he does not want to end up killing Prager. Be on the run for the rest of his life? Clearly a thousand days of probation shit is way better than that. Plus chances are good he'll get picked up, and clearly, given how it's all going to look, no way will he come out winning a self-defense plea, the belief that he was kidnapped. Overpowering Prager, if he can escape without wasting him, does give him the option of holing up somewhere and never going back to Danford. He'd have to ditch the Maverick. Gramma ... Tess ... Mamo. Even Sunny. Somehow, if it comes down to that, he will find a way to let them know he's alive and starting over.

"Hey, Rudy, I know you still got enough oxygen 'cause I can hear your heart pounding all the way up here."

Jesus. The sweat's draining from every body part that's equipped to seep panic.

Shit. When he pushes tentatively on the brake-light panel, it gives enough for him to know with one mighty shove, muffled when they're passing a noisy vehicle, it'll pop out. Thing is, there will be no going back then. Because if no one does the 911 when they see his hand screaming help, the next time Prager stops, he'll see the hole. And that will be it.

Either way, he's got to wait until the right moment. Meanwhile Prager is keeping the speed steady, driving like a man who knows where he's going and what he needs to do.

Maybe Rudy drops off, maybe the fumes have gotten to him, but out of the darkness he hears the roar of something big rattling up on the left. When the noise is at its full rumble, he gives the brake light panel a shove with both hands. It pops the plastic out. It becomes a red flash as it flies up and away. A blast of air hits him. Not more than two car lengths behind there's a silver Lincoln Continental. Some guy in a truck with a .22 in the rack would've been better for a 911. *But.* He sticks his hand out and begins a frantic wave that means "SAVE ME."

■ ■ ■

[ 72 ]

# Gruel

Carla and Angela are sitting on the porch of the Edgewater when Tess pulls up. It's such a dark night, their faces flicker on and off with the neon of the Coors sign. Carla pulls herself into the back seat with Queenie. Tess helps Angela into the front. Maybe one of those little portable steps might be in order soon.

"What's that lovely smell?" Angela says.

"I was just going to ask you the same thing," Carla says. "Only lovely isn't the word I would've chosen."

"It's gruel for the chimps. Gary and I are going to stuff it into tubes that will encourage them to use sticks to get it out once we get the termite mound built. More like living in the wild."

"Gary … ," Angela says.

Tess turns onto the Back River Road.

"Why are you going this route? It's longer," Carla says.

"On my way to pick you up I saw a flash of someone out doing a run along this road, and if it turns out to be Mark Merrick, I want to force him off into a ditch."

"Tess, shame on you," Angela says.

"Well, at least I want to blast him with the horn so loud, it scares the sh — the living daylights out of him."

"You're not really going to do that are you, Tess?"

"No, but it cheers me up just thinking I could."

They begin to watch the road, but there's no flash of anyone loping along. It's so dark, it's hard to see anything beyond the high beams. There's a light on in the upstairs window at the Daweses'.

Angela touches Tess's arm. "Have they heard anything?"

"Tommy's okay. They got an email this evening. Sorry, I meant to tell you first thing."

"Such good news," Angela says.

None of them wants to go any further with where that phrase leads. Nothing from Investigator Riley, zero results on the all-states bulletin. It's come to this: whatever's lurching its way toward them, it doesn't begin with the word "good."

Once the truck reaches Cobb's Road, they are silent.

And when they make the turn onto Chicken Farm, all three of them steel up at the sight of the dark house, even Queenie looks anxious. They've tried leaving lights on, but that doesn't help. Off or on, the rooms are just as empty when they get there.

Tess helps her grandmother mount the porch steps and Carla bangs her rear into the door to open it. Then they halt right there, bunch up: the kitchen's lit by the red blink, blink, blink of the machine. Each waits for the other to be the one to move across the room, to be the one to allow the machine to speak.

Carla turns on the light. Angela sits down. Tess presses *Play*.

"It's me … I'm in Oregon … kidnapped … a gun convinced me to be cooperative. Prager's in jail. Looks like, with a lot of backing from Granley and Jacobs, probation's going to come around. Only bad news: the Maverick's a goner. Police are making arrangements to get me back to Danford. Tell Father Rios to hold my job. See you in a few days."

▪ ▪ ▪

[ 73 ]

# Our Lady of Sorrows Community Fair

Here comes Rudy, hefting a big speaker on his shoulder, past the barbeque pits where it's my job to turn the chickens. He lowers the amp onto the closest picnic table  and lights a cigarette.

"Have to set down my burden," he says. Rudy likes to sprinkle in biblical bits to assure me he's still the con he always was.

Now he gives me a grin. I know exactly what he's going to say next.

"You believe this, Tess, you'll believe anything."

See — what'd I tell you? Wonder and skepticism have been fighting back and forth on Rudy's face ever since he returned from Portland two months ago.

"One more of these mothers of all speakers to go and then the keyboard. Gary's going to help on that one." He wipes his forehead with the bandana that's been hanging from his pocket since Gramma Deluca talked him out of wearing it on his head. "What time we going to play?"

"Right after the Pet Parade, which starts soon. Probably about three."

"The Pet Parade. I don't want to miss that."

We both laugh, but in fact I know he plans to be right on the sidelines giving Mamo and Queenie a look laced with incredulity.

As Rudy bends to lift the speaker, he says, "How about calling the band 'The Far-Fetched'?"

Ever since Rudy, Gary, and I promised Father Rios we'd put together a little gig for the church fair, Rudy's been bedeviling us with pseudo-band names. How about "The Delusions"? How about "The Unlikelies"? "The Fallen Angels"? When Gramma DeLuca overheard that one, she suggested "The Gabriels." Her sincere interest shut him up for a while.

I don't give him the satisfaction of an answer.

Perhaps, like the rest of us, you can ditto Rudy's disbelief. Mamo and I are still walking around in a confused state saying to each other, "Pinch me." Not Gramma DeLuca, though. She claims for her there was always a glimmer. Understandably, Rudy's final forecast was apocalyptic as he hurtled down the Oregon back roads ninety miles an hour in the Maverick trunk, police car sirens screaming in pursuit. Rudy does admit to saying, "Sweet Jeezo save me" about a hundred times.

I watch Rudy and Gary setting up on the small stage over by the Wet Sponge Throwing Game: twenty-five cents a try to hit the middle-school principal, who's got his head stuck out of a hole in a big piece of plywood. Then I go back to turning the chickens, getting them crispy brown using one of the church ladies' secret barbeque sauces.

Off to my right, Gramma's working the crowd, hawking the 50-50 raffle tickets, to split the pot — the church's half to go toward a new roof. "Don't you want to buy six tickets for five dollars rather than just one?" she says to the people milling about eating hotdogs and cotton candy. "Six really ups your chances to win."

Later, after we play, if she hasn't sold enough tickets, she wants Gary and me to act as shills to go around taking her up on this great bargain. "Shame on you," I told her.

Back under the trees Queenie, leashed, lies beneath the picnic table, Mamo on the bench above her. Both of them dazed. I give Mamo an encouraging wave to remind her of her promise to be the lead in the Pet Parade, which I'm in charge of executing. She loads up her return gesture with as much irony as it will hold.

So — here we all are: Startled Participants. Well, not quite *all*. But who knows who still might appear before the final fireworks? One thing for sure: Prager & Co. will definitely not be competing in the Ring-Toss.

2:15. Time for the parade. The animals are congregating with their "masters" in front of the mini-grandstand. Time to pass the responsibility for the chickens over to another volunteer, a lanky kid with a head of spiky hair. Rudy tells me this boy for sure has the Sacred Heart tattooed on his chest.

I go over to gather up Mamo and Queenie to join the other paraders by the stands. With a look of apology, I fasten a large purple bow to Queenie's collar. She gives me an I-can't-believe-this look as well.

Next I gentle-arm the two of them to the front of the group, and the rest of participants begin to fall into a ragged lineup: a scruffy rabbit in a cage being pulled along in a red wagon that's bedecked with Kleenex roses; a black poodle being pedaled forward in a bicycle basket; a haltered small goat threatening to leap on the back of a boy who's bent down in front of it trying to calm a parrot that's shouting obscenities. But mostly there are dogs, about twenty of them, of every variety from AKC pure to the most committed mongrels, all chaperoned by kids, also of every size and shape. Some dogs heel, and others drag their children off into the ditch that borders the parade strip. I blow the whistle and the lineup begins to straggle toward Father Rios, standing about fifty yards down the runway, a large basket full of Fair goodies beside him. Well-wishers, mostly parents, sit in the bleachers waving and sending out soft calls of encouragement. Lots of picture taking.

As Mamo passes me, she rolls her eyes to the sky. "If the Pagan Motorcycle Auxiliary could only see me now," she says.

But no question Mamo's a lot more relaxed now that Rudy's full time at Our Lady's and living in the little apartment over the garage, saving his money to buy a car since the Maverick was destroyed in the chase. Already, after being at the church for only two months, Rudy's painted most of the parish rooms, replaced Father Rio's muffler, and given the riding mower a complete overhaul. All this in addition to his regular cleaning and maintenance duties. But no matter how Gramma cajoles, he keeps saying no to Confession. And "One Mass was enough for me." My guess is she's still in there kneeling on that little prayer rug working on getting Jesus to change Rudy's mind.

Me? I'm almost done with the internship. We built the termite mound with Rudy's help on the welding, and our collection of data has been so fruitful, Gary and I are collaborating on a paper we hope to deliver, with video accompaniment, at the National Zoo Conference in Washington in December. We still knock around the idea of balancing all our brains.

In the background of the barking dogs and sweet cheers from the bleachers, I hear Rudy and Gary testing the sound system — one-two, one-two — on the stage Rudy reinforced to support the three of us, the keyboard, and all the speakers and mikes Gary borrowed from his Ithaca friends.

At last all the paraders have reached Father Rios, who is going down the line speaking to each creature and kid and giving out the gifts. Even Queenie smiles and wags. Mamo gives Father's arm a grateful tug. Fortunately, though the kids on the planning committee pressed Rios to do a blessing of the animals, he said that wouldn't be possible since this rite is traditionally done only in the fall. No sermonette is good. Though Queenie and Mamo have gone along with the parade, a blessing might have caused them to make a surprise exit.

Okay, there's the signal from Gary that it's time for me to go test my mike, to make sure the sound's right on the keyboard. We've done quite a bit of practicing, carefully choosing songs that will in no way offend any of the God-fearing who'll be in the audience, and we've set up the order of music so the crowd will have to start moving to the beat, plenty of room to dance. Father Rios has promised he'll get them going.

I step up on the stage.

"Hey," Gary says.

"Ready or not," I tell him.

With his guitar swinging from his chest, Rudy backs up close to me, and sotto voce, away from the mikes, says, "How about 'The Apple-Pickers'?"

I just give him a loving smile, heavy with warning, and play a few testing bars. Then I one-two, one-two my mike. After testing, testing, testing some more, Gary signals his friend who's doing the sound board that we're all set.

People surge toward the stage. I look out over the crowd: Rozmer and his son, Gabe, right in front. Off to the side, standing together: Ben Jacobs and William Granley, Attorney at Law. Nooley and an NA contingent. And way in the back, Charles Dale and Darlene, their baby suspended in a pouch on Charles's back.

Sure, many of us know our lives are only one phone call away from a crash and burn or something malignant on the MRI. Rudy still hates his sessions with Frozen Ida, and probably he flushes his meds down the toilet. He's still *X*-ing off the nine-hundred-plus days of going by the book. Believe me, we commiserate with the Lady of Sorrows, confirm without any disclaimers it's one day at a time.

You know, there were years when I'd have named our trio "The 911's," or maybe "The Don'ts," but the title I'd come up with now might be so sappy with hope, Rudy'd wish he'd never started this game. Though I've never found the right time to tell Mamo and Gramma about Billy, to talk to Rudy about any of it, and though Sunny isn't likely to appear, beyond that, at this very moment, I *do* believe anything. Almost. I wouldn't be surprised, before this set's over, to see Mark Merrick come running by with a Jew's harp in his pocket, Mamo and Gramma up here doing backup vocals.

For the kickoff, what I want to say is "Rudy, this first song's for you," but since I know he wouldn't like that, instead I give him this aside: "If you swing into that Jeezo song, I'm going to announce a sacred name for this band that'll make you want to go hide in the crawl space for the duration."

With that final threat, I lean into my mike and yell the next thing that's on my mind: "Hello out there. Without further ado, this is what I want you to know on this blue-sky day: We are so believably happy to see all of you here."

And we're off and away: Rudy on guitar, Gary on fiddle, me on keys.

▪ ▪ ▪

*Doing Time Outside*

# Epilogue

Jeezo, seems to me, we
got a heavy dose of women-hovers
more mother-pleads than any man needs
no matter how your good book reads
dragged, ragged by their tears, their fears
the mind-grind of their gears,
one foot on the brake, the other on the gas
of don't and do
allowing no sass — me be me, you be you

Jeezo, not to compare the trouble double
headed your way to my measly lower station
stashed mostly with aggravation
making me daily wail my poor-me low-budget white-boy blues
self-inflicted conflicted convicted, me paying my dues

still I got to say — strange your pop
the biggest CEO-cop
sending you on a mission
any kid who watches T-vision
even one loony tune day
can say what he's selling
what you're telling
is going to get you jailed nailed and tombed-down for good
no matter how many tales they later tell in your hood

To save all us sinners? You really cred that? To be his right-hand man?
Me? I'd rather take my chances on a few more dances with a good girl band.

▪ ▪ ▪

## Acknowledgments

Always I am grateful for the comments of my West Kortright Centre and Cedar Key writing groups and the opportunity to read excerpts of this novel during the open mike sessions at Word Thursdays in Treadwell, New York. My thanks for the gift of time without interruption granted to me by the MacDowell Colony, the Saltonstall Foundation, and Blue Mountain Center. My thanks also to Alice Tasman of the Jean V. Naggar Literary Agency for her energy and support. And finally much appreciation to other writers who have critiqued the work along the way: Charlotte Zoë Walker, Wayne Somers, Rose Mackiewicz, Forrest Bachman, Kim Ilowit, and KK Dewart. And a final toast of gratitude to Adam Rozum, the designer, and Robert Colley, the publisher, of Standing Stone Books.

Ginnah Howard's stories have appeared in *Water~Stone Review, Permafrost, Portland Review, Descant 145, Eleven Eleven Journal, Stone Canoe,* and elsewhere. Several have been nominated for a Pushcart Prize. Her novel, *Night Navigation* (Houghton Mifflin Harcourt 2009) was a *New York Times Book Review* Editors' Choice. The National Alliance on Mental Illness of New York State gave Howard their Media Award for work on behalf of those with mental illness and their families. For more information visit: **www.GinnahHoward.com**